LUCY NEAL:

OR,

NEGRO LIFE, LOVE, MIRTH, AND CHARACTER.

A Novel.

" I came from Alabama, my massa's name was Deal,
He used to own a yaller gal, dey called her Lucy Neal."

. LONDON :

PUBLISHED BY E. LLOYD, AT THE OFFICE OF THE " ILLUSTRATED EDITIONS
OF STANDARD WORKS," 12, SALISBURY SQUARE, FLEET STREET.

1847.

PREFACE.

THE great amount of public curiosity recently awakened with respect to the lives, habits, manners, and characteristics of the negroes, encouraged the Publisher of LUCY NEAL, to believe that a work of fiction, such as the present, which should weave up in the form of a narrative such information regarding the peculiarities of that strange, and in many respects picturesque and entertaining, race would be acceptable to the Public.

That this calculation was based upon correct data has been evinced by a very large demand for the work, and the lavish encomiums of the press.

And although the romance of LUCY NEAL is, as respects the incidents, a romance, it is not so in every sense in which that term may be used; for it presents a true and living picture of what slavery is in the United States of America—a country in which there is more real pride, aristocratic feeling, and the oppression of class upon class, than in any other spot of the habitable globe. And yet that is, *par excellence*, the much-boasted land of freedom !

The melancholy and pathetic end of Cesar is a true incident, and occurred at the conclusion of one of those risings of the slaves which from time to time have contributed to make so sanguinary a page in the domestic history of America.

Let us hope that the time will soon come when the condemnation of the whole civilised world will be sufficient to overcome our transatlantic brethren's passion for dollars, and that the American flag will no longer be considered to represent by the *stars* that they are only in the twinkling twilight of civilisation and common honesty, and by its *stripes* the lashes that the " free and enlightened citizens" bestow on the backs of their slaves.

With these few observations with regard to the tendency and feelings of the present work, we dismiss it to the public, hoping, likewise, that there is sufficient stirring interest in its pages to gratify the most ardent lover of the romantic.

LONDON,
April, 1847.

LUCY NEAL;

OR, NEGRO LIFE, CHARACTER, MIRTH, GRIEF, AND LOVE

BEING THE VERITABLE HISTORY OF LUCY NEAL AND CESAR BOBB.

"Dey bore her from my bosom, but de
  wound dey cannot heal;
And my heart, my heart is breaking, for
  I lub'd sweet Lucy Neal.
Oh! yes, and when I'm dying, and dark
  visions round me steal,
De last low murmur ob dis life shall be,
  sweet Lucy Neal!
Oh! poor Lucy Neal, &c.'

CHAPTER I.

THE COLOURED BALL.—THE DECLARA-
TION.—A NIGHT ON A SUGAR PLAN-
TATION.—ADOLPHUS DEAL IN A
FIX.—THE PLOT.

Now ladies and gentlemen, hi
hi! hi! all ob you shall see what
all ob you shall see, hi! hi! hi!
Dis is de greatest ob curiosities ob
de Fancy Ball. Get out ob de way
ob de master ob ceremonies, you black fellow, will you?
Now ladies for de grand cocoa dance—down de middle, and up
again—cross hands—go round two times—set on de right leg,
and den up de middle again, hi! hi! hi! Get out ob de way,
you black fellow, anybody would think you was used to no good
society, hi! hi!

No. 1.

It is night, and the master of the ceremonies, at a coloured ball, in Georgia, is fully pursuing his important avocation in clearing a space amidst one of the strangest motley throngs that were ever assembled together, for the dancers who were ready to commence.

The room, if room it could be called, for it was in reality a large shed, was fitted up with considerable ingenuity and taste, so as in a great measure to hide the roughness of its aspect, and give it very much the air of a ball-room. ·Broad leaves of the large succulent plants indigenous to the soil stopped up any unsightly crack in the ceiling or walls, while bright flowers, plucked from the luxuriant hedge-rows, blazed in all their enchanting colours from every corner.

But if the floral decorations were marked and magnificent, and such as more northernly regions might hope in vain to produce, the dresses of the visitors to the Coloured Ball completely threw them into the shade by the brilliancy of colouring they displayed.

There was an announcement outside, which ran as follows :—

" Ladies and gentlemen is expectorated to come in full dress to the Coloured Ball, and not to spit on the floor.—N.B. No niggers admitted."

Of course such an announcement as this had convinced everybody of the select character of the entertainment, and accordingly, to do honour to it and to themselves, the guests had come arrayed in most rainbow hues. A white ground, with broad, bright, pink stripes, was the prevailing character of the gentlemen's unaccountables ; while the ladies affected very much a dress of bright yellow, occasionally with crimson spots, each about the size of a moderate pot-lid. Some of the gentlemen wore white cotton gloves, but with those who could not very well afford to revel in such luxuries, it was a custom to carry a good-sized piece of chalk, with which, previous to every dance, they gave their hands a good rubbing, which answered the purpose amazingly well, and was considered perfectly genteel and proper, " particular" as the master of the ceremonies observed, " when de ladies and gentlemen get all over ob an inspiration."

" Make way for de dance," shouted several, and the musicians, consisting of a blind man who played the violin, and a boy who beat away upon a drum, without the slightest idea that in performing his part in the band anything was necessary but to make a noise, struck up.

The ball had already lasted a couple of hours, so we may well imagine that the hilarity was at its height ; and from the exploits of the two dancers who now came forward, it was quite clear that either they must have reserved themselves for that exhibition, or that they were in the most wonderful spirits. The springs, the evolutions, the rapid movements, and the strange gesticulations, brought down thunders of applause ; and when the measure was over, and some one bawled in the blind and half deaf violinist's ear that he might leave off, there was a loud and general clapping of hands.

The coloured gentleman led his partner to a seat, and then previouly to the next dance, a general conversation ensued.

" Well, Miss Cleopatra," said one gentleman, " how you do ? Don't you think that de stocricy ab mustered pretty strong ?"

" Bery Jem, bery, Dandy Jem."

" Oh ! Miss Cleopatra, don't you call me by dat name, you is de dandy ob my heart, Miss C."

" What will you take, Miss Dinah Cave ?" whispered another.

" Nothing," was the nymph's reply ; " but I want you to take something bery partic'lar indeed !"

" What might dat be, Miss Dinah? you know I ab honour to be your humble servant, and will take whateber you like, Miss Dinah."

" Take yourself off, then."

" Oh, gar ! hi ! hi ! hi ! You could not say more if I hab misfortune to be a nigger like Anthony, hi ! hi ! hi !"

Before the young lady had time to make any reply to this cruel taunt upon the individual who was not present, but who was really the object of her fond attachment, there was a general motion in the place, and the master of the ceremonies called out,—

"Room, for Cesar Bobb and Miss Lucy Neal!"

The announcement of these names was followed by loud applause, and in a few minutes a space was cleared in the centre of the apartment for the dancers; and Cesar Bobb, a young, good-looking negro, led out a slight, handsome girl, whose brilliant teeth, sparkling eyes, and animated countenance, excited universal admiration. To be sure the ladies could not, for the life of them, see anything in her, but the gentlemen were perfectly enthusiastic in their applause, in acknowledgment of which, Lucy Neal curtsied with a grace that would not have disgraced St. James's.

And how proud and happy did Cesar Bobb look with his beloved Lucy's hand in his— the Lucy Neal whom he loved so fondly, and for whose freedom he was laying by all the earnings which he could of right call his own; and every cent he received for hard work during those hours when the business of the plantation did not call upon him to toil for Mr. Deal, his master.

And well worthy was Lucy of so much devotion—well worthy was she of such a heart as Cesar Bobb's, which although it did beat within a bosom covered by the dark skin of a tropical clime, was none the less a true, a noble, and a manly one; for he loved Lucy Neal with a devotion and a purity that had elevated him by the very ennobling influence of the heaven-born passion, far, very far above the station in which an evil destiny had placed him. They both belonged to Mr. Deal's estate. (How that word *belonged* grates upon English ears!) They were both slaves—slaves to a man far beneath them in intellect and in feeling, and in all which tends to make the human character great and estimable. But our business just now is with the dance at the Coloured Ball, and we would not anticipate anything which will present itself vividly to the mind of the reader during the course of this most eventful narrative.

Negroes are passionately fond of dancing; and the attention which was now bestowed upon the couple who occupied the floor far transcended that which had greeted the previous exhibition, and well did they deserve this homage of silence and attention, for although each of them was probably more intent upon the other's action than upon their own, the dance was really executed with inimitable precision, and we must add grace.

First, it commenced with a slow movement,—a movement which had more to do with the figure of the dance than with the steps; but the old blind violinist knew what he was about, and he gradually increased the quickness of the time, while the boy belaboured the drum with a perseverance which threatened its utter and unconditional destruction.

And, then, it was something indeed to watch the nimble feet of the dancers; to see how Cesar Bobb banged the floor with his heels, producing a distinct rat-tat at every movement; and it was something, too, to see Lucy Neal's twinkling feet with yellow sandals darting hither and thither, and producing such difficult steps and evolutions, the like of which was scarcely ever seen.

A murmur of congratulation and of admiration arose from the throng of guests at the Coloured Ball: the blind man played away at the violin as if his life were a stake, and solely depended upon the rapidity with which he succeeded in executing the strains that came shrieking and screaming out of his old instrument. The boy who was beating the drum redoubled his efforts until his face assumed a shining greasy aspect; and then, suddenly, Cesar Bobb taking Lucy Neal by the tips of her fingers, twirled her round for a few moments in the rapid evolutions of a pirouette, and then he caught her in his arms, and carried her to a seat.

The clapping of hands was loud and long; and the gentlemen were enthusiastic in their praises of Lucy Neal, while the ladies thought Cesar Bobb the best ob berry fine dancers,—hi! hi! hi!

An old lover of Lucy Neal's, who had looked on with frenzied eyes, thought h would steal a march on Cesar Bobb by bringing a cup of sweet, which is composed of expressed lime-juice, made palatable with syrup to the exhausted fair one, if we may use that term to one of Lucy Neal's complexion.

"Well, Cesar," he said, "berry good dance, indeed,—hi! hi! Me tink you little lame in left leg, Cesar."

"Tank you all de same; de lameness be in de corner of your right eye, Carlos."

"Berry good, berry good! Perhaps Miss Lucy Neal will take a drop ob sweet."

"Berry much obliged," said Cesar Bobb, as he took the proffered cup himself from the hands of Carlos, "berry much obliged,—hi! hi! hi! Bless my heart and life, dis sweet looks as if some nigger had been looking at him and dropped evil eye in it."

One of the windows of the long barn or shed, which composed the ball-room, was partially open, and towards that Cesar Bobb threw the contents of the cup, little suspecting that it would go slap into the face of the Rev. Tobias Slankey, a missionary, who had just arrived for the purpose of persuading the coloured people to give up their ball, and join him in a psalm over the remnant of their festivities.

"Murder! damn it," cried the reverend gentleman, "who has thrown that into my pious face? ye sinful wretches, ye savages, do ye want to murder a labourer of the Lord's? Fall down on your blessed knees, all of you, and own yourselves cracked vessels."

The lugubrious aspect of the preacher, as he now attracted universal attention to himself, caused a great shout of merriment, for Mr. Deal's estate was one of those upon which but little encouragement was given to the methodistical fraternity.

"Mark my words, Cesar Bobb," added the Rev. Tobias, "I know you,—you shall repent of this as sure as you're a living man."

"Why, Massa Slankey," said Cesar, "you put your face at the window and hab got de sweet by accident; and as for threatening,—hi! hi! hi!—I hab quite as leab you did that as anyting else,—for,—hi! hi! hi!

Habn't I by my side my sweet Lucy Neal,
Be off, you Massa Slankey—how happy I do feel!"

"Don't anger him, Cesar," whispered Lucy, "don't anger him; for if you do, he will certainly say something to John Grubson, the overseer, and we shall all get nto trouble."

"Hark you, Cesar!" said Carlos, assuming a valorous air, "did you mean to 'sult me, sir, by throwing ob de sweet in de face of Massa Slankey?"

"Yes, I did."

"Berry good, Massa Cesar; then me tell you what I do."

"What you do, you nigger?"

"Nothing at all.—Hi! hi!"

The preacher had withdrawn from the window, and the little altercation that had taken place between Cesar Bobb and Carlos had terrified Lucy Neal, who, when she saw that the preparation was being made for another dance, whispered to Cesar that she felt the air of the ball-room too much for her, and wished him to make way with her into the open air for a short time. This was accomplished without much difficulty, and in a few moments they stood beneath the cloudless sky and in the soft twilight of that nearly tropical light.

Far and wide before them were the sugar and cotton fields belonging to Mr. Deal, while long regular rows of huts skirting the horizon showed where the habitations of the slaves of the plantation were.

Some distance to the right was a low, long, irregular-looking house, the roof of which was covered with a deep overhanging thatch, and from the windows of which glanced lights at intervals. Some beautiful trees, evidently planted with a view to picturesque effect, grew around this mansion, and a considerable portion of ground adjoining it was enclosed by a strong paling.

This was the house of the Deal family, the owners of the estate; and as Cesar looked upon it and then glanced towards the long line of little low huts that marked the slave habitations, he turned to the girl who was resting on his arm, and spoke with an emotion which he could not conceal—

"Lucy Neal, I came from Alabama, and weary wid de salt tears was both of my eyes when first I saw de Deal estate: all was sad, and dark, and uncomfortable, and I heard de sound of de lash in de hands of John Grubson, Massa Deal's overseer. I thought of running away—I thought of killing myself, and so purchasing my freedom with my blood; but den I saw you, my sweet Lucy Neal, and de dark thoughts passed away. Lucy Neal, I lub you!—I lub you, Lucy Neal!"

Lucy clung closer to him, and he heard her sobbing.

"Oh Cesar! recollect," she said, "that we are slaves; recollect, Cesar, that we are the property of another—that all our thoughts, all our actions, are enslaved—we dare not love."

"Not lub, Lucy Neal! De wood-pigeon lub its mate, and de soft curlew sing de melancholy song among the mangoes, and shall we not lub?"

"You are right, Cesar—you are right in what you say, but still I repeat that we are slaves—it has been my misfortune—alas! I thought it once a great advantage to have been born in a family in Carolina, who were very kind to me, and taught me many things which slaves know not, and from all their teaching, Cesar, has arisen—along with a knowledge of what it is an ardent desire to possess—my freedom. Is it because my skin is of a darker hue than that of young Mistress Deal, that I am to be a slave?—is it because I'm of the colour that God made me, I am to be the property of one he likewise made at His own good pleasure? Oh, Cesar! Cesar! it is the humiliation of slavery I feel, and that brings these tears to my eyes."

"Hush, Lucy, hush! You hab placed a hot coal in my heart—hush, Lucy Neal, and listen to what I hab got to say to you."

"I will listen, Cesar—say on."

"Well, Lucy, from de first moment I saw you, I lubbed you. I said to myself I shall never lub another, and what is my freedom without de freedom of Lucy Neal? Dis is not de worst estate to be upon, dere is some time to earn money, and in course ob years to buy de great ting—freedom. Lucy, you shall sabe all de dollars dat you can, and shall sabe all de dollars dat I get, for your freedom, Lucy—for your freedom."

"But what is to become of you, Cesar? do you think I could permit you to sacrifice yourself in such a way?"

"What you mean by sacrifice, Lucy Neal? If you hab your freedom I shall gib Massa Deal de slip, we will get to de coast ob a free state, and go to old England."

"I fear, Cesar, that this scheme is wild and impracticable; do not think of it, for at all events it is extremely dangerous. You know that it is not the value of a single slave which induces the owners of a plantation to spend hundreds of dollars in his recovery, but it is for the sake of example. I should never sleep in peace again, Cesar, if I really thought you entertained so fearful a project."

"And do you tink ob me enough, Lucy Neal, not to sleep if anyting hab happened to me? Dat is enough to make my heart double de size. I defy Massa Deal and all de oberseers in de world."

They had been strolling gently onward, during this brief conversation, and were now at a considerable distance from the ball-room. Lucy was about to make some reply to what Cesar had last said, when she fancied she heard a slight rustling among the sugar-canes to their left, and after a moment's pause, then she spoke hurriedly,—

"Cesar, you have said that you love me; if you really do, let me beg of you to let me go back to the ball-room at once, and alone. I fear we have been watched, and I am most anxious to ascertain who it is that has done so. Do not refuse me—do not refuse me, Cesar; I know what you would say, let me go, I implore you to let me go alone."

"I tell you what it is," cried Cesar, "I know dat young rascal, young Massa Adolphus Deal, look at you as if he lub you. Tell me, Lucy, if he speak to you, de damned white rascal, and I shall be under de agreeable necessity ob screw his neck."

"Hush—hush, Cesar! every word you say is fraught with danger—farewell now, and rest satisfied that you shall know all."

Lucy Neal darted from him in the direction of the ball-room, leaving Cesar to watch her form as long as he could, and in the dim light trace her fluttering garments.

CHAPTER II.

THE RESCUE.—A FRIEND IN NEED.—CESAR'S DANGER AND THE ESCAPE.—
MR. SLANKEY IN TROUBLE.

LUCY NEAL felt certain that her sense of hearing had not deceived her, but that some person had been lurking among the sugar-canes and probably overheard the very incautious remarks made by Cesar Bobb; remarks which certainly, if they were taken to the ears of Mr. Deal, would bring down upon him the unmitigated vengeance of the slave-owner.

She likewise had her own fears—fears of a sterner character than she chose even to communicate to Cesar, and as she darted onward with great rapidity, she more than once fancied she heard the sound of footsteps behind her, and occasionally paused to assure herself, if possible, that such was not the fact.

She was astonished at the distance she had gone during that brief conversation with Cesar, but Love is not a very accurate chronologist, and that brief dialogue had really been much longer than Lucy Neal imagined.

About half the distance had been traversed between the spot where she left Cesar, and the long shed in which the Coloured Ball was held, when she heard a voice behind her calling upon her imperatively to stop.

Habitual dread of those who had arrogated to themselves the title of "master" caused the young girl to shrink aside, and in another instant, in the dim light, she perceived the coarse, ungainly figure of Slankey, the preacher.

"Ah, ah! heathen!" he cried; "wretched heathen!—am I to be the chosen instrument to bring you into the ways of grace—speak, ungodly lover of dancing—speak!"

"I am no heathen," said Lucy; "I was brought up a Christian, and a Christian I am—perhaps a better one than many who arrogate to themselves the title."

"Wretched girl! have I come thousands of miles and deserted my native land—where in Exeter Hall I was a shining light, and where in the Chapel of Little Bethel, at Camden Town, I used to freeze up the hearts of sinners—have I come all this distance to be contradicted?"

"It is immaterial to me," said Lucy; "all I require is that you let me pass."

"Nay, stop, maiden, stop! although your skin is black you are comely to look upon—and—and as there's nobody listening, I may as well tell you that I love you—Lucy Neal—I do you the honour of loving you. Keep this a secret—I will give you money, and you shall be mine—mine, Lucy Neal."

Making a curious, slobbering noise with his mouth, the holy man advanced towards Lucy, who shrunk back with horror from his contaminating touch.

"Approach me not, approach me not," she cried; "my cries shall bring assistance."

"Nay, nobody will hear you."

"Off, sir! I say—beware—there is a Heaven above us which will not look down calmly upon such wickedness as this."

"What! am I to be repulsed by a black girl?"

"Yes, and doubly repulsed—oh, shame upon you!—to pretend to be a minister of that Heaven which knows and acknowledges no sin, and thus to address the words of passion to me. I have heard you exhort trembling mortals to repent, and now I, a young, timid girl, bid you repent and try to make your peace with Heaven.'

"This to me?"

"Yes, advance but another step and my cries shall reach Mr. Deal's house."

"Hark ye, girl! this is the worst night's work that ever you did—I'll be revenged as sure as my name is the Rev. Tobias Slankey—I am not one to be rejected upon slight grounds. You will repent of this."

"It shall be my business in the morning to tell my master."

"Tell him now," said the preacher, "your young master, Adolphus Deal—I hear his footstep—tell him now."

"Is it all settled," said a young looking man, of rough and brutal exterior, and about as ugly as anybody possibly could be, suddenly stepping forward—"is it all settled—have you told her, Tobias, that I condescended to take some notice of her?"

"Verily have I, Master Adolphus," said the preacher; "but she is obstinate, dreadfully obstinate, and will not listen to reason."

"Oh! pooh, pooh! nonsense! Lucy Neal, you understand me, you are pretty, I shall patronise you."

"Good God! what is the meaning of all this?" cried Lucy.

"Ha! ha!" whispered the preacher in her ear, "what do you think now of the state of affairs; where's your protector, and why don't you make your complaint?"

"Come, my pretty coloured wench," said Adolphus Deal, "we shall understand each other better by-and-by. I told Mr. Tobias here to bring you to my lodging in the left wing of the house, but somehow or another he has been a long, while about it."

Adolphus flung his arm round her waist, and was in the act of pressing her close to him, when a strange yelling sound came upon the night air, which might be human, but which certainly bore but a faint resemblance to that character.

"What is that—what is that?" cried Adolphus.

"Hush, hush!" cried Lucy Neal, as she clasped her hands, "I heard that cry once in Carolina, it was said there to belong to a spirit called the Mangoni, and who haunted some plantations, spreading terror and destruction among those who oppressed their coloured population."

"Nonsense, nonsense," cried the preacher, "an idle tale: Master Adolphus, I have to tell you that I surprised this maiden along with one of your slaves, by name Cesar Bobb."

"Indeed! the scoundrel shall smart for it in the morning."

"No, no, no," cried Lucy Neal, "not on him let vengeance fall; spare him, oh spare him; Mr. Deal, allow me to go back to the Coloured Ball and let the proceedings of this night be forgotten."

"That's a likely idea," said Adolphus Deal; "you shall be mine, Lucy Neal, and your opposition only fixes me more firmly in my determination. Tobias, just lay hold of her arm: we shall soon get her along."

"Do you think," whispered the preacher to him, "it's exactly prudent to use force?"

"Prudence be hanged! I'm partner with my father in the plantation, and I suppose I may do what I like with my own."

"No, no!—Mercy, mercy!—I appeal to you, Mr. Deal—to your better feelings—to have mercy upon me. This is an outrage which your father, your mother could not sanction; you have a sister too, who would blush to own you as a brother, were you guilty of this most dastardly and infamous act. Help, help! Oh, help!"

Scarcely had this cry time to raise an echo, when a fearful yell, like the shriek of some demon just escaped from bondage, burst upon their ears, and from among the sugar-canes there rushed a figure of tremendous height, with a most hideous countenance of enormous size, apparently covered over with small tufts of red wool, while the eyes glared with a strange phosphorescent appearance. The preacher and Adolphus Deal were paralysed with fear, while Lucy Neal sank upon her knees, clasped her hands, and scarcely knew whether to be thankful for this singular interference or not.

The huge being, with two strides came up to the startled group, and stretching out one brawny arm, he seized the lank hair of the preacher, while with the other he dashed off the cap that Adolphus Deal wore, and grappled him by the coarse red locks, resembling a door-mat, that were upon his head.

In another instant the singular apparition dashed their faces together with a force that made them recoil several yards from each other, and lay trembling and bleeding upon the ground. It then uttered some words in a language which Lucy Neal did not understand, and dashed off again among the sugar-canes.

It is a doubtful point whether Lucy Neal was not more alarmed at the singular apparition which her cries had summoned to her assistance, than she had been at those who so atrociously attacked her; for although she herself had threatened her assailants with some sort of visitation for their injustice towards her, she had been far from expecting such succour.

For a few moments she remained in a crouching attitude, to all appearance as incapable of motion as young Master Deal and the Rev. Tobias Slankey, neither of whom were in a condition to impede her progress now, if she herself had nerve enough to continue it.

This physical prostration, however, on the part of Lucy Neal, was but temporary, and after a silence of a few minutes' duration she roused herself to action, and with a cry of terror rushed onward again fleetly towards the large, irregular building where the ball was taking place.

It soon, however, appeared to her as if one of her old enemies must have recovered sufficient strength and recollection to pursue her, for she heard behind her the rapid sound of footsteps; once only she paused to listen, in order to be quite certain that her fears did not deceive her, and then terror added wings to her flight.

Whoever it was, though, who, amid the darkness of the night, thus rushed upon the footsteps of Lucy Neal, was swift of foot, and although she knew that few upon the plantation could compete with her in fleetness, she yet had the horrible consciousness that her pursuer was rapidly gaining upon her.

This certainly, while it for a time increased her speed, brought with it an amount of mental agony which soon reacted upon her physical energies. She glanced repeatedly behind her, to see if she could note anything decisive as regarded the character of her pursuer, but all she could see was a dusky form following along as if impelled by wings.

It was upon one of these occasions that the young girl caught her foot on some projection of the ground, and, after plunging forward a yard or two, she fell.

A shriek came from her lips as she felt a hand upon her arm, but what an exquisite relief it was to hear the well-known voice of Cesar Bobb exclaiming—

"Lucy, Lucy, what is de matter? You hab gib me such a run to-night as hab left no breath in me."

"Oh, Cesar, is it you—is it you indeed? Let me look upon you by the faint night light, and see, beyond the possibility of a doubt, it is you."

"Why, Lucy, what hab happened? You tremble like the soft leaves of de monca tree. I heard a cry, and I crossed de plantation and come after you. What hab happened, Lucy? tell me all."

"Yes, Cesar, yes, I will tell you all; but it must be upon one condition, and that is, that you will take no step in the business which I shall not sanction."

"I promise all—ebery ting—if you but tell me all."

Lucy then, as shortly as was consistent with the facts, informed Cesar of her perilous adventure, and of her singular and most unexpected deliverance. Probably a natural reserve, and a wish not sufficiently to excite the indignation of Cesar, so that he might become unmindful of his promise, induced her, in her narrative, to deal more leniently with both Adolphus Deal and the rev. gentleman than they deserved.

Had she said, however, but half of what she did, it would have been amply sufficient to rouse to the full the indignation of Cesar Bobb.

She could see his eyes glistening in the faint light, and when he spoke, his voice was so altered, that she could scarcely recognise it as belonging to the same person who could speak so softly to her of the affection which formed part and parcel of his very nature.

"I will hab revenge," he cried—I will hab revenge! "Dey may call me a slave, but dey shall hab a tale to tell of what de slave did under cruelty and oppression, and how he vindicated de honour which his masters knew not. I will hab revenge!"

"Cesar, Cesar," said Lucy, "is this the way you keep [your promise towards me? The narration of this night's proceedings should not have passed my lips if I had thought that promise was so soon to be forgotten."

No. 2.

"But, Lucy, you would not hab me in silence submit to dis?"

"Be satisfied the outrage was avenged, and that, too, by a being surely not of this world. I dread to think of the strange and powerful appearance that so opportunely took my part."

"No, no, Lucy—no, no—I must hab revenge! Since Adolphus Deal came on de plantation, all hab gone wrong. Massa White, de late oberseer, who would sometimes say a kind word even to a slave, was sent away, and John Grubson came, and since den the sound of de lash hab been heard upon de plantation."

"Yes—yes, Cesar; but our master, Mr. Deal, is not a bad man."

"No, Lucy—not a bad man, but de next thing to it, for he be weak enough to let other men be bad men about him."

"Now, hear me, Cesar, and I will make a proposition to you which ought to satisfy you: on condition that you take no steps yourself in this affair, I will promise to-morrow morning to go to the great house and make a complaint myself to Mr. Deal; he will, I think, afford me redress, more particularly too as I shall ask for nothing but protection—a word from him must stop a repetition of such a scene as that which has occurred to-night."

"Den you will promise, Lucy, to meet me here to-morrow night—one hour after sunset, when de day's work is ober."

"I will, Cesar, I will."

The events of that night seem to have established a much greater amount of intimacy between Lucy and Cesar than they had enjoyed before—a common sense of danger had now associated itself with their affection, and there needed no further explanations between them to prove that henceforward, even if their paths in life should be distinct and separate, their hearts would be together.

<hr />

CHAPTER III.

ADOLPHUS'S TREACHERY,—THE PLOT.—THE ALARM.—A NEW CONFEDERATE.

So severe had been the chastisement that Adolphus Deal and the preacher had received at the hands of the powerful and mysterious being who had made the practical experiment to ascertain which of their heads was hardest, that they lay for full a quarter of an hour without sense or motion.

It was Adolphus Deal who recovered first; for, although he had been terribly bruised, he seemed not quite to have suffered so much as the Rev. Tobias in the encounter.

He sat up and looked about him with a bewildered air for a few moments, but with a return of consciousness about all was sure to come a return of memory, and then he recollected how he had suffered by the preacher having been converted into a battering-ram by somebody of such power and strength that they could not be resisted.

Such persons as Adolphus Deal, if the individual be not present upon whom they would wish to reap their vengeance, generally look about for somebody else upon whom to expend some of their bottled-up wrath.

Who so ready then as the Reverend Tobias Slankey, who lay quite unresistingly upon his reverend back, with a tremendously black eye, and a stream of blood welling slowly out of his pious nose?

"It's all through your bad management, you methodistical thief," cried Adolphus Deal, as he struggled to his feet, and bestowed upon the reverend gentleman such a hearty kick that it went far towards his recovery—another and another of such salutations thoroughly roused Mr. Slankey, who roared out murder in stentorian accents; and then Mr. Adolphus Deal, finding that the exertion in his then present condition brought on a furious headache, sat down upon the ground and groaned aloud.

"What did you kick me for?" cried the Reverend Tobias, "I didn't do it—oh! my nose; it's smashed quite flat, and I'm quite sure that one of my eyes is gone: it must have been the devil himself."

"If it was," said Adolphus angrily, "it was all through you."

"Really, Mr. Deal," replied the preacher dolorously, "I'm to be pitied, I think, rather than accused—here's an object I shall present to my pious congregation—a nose, I do think, hammered quite flat, and one eye—I'm ruined and undone. Mr. Deal, I ask you for vengeance."

"Vengeance," half shrieked Adolphus, "yes, you've hit the right nail on the head there. I will have vengeance—just find out for me who it was, and you may make yourself quite easy about the vengeance."

"Mr. Deal, it seems that instead of kicking each other we ought to make common cause in this affair to find out who it is that has treated us so scurvily— Alas, alas! woe is me! I was going over to see Mrs. Macpherson, the charming and pious widow, at the Blue Bottle estate, to-morrow; but how can I go deprived of my nose's fair proportions and one eye?"

"Bother your nose!"

"Ah! Mr. Adolphus Deal, you were born to riches, and it don't matter to you whether you have a nose or not; but I, who have to scramble my way through this vale of tears, require every possible assistance. Dear me, I find I can hardly stand —I'm quite giddy; excuse me, Mr. Deal."

As he spoke, the Rev. Tobias Slankey took care to fling himself backwards upon Adolphus Deal, knocking that young gentleman over, for he had been sitting on the ground, and could not help himself; and Mr. Slankey, being much the largest and heaviest man of the two, nearly crushed Master Adolphus to death, before he condescended to get off him.

Probably Mr. Slankey's sudden giddiness arose from a vivid recollection of the kicks he had received when he had not exactly been in a state to resent them, and he took this method of paying off Adolphus for that piece of treachery.

Of the two now, the preacher was much the more able man, and, with many expressions of commiseration, he lifted up Adolphus, and led him carefully towards his home.

Young Deal said but little now—probably he fully understood the nature of his obligations to the Rev. Tobias Slankey, but thought that some more fitting time than that would be the best for reminding him of them.

"Truly," said the preacher, as they proceeded onward towards the large house inhabited by the Deal family, "truly, this night's proceedings have not been of that satisfactory character we could exactly have wished; but then, as I say, Master Deal, we must make the best of the affair—do nothing rashly, but let us consult over it to-morrow; and, probably, we may devise some means of yet accomplishing all you wish, and of having ample vengeance for the past. We had better be friends, Mr. Deal—do you see that we had much better be friends? for we may do each other a mischief if otherwise; while two heads are always better than one, in devising mischief against other people."

Adolphus did not speak, and the preacher continued, after a moment's pause, saying,

"Besides, you know, Mr. Deal, that it's absolutely necessary for the peace and safety of you and your family, that you should find out who and what it is has marred this night's work."

"Tell me," said Deal, in a low tone, "do you think it was anything human?"

"It felt uncommonly like it—I never had such a clutch taken of me before; it seemed about as strong as a steam-engine, and though, doubtless, there are immaterial things upon the earth, I don't think anything but flesh and blood could have served us as we have been served to-night. Is there a slave upon the estate could have done it?"

"Not one—not one—the height was prodigious, and the face—did you see the face ?"

" I saw something like a face strange and horrible."

"Yes, strange and horrible indeed. I shall not soon forget it; but I don't feel myself capable of talking of it now—meet me in the morning, Slankey, in my own private office, where, by the will of my father, I am forced to seem to be transacting business; meet me there, Slankey—but not before ten, for I shall not be stirring ; and, in the mean time, say nothing—be assured that, if I wait, it is that my revenge may be complete and ample."

" And it will not be amiss," said the Rev. Tobias, " that we take John Grubson into our council—a very worthy man, and, I should say, one who would stop at nothing, provided the price were sufficient."

" Agreed! John Grubson knows the estate better than either of us, and he may give some useful hint on the affair.   Good night—good night !"

CHAPTER IV.

CESAR AND HIS FRIEND.—MORNING AT THE PLANTATION.—THE SLAVE-DRIVER.

CESAR BOBB had been satisfied before he took his eyes again off Lucy Neal that she was in comparative safety : she did not go back again to the Coloured Ball, but allowed Cesar Bobb to escort her as far as was prudent towards a long range of huts, where the female slaves slept.

With mutual good wishes then they separated, and Cesar, although he was in almost too great a state of excitement to think of sleep, repaired to his own quarters.

He had been sufficiently long upon the estate to receive the indulgence of having a hut to himself, to which was attached a little patch of garden ground—the sale of the produce of which, at a neighbouring town, constituted one of the ways and means by which he hoped to save sufficient money, in course of time, to purchase the freedom of his beloved Lucy Neal.

It was with a heavy heart on this night that he opened the little wicket gate, which would lead him across the garden to the hut he had mainly built for himself. The brief night of that clime had almost passed away, and a strange, yellow, mysterious sort of radiance was slowly lighting up every object, while, at the same time, he could hear the soft sighing of a morning breeze among the cotton trees and sugar canes, which spread far and wide in almost every direction.

Upon this occasion—and perhaps it was the only one—he did not cast a look of approving pride upon the little enclosure through which he passed, but he took his way in silence direct to his cottage.

Of course its interior was much darker at that time than its exterior, but Cesar Bobb's eyes were good and clear, and he had not taken two steps into his dwelling before he became aware that there was some one present in it besides himself.

Upon any other occasion, Cesar Bobb would hardly have felt any degree alarm at this circumstance, because he was on sufficiently good terms with several of the slaves to warrant them in taking the liberty of going into his dwelling, when he was from home, and there waiting for him.   At that time, however, the events of the night had naturally brought on a considerable amount of excitement, and he cried in a harsher tone than usually came from his lips,—

" Who is there ?   Speak—speak at once, who is there ?"

" What, Cesar Bobb !" said a voice, " you not know your ole friend Pompey— poor ole Pompey—hi, hi, hi !—so damn ole he not worth his keep—hi, hi, hi !"

" No, Pompey—Goramighty bless me, I didn't know you, Pompey—any news, Pompey—sit yourself down—take a cup of sangaree, Pompey ?"

" Hi, hi, hi! Massa Deal may take a cup of sangaree, but not poor ole Pompey

—damn ole Pompey. I tell you what, Cesar, I've had a dream, so I thought I'd come to your hut, and ask you all about it—hi, hi, hi!"

"A dream!"

"Yes; I'll tell you what it is all about—I thought Massa Adolphus Deal, he make lub to Lucy Neal."

"De debil! You dream dat too late, Pompey—he hab make lub to Lucy Neal. But, Pompey, you ole man—now you come from Alabama like me—did you eber hear ob de *Mangoni*—tell me, Pompey, did you eber hear of de *Mangoni?*"

The old negro laid his hand upon Cesar Bobb's wrist, and held him for a moment with such a grip that it was almost too painful to bear, as he asked,—

"Hear ob de Mangoni—hear ob de Mangoni, you ask ole Pompey—yes, yes, yes—de Mangoni revenge for poor black fellow. De Mangoni coloured man's friend—de Mangoni tall and strong, and at de moment when not expected, but when de voice of de coloured people call out in de wilderness, and den white Christian—hi, hi, hi! de white Christian is de oppressor, he will come—yes, den de Mangoni come."

"I was brought away a boy from Alabama, and I am still young. I had heard ob de Mangoni, but neber beliebed it, Pompey, till to-night."

"Not belieb de Mangoni, Cesar! dat was berry wicked."

"No, Pompey; how could I eber belieb dat dere eber was a protected spirit to de coloured man when I've seen his flesh torn by de tong ob de oberseer's whip—when I've seen de wife he lubbed dragged from his arms to be sold and carried far from him—when I've seen his little children purchased before his face, and he struck down to the earth by a blow because he presumed to weep. Can you tell me, Pompey, dat dere is any protection for de coloured man—for de poor slave? Why, Pompey, my own sister was dragged into bondage, and den murdered—murdered because she sought dat which belongs to all—liberty. Where was de Mangoni den? I ask you, where was de Mangoni den?"

"Peace, peace," cried old Pompey, "peace; de Mangoni take his own time, and his own pleasure; but, Cesar Bobb, I hab advice to gib you. If it be true dat young Massa Deal do lub Lucy, you must submit—you must not oppose, you are but a slave, and she is but a slave."

"Pompey," said Cesar, as he rose, "Pompey, you hab been good friend to me since first I came on de plantation, and many kindnesses I hab had from you. You're an ole man, and hab got timid; but if you tink dat I will submit to hab my Lucy torn from me, you are mistaken. I want no such advice, Pompey."

"But what can you do?"

"Die in her defence."

"You would!" cried the old man with energy, "you would, Cesar? De man who would die for one he lubs may well lib for her. I did not mean dat you should submit. I only gab you dat advice to see what effect it would hab upon you. You hab answered after my own heart, Cesar; and now I tell you, even I, ole Pompey, dat you shall not die for Lucy Neal, but lib for her."

Without waiting for a reply, the old man rose, and with his bent form walked hastily to the door, and disappeared from the hut.

*   *   *   *   *   *

It is morning upon Mr. Deal's plantation; the brief night has passed away, and a bell is tolling to summon the slaves from their places of rest, in order to resume their labour.

The sun is but just skirting the horizon, but its slant beams are full of fire, and the air is becoming thick and hot, as the misty vapour which enshrouded all things at a very early hour rolls away. In a very few minutes troops of slave of both sexes and of all ages might be seen hurrying from the long range o wooden huts in which they dwelt, and proceeding to their different field occupations.

The bell ceased its monotonous sound, and then there issued forth from the wing of the principal mansion on the estate a tall man of coarse features, attired in a jacket and wide trousers of nankeen, while a straw hat with a prodigious brim shielded his countenance in some measure from the direct rays of the sun.

The expression of this man's face and the shape of his features were so decidedly Scotch that there was no mistaking him for any other countryman, and when he spoke, his language at once betrayed that he belonged to that land of pride, poverty, and selfishness.

A young negro boy handed him a long, lissom-looking cart whip, with which he executed three smart cracks in the air, each as sharp and loud as the report of a pistol—as a kind of warning to any stragglers who might not yet have come from the huts to commence their daily avocations.

This was John Grubson the overseer, certainly a man, take him for all in all, the like of whom nobody, who once knew much of him, ever wished to see again.

The comparatively mild sway of the former overseer had stripped slavery of much of its horrors, but John Grubson had made a proposal to the Deal family which was captivating to them, inasmuch as it made the overseer's salary dependent upon the proceeds of the estate.

Probably Mr. Deal himself would scarcely have listened to a proposition which his own common sense must have told him greatly hazarded the happiness of the poor beings who were committed by circumstances to his charge ; but then Mrs. Deal was a great showy woman, who never thought she had silks and satins enough, and Miss Deal was a young lady, whose expenses certainly far outran the allowance which Mr. Deal had thought sufficient for her.

Need we say, likewise, that Adolphus Deal was an extremely likely person to require as much money for his extravagance as he could possibly get, so Mr. Deal yielded to the proposition of John Grubson, backed as it was by his son and wife, although it certainly went against his own better judgment.

It was rather singular to observe how the lad who had handed John Grubson the whip, kept amazingly close to that individual—so close, indeed, that had the overseer, in the waywardness of his temper, wished to inflict a blow with the whip upon the lad, he would have found it impossible to do so.

Probably the little negro knew his customer, and, that he was in the habit of being so facetious occasionally, he kept a wary eye upon the countenance of Grubson, and it was not until he saw that the overseer's gaze was intently fixed upon some stragglers, who were creeping out of one of the log-huts at a distance, that he ventured to make a sudden start, and scamper off among the working gangs in the fields.

Grubson paid no attention to the escape of the boy ; he knew that he had the little wretch in his power, and that any power he chose to inflict upon him, would keep amazingly well till a more fitting opportunity.

He took from his pocket a small perspective-glass, and looked intently at the few negroes who were last in coming from the huts, so that he might identify them.

" Ha !" he said " I know them,' and then he rather implied than uttered what he would do, by giving the whip another crack in the air, after which he was about to walk off, when some one touched him on his shoulder, and turning round, he beheld his young master, Adolphus Deal, certainly looking a great deal the worse for his last night's adventure.

"Bless me, sir," said Grubson, with his Scotch accent, "what has happened?"

" Happened, be d——d !" said Adolphus, " come into my private office, I want to speak to you."

Grubson cast a longing look at the slaves and then at his whip, and then muttering to himself, " Well—well, all that'll keep," he turned to follow his young employer, for he looked upon Adolphus Deal much more in that light than he did his father, into the private office, which specially belonged to that specimen of humanity.

When they reached there, John Grubson, something to his discomfort, found the preacher there, for he certainly had no partiality towards Mr. Slankey ; but Adolphus Deal very quickly let him see that whatever was the subject-matter of discourse, the Rev. Tobias Slankey was to be made a participator, and consequently that it behoved him, John Grubson, to behave at all events with common civility to that uninviting individual.

"Look at me, Grubson," cried Adolphus, "look at me; did you ever see any body in such a state?"

"Ay," said the Rev. Tobias, "and when you have done, Grubson, looking at Mr. Deal, I shall trouble you to look at me,—and I shall ask you, if ever you saw a chosen vessel in such a state?"

"Why, certainly," said Grubson, "you both seem as if you had been in the wars; pray what has happened?"

"Did you ever hear of any thing or person called the Mangoni?"

"There is a superstition among the slaves of something of he kind; it is a kind of spirit, which they say interferes for their protection; although I certainly never heard of it doing them any good."

"At all events," said Adolphus impatiently, "it's to this inf rnal Mangoni, by it who it may, or what it may, that we owe our present position; but that can't be helped. Do you know a slave called Cesar Bobb?"

"Yes, a likely young fellow enough, but now and then inclined to be trouble-some, and more especially so on account of a young girl on this estate, called Lucy Neal."

"There, you've hit it!" added Adolphus, with an oath; "you may as well know it at first as at last, Grubson, that I like the girl, but I fear this confounded Cesar Bobb stands in the way."

"Then we'll soon make him stand out of the way," said Grubson. "The idea of a slave making himself troublesome in such an affair. What will the wll come to next, I wonder? Why they'd hardly believe such a thing in Scotland."

"Ah, but the girl has scruples likewise; you'd hardly believe it, but she repulsed me—ay, just like as if she had been a European."

"Indeed! Why don't you take the whip, and bring them all to reason?"

"Why, the fact is, my father has some prejudices, and you know that in Mr. White's time, the overseer that was here before you, the slaves had everything a great deal too much their own way; marriages used to be encouraged among them, and some foolish promises were given about not separating families, and so, what with one thing and another——"

The door at this moment was opened, and a servant of the household appeared, who said,—

"Massa Adolphus, if you please, Massa Deal want to speak wid you 'bout Miss Lucy Neal."

"With me! What's the meaning of this? Where is the governor?"

"In him own room—hi, hi!—Goramighty, sich a row 'bout Miss Lucy Neal."

"By Heavens!" muttered Adolphus, "she has actually had the infernal insolence to make a complaint. Come with me, both of you, we'll soon see the end of this; it's something new, I think, to be sent for to answer the charge of a slave; but come along, you'll understand it better by being present, Grubson."

CHAPTER V.

MR. DEAL'S JUSTICE.—MRS. DEAL'S MATERNAL SOLICITUDE.—THE PROMISE AND THE THREAT.

It was indeed true, notwithstanding John Grubson and Adolphus Deal thought it such a wondrous piece of insolence, that Lucy had indeed gone to his father to prefer her complaint concerning the last night's proceedings.

We have before remarked that Mr. Deal was rather a weak man than a wicked one, and whatever abstract notions he might have upon the subject of slavery, he had been accustomed all his life to derive a large income from his West Indian property; that he certainly had not the slightest intention of giving it up in consequence of any philanthropic notions about slaveholding.

He had always encouraged his slaves to bring their grievances to him, and though, under the rule of John Grubson, he saw much less of the few hundreds of beings in whom he claimed a property, than he had been in the habit of seeing, yet when Lucy Neal came and said she had a complaint to make, he did not like positively to refuse to listen to it.

Lucy's story had been simple and concise. She informed him how she had been at the Coloured Ball, which was held by special permission, and concealed nothing. She told him how she had walked out into the cool air with Cesar Bobb, and then how, after they had parted, she had been attacked by the preacher; and secondly, by Adolphus Deal."

Up to this point Mr. Deal's indignation had been sufficiently aroused to make Lucy fully hope and expect justice at his hands, but she saw the struggle that took place in his heart immediately that his son became implicated.

Upon that head she spoke, saying,—

"I ask for nothing, sir, but protection. I want nothing done—no censure, no reproval ; but, I want protection—that protection which we have all hitherto enjoyed from you. I want you to say, sir, that, although I am a slave, you will protect, and that I shall not be made a victim of, even by your own son."

It was at this moment that Mrs. Deal entered the apartment; and she saw by the vexed look of her husband, and the attitude of the young girl, that something more than common was going on.

"What is this?" she exclaimed, in a haughty tone. "More complaints of slaves! I thought we had done with all this since Mr. Grubson came, and the estate was kept in better order. What is it now?"

"Peace, peace," said Mr. Deal, "the girl is right enough. Lucy Neal, I will redeem the pledge I have frequently given to all who labour on my estate, you shall be protected. I will tell my son in your presence that I will not suffer him to persecute you."

"Our son!" exclaimed Mrs. Deal. "Do you mean Adolphus?"

"I am sorry to say that I do mean Adolphus. He and another have been annoying this young girl with solicitations which she has a right to resist, if she please."

"Oh, stuff, stuff! I don't believe a word of it. These creatures are always too forward. Go away, girl, go away, we can't be troubled with you, we don't believe a word about it, and, if it were true, it would be more your place to come to me, than to trouble Mr. Deal with such affairs."

"I did not come to you, madam," said Lucy, "because I did not think I should have justice at your hands. You're blind to your son's faults—you have aided and abetted him in more than one cruelty and act of oppression. I came, therefore, to my master."

This was an uncommonly true speech, but, sad to say, like many such, most uncommonly imprudent, for from that moment Lucy made a bitter and irreconcilable enemy of Mrs. Deal.

"There," cried that lady, in a violent rage, "there, Mr. Deal, all through your indulgence to negroes, I am to be insulted! Things have come to a nice pass indeed, when a slave under my own roof is to speak to me in such terms. My father, who kept one of the largest plantations in Bermuda, would have flayed her alive for half as much."

"Yes, missie," said a negro, who had come into the room on some domestic purpose, "yes, missie, hi—hi—hi! Your fader was called old bloody Tomkins, hi! hi! hi!"

"Silence—silence," said Mr. Deal. "This girl is right or wrong in her accusation, and that is all we have to do with. So that she gets justice, it is no matter whom she comes to for it."

"But am I to be insulted?" screamed Mrs. Deal.

"If I were you," said her husband, "I would carefully ask myself if this girl were right or wrong in what she has said."

Mr. Deal's tone was of that character, which led Mrs. Deal to the opinion that whatever might be his regret at the circumstances, he considered Lucy was tolerably correct in what she had said of the overdue partiality of Mrs. Deal for the beautiful Adolphus.

Rage for a moment or two choked the lady's utterance, during which Mr. Deal had given instructions to the negro, who apparently had such a lively recollection of old bloody Tomkins, Mrs. Deal's paternal relative, to search for Adolphus, and tell him to come to that apartment.

It was thus that the message found its way to the three worthies in the little office, and in a few moments they made their appearance in Mr. Deal's apartment.

"Here are more parties," said that gentleman, "than I asked for; but I don't know, Mr. Grubson, that I should not have sent for you, and as for you, Mr. Tobias Slankey, I am glad you are here to answer a charge which is brought against you."

"Against me! what dreadful wickedness!"

No. 3.

"That we shall see : the charge is made, and it is for you to rebut it ; at the same time, you must recollect, that I warned you off my estate some time since."

"I'm a chosen vessel, I'm a chosen vessel; of course the devil puts it into people's heads to say things against chosen vessels : what has the evil one got now to remark ?"

"And you, Adolphus," added Mr. Deal, "how is it that you have forgotten what was due to yourself as well as to me ?"

"I don't know what you mean, father,—what's it all about ?"

'Ah !" said the reverend gentleman, "there we have them,—what's it all about ? ask Satan, in the shape of a black girl, what's it all about."

"This young girl Lucy Neal has told me a story which your appearance tallies with most wonderfully."

"Appearance !"

"Yes, both you and this preacher exhibit injuries such as from her narration I should conclude you were likely to have received : now mark me, Adolphus, I do not wish any contention upon this affair, or even that you should suffer more mortification than is absolutely necessary, but once for all, I tell you I will not have the slaves upon my estate persecuted. You understand what I mean, and as to you, Mr. Slankey, I again warn you off my property, and if after this I catch you upon it, I shall institute a prosecution against you."

"Stop a bit, Mr. Deal," said the Reverend Tobias, "I can tell you the reason of all this. This charge is trumped up because Mr. Adolphus and I overheard a slave of yours, called Cesar Bobb, proclaim his own intention to run away, and inciting this young girl to do so likewise."

"No—no," cried Lucy, "he did not incite me."

"She all but confesses it."

"It is my pleasure," said Mr. Deal, "that no more be said about this business. I have no doubt whatever of the truth of what the girl has said about you two ; and I cannot perceive, Adolphus, although you look so triumphant, that the seduction of my female slaves is to follow, because they express an intention to run away ; probably those circumstances may be cause and effect the other way. And now go away, all of you ; and understand me fully, I will not have this young girl persecuted, and I particularly direct her to come to me if anything of the kind should occur, and she shall be protected, and remember, Mr. Slankey, you leave my estate."

Mrs. Deal had sidled round to the back of her husband's chair, from whence over his head, she, by telegraphic signs, intimated to Adolphus, that he need not mind what his father said about the affair, however, he might pretend to do so, and certainly he did great credit to the education which she had bestowed upon him.

Lucy had obtained her object, protection for herself ; and what was more, the only charge which could be brought against Cesar Bobb, and which might have involved him in some danger, had been duly made and passed away.

She rushed like a young antelope from the house to the plantation, her countenance beaming with satisfaction.

But what a marked contrast was presented by those, whom we may well call the conspirators, as they left Mr. Deal's apartment ! Adolphus had well understood his mother's signals, and leaving John Grubson and the preacher to walk from the house, and talk over matters as they liked, he went round to another entrance with a view of holding a confidential council with his mother.

Mrs. Deal thought it a very hard case that such a beauty as Adolphus should be crossed in any little bit of pleasantry he might project on the estate.

CHAPTER VI.

THE EXECUTION.—CESAR BOBB'S ANXIETY.—THE EVENING COMES AGAIN, AND
THE MEETING.

ONE may easily imagine with what intense anxiety Cesar Bobb waited during the whole of the day, to know how Lucy Neal had prospered in her application for protection to Mr. Deal.

It was the custom on that estate, although not universally so, as regarded slave property, for the male and female gangs of slaves to work at different portions of the field, so that poor Cesar had no opportunity of getting sufficiently near Lucy Neal to ask her a question upon the subject.

Perhaps, under ordinary circumstances, he might at some time of the day have managed this much, but as it was, he could well see that John Grubson kept a more than usually strict eye upon him.

An incident occurred during the course of the day likewise, which, if anything could have tended more than another, to increase Cesar Bobb's desire to run away, was just what would have had that effect. The neighbouring estate belonged to a Mr. Samson, who was some such another as Mrs. Deal's father, and was quite as much entitled to a sanguinary addendum to his name.

From that property a negro had absconded, and was during the course of the morning brought back to undergo whatever punishment Mr. Samson might project.

This punishment consisted in being tied hand and foot, and smeared all over with molasses, so that myriads of insects came from far and near, and completely covered up the unhappy wretch, penetrating his skin in every possible way with their powerful stings, until his blood mingling with the molasses, made a frightful repast for millions of the insect creation.

This execution, for it could be termed nothing else, inasmuch as the poor wretch died before sunset from exhaustion, took place upon the very verge of Mr. Samson's estate, so that it was witnessed by almost all the slaves on the Deal property.

It probably did strike terror into many, but Mr. Deal, if he had seen some of the flashing eyes that exchanged looks during the progress of that day, would have very much doubted the good effect produced among his own slaves, at all events, by such a spectacle.

John Grubson, too, thought it would be just as well to improve the occasion, as the Scotch Presbyterian preachers have it, and he accordingly applied the whip on that day with a more than usual vigour.

The longest and weariest day that ever shone out of the heavens must have an end at last, and most welcome was it to every one on the plantation to see the soft shadows of evening creeping on, and to know that toil was over.

The regular day's work closed immediately that the sun's disc dipped below the horizon; then it was that the bell again tolled, and that the slaves had time, if they chose so to occupy it, to do a little work in their own land allotments.

We may well imagine that it was little indeed Cesar thought of doing on that evening; but, on the contrary, he hastened to the spot where he had appointed to meet Lucy Neal, burning with impatience to hear from her lips an account of her interview with Mr. Deal.

He was much earlier than the time appointed, and the leisure he had he carefully employed in scrutinising the spot, and listening intently with the hope of detecting if any person was playing the eavesdropper upon his privacy.

With all the acuteness, however, that he could bring to this task, he did not succeed in discovering any one, and he leaned against a tall tree, waiting impatiently for the arrival of her whose fate he felt henceforward would be his fate, and for whose sake he was ready to do and dare as much as ever a hero of tale or legend did or dared, for the fairest she of Christendom.

Dark thoughts swelled in his breast, as he thought over what he was and what he might be ; he knew to a fraction how much money he had hidden beneath a stone in his little garden,—a more sad reckoning still; he knew to a fraction how much more he required before he could, with the slightest probability of its acceptance, think of making an offer for the freedom of Lucy Neal.

The time appeared frightfully distant, reckoned by the past, before this could be accomplished. His heart almost died within him at the sorrowful contemplation.

But soon other and better thoughts possessed him, for through the dim night air he saw, flittering like some gentle spirit towards the trysting-place, his own Lucy Neal.

In a few moments she reached the spot, and now, for the first time, she did not chide Cesar because he clasped her in his arms.

Their conference at first was very hurried, for she had much to tell him, and when he became quite exultant at the tide affairs had taken, and at the protection Mr. Deal had promised, she gently checked him, saying in her own soft tones—

" I am sure I did right in making known to Mr. Deal what had happened, and likewise I felt, Cesar, that by so doing I could not make our situation worse, but I doubt much if I have made it better ; our enemies are as bitter as ever, but they will proceed with more caution, perhaps."

" I do defy dem all while I hab you by my side, my sweet Lucy Neal."

" 'Tis well to defy them, but still not well to be too confident. I pray you therefore, Cesar, to be very careful in what you say, and what you do ; those who are enemies to you will watch now with the greatest perseverance for some means of doing you harm ; they will think no toil or trouble is sufficient, and perhaps some plot may be laid even for your destruction, for it is grievous to think what wickedness will stoop to."

" Fear nothing, Lucy, I will be careful, and is not de Mangoni 'pon our side ?"

" I dread, Cesar, to think of that terrible visitation."

" Do not dread de Mangoni, did it not rescue you ? and be it what it may, it hab my best tanks, and now, Lucy, I must tell you that it will be three years, three lucky years, too, more, before I can go to Massa Deal, and say, here is de dollars for de freedom of Lucy Neal."

" Heed not that—heed not that ! think of yourself, Cesar, and not of me so much. What would my freedom be without yours ?"

" If you were free, I could——."

" Hush, Cesar, hush ! make no imprudent declarations ; one of such has been already overheard, much to your prejudice ; we don't know what spies may be lurking near us now,—say nothing—say nothing."

Cesar was not so foolish as not to feel the full force of this appeal ; and at all events whatever mental resolutions he might come to, one thing was perfectly clear, and that was, that he had better keep them to himself, insomuch that although he had well searched, as he thought, the spot, he of course could not arrive at a positive certainty that he was not watched.

" Lucy," he said, " I will be prudent for your sake, and not one word shall pass my lips dat Adolphus Deal can take hold ob to my prejudice—hush ! what sound dat?"

They both listened, for certainly some sound had come from among the trees, and thick bushes close to where they stood.

And silence continued for the space of about a minute, and then something came rustling among the leaves of the tree nearest to them, and a stone fell at their feet. Cesar picked it up, and saw that a piece of paper was folded round it, but the blessings of mental culture had not reached Cesar in sufficient abundance to enable him to read, so he handed it to Lucy Neal, who deciphered upon it the words,—

Beware of Snake Hollow !"

That was all, but the warning was significant enough, for the Snake Hollow was a piece of ground lying in a low swampy place covered with reeds and coarse luxuriant vegetation through which Cesar had to pass in his road homeward to his hut.

It was true enough that he need not traverse that route; but as it was by all means the most direct one, the caution, let it come from whom it might, could not be said to be thrown away.

"I told you as much, Cesar," exclaimed Lucy Neal. "Danger yet threatens you; you have foes abroad, and for my sake let me implore you not to return to your hut by Snake Hollow."

"Fear noting, Lucy; to be forewarned is to be forearmed, and you may depend dat I shall escape. You must promise to meet me here ebery night."

"Scarcely every night, Cesar, but every night that I can you may depend upon my being here; you know I have to assist Dinah in a world of things, and we have but little time: there are lands which I have read of, where there is long twilight after the sun has set, but it is not so with us; darkness drops down at once, and it is only by the night-light that people work."

"Dat is true—dat is true; and I too hab to raise de fruit and de vegetable to get dollars to lay up in store for your freedom, Lucy Neal."

Lucy in vain tried to get a positive promise from Cesar, that he would not return to his hut by Snake Hollow, but it was evident he had some idea of his own upon that subject, and, although he promised every kind of care and diligence, she could not get him positively to say that he would not traverse that route.

She felt that it would be useless to attempt to extort from him a promise, and perhaps with some confidence in the mysterious being who had already protected her, and to whom likewise she attributed the warning scrap of paper that had been coiled round the stone, she bade Cesar adieu.

He looked after her slight agile form as far as he could see it, and when it was completely lost to him in the darkness, and deep shadows likewise, which were thrown by the tall trees, he turned himself to pursue the route which lay open to him.

"Yes," he said, "I will go through Snake Hollow, but I will be careful—I will show dem a trick I learned in Alabama, and find out what de danger is."

CHAPTER VII.

THE ATTEMPTED MURDER.—MR. SLANKEY'S MISHAP.—THE RUIN AT THE HUT.

FOR some few minutes after Lucy Neal had left him, Cesar appeared to be ruminating over the step which it would be advisable first to pursue, and then suddenly apparently making up his mind, he walked into the wood close at hand, and taking a knife from his pocket, he cut a long thick bough from one of the trees, and with that in his hand he walked hastily onward to his destination.

Snake Hollow, which has been already frequently mentioned, was a desolate and uncomfortable-looking track of land, from some cause or another, certainly not from drainage: it was always damp, and hence a thick undergrowth of all kinds of rank vegetation grew up about it, making it a place not at all desirable to pass through, inasmuch as it was the resort of many of the most ferocious of the insect tribe, and more than once some rather ugly specimens of the snake species had been observed, coiled up among the bushes.

It was from this latter circumstance, that it took its name—Snake Hollow, and it was generally avoided by the negroes, who had a notion that it was an unlucky place to pass through, and so it certainly was, if by any accident a tolerably-sized specimen of the serpent tribe laid hold of the passenger.

But these were not fears which induced Cesar to forego his intention; he did not question for one moment but that there was danger,—that he fully believed, and his great object was to know as nearly as possible the shape it would assume.

His proceedings, as he approached Snake Hollow, will appear to be rather singular, but we shall soon find that he has good reason for what he is about.

Before he fairly reached the spot, he took off a jacket that he wore, and so fastened it, and buttoned it, and tied it about the bough of a tree that he had cut down, that with the exception of a head, it represented the bust of a man pretty tolerably. He then placed his straw hat above that again, and keeping the singular-looking apparition he had thus constructed in his hand, he came quite on the margin of Snake Hollow.

Then he immediately commenced singing, in a loud tone, so that there should be no mistake about his identity,—

> " I hab no oder lub just now,
>   But oft wid transport feel,
> How dear to all my heart and life
>   Is my sweet Lucy Neal.
> Her heart is whiter dan de snow,
>   Young Cupid set his seal
> On de rosy lips and flashing eyes
>   Of my sweet Lucy Neal :
>   Oh, my sweet Lucy Neal,
>   If I had you by my side,
>   How happy I should feel !

> " I see her 'mong de sugar canes,
>   My lub I can't conceal,
> But creeping close, I whisper then
>   Oh, my sweet Lucy Neal.
> De oberseer oft come by,
>   His whip he do reveal,
> But little heed I dat sharp crack,—
>   I tink of Lucy Neal.
>   Oh, my sweet Lucy Neal,
>   If I had you by my side,
>   How happy I should feel !"

" Hi ! hi ! hi ! bery good song, and bery well sung. Goramighty, I could make lots of poetry about Lucy Neal. I lub her, and she lub me—

> " Oh, my sweet Lucy Neal,
>   When I hab got you by my side,
>   How happy I do feel!

" I wonder," muttered Cesar to himself, " whether any dam rascal hab heard all this ?"

He had now got fairly within the precincts of Snake Hollow, and he stopped to listen for several minutes before he proceeded but he heard nothing ; a stillness deep and profound reigned on the spot, and Cesar almost began to think that the warning was superfluous, or at all events that, if any attempt against him had been projected, the parties had given it up again from some cause or other.

This stillness, however, profound as it was, did not induce him to forego the caution which he had made up his mind to exercise, nor the Alabama trick which he had talked of playing, and which consisted of this :—

The light in this Snake Hollow was so very dim, that certainly nothing but the dusky bulk of any human figure moving through it could have been observed even by the keenest eyes, and Cesar had no reason to suppose that his enemies possessed anything beyond the ordinary amount of visional acuteness.

He cautiously stooped down until he got fairly upon the ground, but as he did so, he kept elevating the mock-figure until it supplied his place, and as the tall grass and strangled brushwood was in every place sufficiently high to reach a man's knees, the delusion was a very perfect one indeed.

As Cesar crept along, he held the figure so nicely adjusted that it just took the movement of a man walking, and he increased the delusion by ever and anon bursting into the burden of his love ditty regarding Lucy Neal ; now and then laughing too in the manner peculiar to his race, and altogether affording the fairest opportunities for his recognition, that any one who was lying in wait could have possibly wished.

In this manner he had traversed about half the space called Snake Hollow, and had just come opposite to some very thick brushwood, when bang went a gun-shot and that again was immediately succeeded by another.

In an instant Cesar's cap which he had placed on the top of the bough fell to the ground shattered by two or three bullets ; and, raising a strange unearthly kind of shriek, Cesar let the bough drop to the earth, and then waited calmly and silently for what should occur next.

" Ah ! my fine fellow," said a voice, " I think I had you there—you'll be no more trouble to anybody, confound you—a nice thing indeed that a chosen vessel, such as I am, should take a fancy to a pretty black girl, and be annoyed by such a fellow as you."

So saying, the Reverend Tobias Slankey—for it was he who had fired the shot—strode forward from his hiding-place towards the spot where he had seen, as he supposed, the figure of Cesar Bobb fall to the ground.

It was quite evident he considered he was advancing to a dead body, or at all events to a sufficiently disabled man to offer not a particle of resistance, and indeed from what he said might be very well gathered what he thought upon the occasion.

" I think I nabbed you," he muttered, " for I flatter myself I'm a tolerably good shot ; but still there's nothing like being quite sure, so I'll just get a light and see for myself ; I think this ought to be a good lesson to those dammed black fellows not to interfere when chosen vessels take likings of their own."

The Reverend Tobias Slankey knelt down by the side of Cesar, and after some fumbling in his pocket he produced a phosphorous box and some matches, one of the latter of which after several ineffectual attempts he succeeded in igniting.

Scarcely, however, had the smallest blue flame began to issue from it, than with a strange unearthly scream, just such an one as he had uttered when he pretended to be shot, Cesar sprung up and grappled with him. This attack was so sudden and unexpected that the preacher, although a powerful man, could make no resistance, and in another moment Cesar was astride upon his back pressing him face downmost to the ground, to the great danger of his suffocation among the mass of weeds in which his head was getting fast embedded.

" I am de Mangoni," growled Cesar, in a deep, hollow voice. " I am de Mangoni ; you mistake me for Cesar Bobb, but he went home another way."

The Reverend Mr. Tobias made no reply, for, to tell the truth, he could not, nor was his sense of acuteness much enlivened by some hearty cuffs which Cesar gave him as he lay.

" Do you hear ? I am de Mongoni, and as you wanted to take de life of one of my people, I must skin you."

The reverend gentleman was still silent ; he did make a faint attempt to speak, but the moment he opened his mouth, Cesar gave his head a job downward, so that he was half choked with sand, and rendered more incapable than ever of making the slightest appeal for mercy.

It was well for the Reverend Mr. Tobias Slankey that Cesar's victory over him had been so complete, for otherwise there can be very little doubt that he would have come by his death. As it was, however, his assailant, although he had ample provocation to do so, evidently shrunk from taking the life of a man who was so completely in his power.

An assassin deserves no quarter, and probably Cesar felt that such was the case, but at the same time the generous spirit of the young negro shrunk from perpetrating what looked like a murder, although in reality it was but a just execution.

" You villain," he said, " de Mangoni wishes to know who set you on to dis matter—eh, who set you on?"

Mr. Slankey was past speaking now, for along with a lot of wet sand several insects had got into his mouth, and he laid his hand upon something that felt so much like the back of a snake that he fairly fainted away.

"Eh, what you say?" cried Cesar, as he gave his reverend opponent's head another punch; "what, you say noting?—Goramighty, he hab faint away or go dead; no, no, not dead—chosen vessels take a lot ob killing, Let me see, what hab I got to do now? Hi! hi! hi! When we all come up at the last judgment, he'll say it wasn't him. Hi! hi! I must put one mark upon him."

Cesar then turned the preacher over upon his back, and kneeled upon him, so as chold his head jammed between his knees; he reached out his hand for the gun which Tobias Slankey had laid out of his hand in order to procure a light.

He took from the lock a small flint which had a sharp, serrated edge, by the aid of which Cesar succeeded in carving a cross upon the Rev. Tobias' forehead, taking care to go as deep as the bone in the process.

If anything was calculated to have a revivifying effect upon the reverend gentleman, this certainly was, and he kicked enormously, which, however, had not the slightest effect upon Cesar, who sat grinning upon his chest like an incubus.

It was a double-barrelled gun—both had been discharged; but a very little searching in Mr. Slankey's pious pockets revealed a powder flask more than half full, and Cesar, pressing the spring, very liberally sprinkled his forehead all over with it. Then, as if for a wager, he rubbed it into the wound, thus making sure that the cross would remain indelible as a frontispiece to the pious countenance of the chosen vessel.

In vain now Mr. Slankey roared and spluttered, fought and screamed; all he got by such opposition consisted in sundry cuffs on both sides of the head until he was silent. Then, placing his mouth close to Slankey's ear, and making a hollow tube with his hand, Cesar shrieked in deafening accents, "De Mangoni—de Mangoni—remember de Mangoni!"

In another instant he was gone, and at a pace which would have defied pursuit, had the preacher been in a condition to undertake it. He went towards his own dwelling.

Not long was Cesar in reaching there, but he almost staggered beneath the blow which Fate then gave him. His trim little garden, in which he had taken so much pride, and from which he expected to raise the dollars with which to emancipate Lucy Neal from slavery, was a ruin; some ruthless hands had been there, and everything was destroyed.

CHAPTER VIII.

ADOLPHUS AT HOME.—HIS IMPATIENCE FOR SLANKEY.—POMPEY'S MESSAGE.—
THE EXPEDITION TO SNAKE HOLLOW.

WHILE these affairs were being transacted, Adolphus Deal was not idle, although, in reality, he was an idler in every sense of the word.

He had no just or profitable occupation; and if it be true that Satan—provided there be a Satan, which in these days is getting rather a doubtful proposition—always finds some work for idle hands to do, according to Dr. Watts, he certainly cut out a very pretty piece of business for Master Adolphus Deal, and we may suppose that gentleman waiting for its consummation.

But, first of all, we may as well state that Adolphus found his mother a great aid and assistance in all his gentle and pleasant desires and amusements.

After the interview which had taken place in the morning between him and his father, it must have been a great comfort for him to find his mamma of so extremely different an opinion.

In fact, the real truth was, that Mrs. Deal was an eminently and grossly selfish woman, and she did not at all see why her gratification, or the gratification of her son, should be impeded by what she considered ridiculous scruples; so that when, n obedience to the telegraphic signals he had received, Master Adolphus made his way to his mother's apartment, she was loud in her invectives against his father, or what she called taking part with the blacks against his own flesh and blood.

"And, my dear," she said, "as for that hussey, Lucy Neal, it shows what a brazen-faced thing she is, to have the impudence to come and make a complaint at all about such a matter."

"Yes, bother her!" said Adolphus; "but, you see, the vernor takes part with the blacks."

"He does, my dear, and it's a wonder to me if it don't come over to him one of these days; but as for that Lucy Neal, I'm disgusted with her—pretending to be so mighty modest, indeed."

"Yes, it's all gammon, of course."

"Of course, it is, my dear; and, what's more, if she had been so modest as she pretends, she ought to have put up with anything rather than come and spoken upon such a subject."

"Yes, that's my idea."

"Well, never you mind, my dear; just you be quiet for a little while, and we'll soon see what's what, and whether these blacks are to give themselves such airs and graces or not; it's really dreadful to think of it—a parcel of low wretches of slaves, of course, made on purpose by God Almighty to wait on other people, and coloured black, so that there should be no mistake about them."

"Yes, of course; that's my idea."

"And a very proper one, too, Adolphus; but, however, as I say, don't you mind about it—just let this little affair blow over, and all will be well."

"I will, only I'll serve out somebody that I know."

"Well, my dear, of course, it's natural enough that you should serve out some people; only, if it's any of these black fellows, all I've got to say is, mind you don't get hurt."

"Oh, I'll take care,—you may depend upon that."

"Hush, don't say anything before your sister Marianne—I hear her coming."

The door opened, and Miss Deal, of whom we have really not much to say, made her appearance. She was a very average sort of young person, without any very good qualities, and without any very bad ones; fond of dress, and most unquestionably looking for a husband.

She was rather showy in appearance, and she certainly had to some extent a leaning towards her mother's opinion, that the blacks were expressly created to be the slaves of Europeans, and that they were so coloured on purpose to make up a proper distinction.

She probably might have shrunk from fancying that the young girls upon the estate were to be sacrificed to Adolphus's pleasure, for that was an opinion which only Mrs. Deal's mature judgment could master.

Adolphus was not anxious that his sister should ask him any questions with regard to his disfigured face, whereon appeared sundry contusions, so he made the best of his way out of the apartment upon her appearance, and again repaired to his own room, to concert measures with his confederates, Slankey and Grubson, for the accomplishment of his purposes.

Adolphus had great hopes that the preacher and John Grubson, between them, would be able to do something that would place Lucy Neal in his power.

What was the result of the various consultations that took place that day between the conspirators, as they fully deserve to be called, we shall be able to discover by the circumstances consequent upon them, without troubling the reader of this most veritable narrative with all the *pros* and *cons* that heralded those events.

Suffice it that Adolphus, acting, no doubt, under judicious advice, did not make any effort the whole of that day to disturb the security of Cesar Bobb, or press his suit upon Lucy Neal, who was not without her apprehensions that he would do so, despite the injunctions of his father.

The whole affair had now, however, assumed such an aspect, that it certainly behoved Master Adolphus to be a little more careful than usual. To be sure, he knew that his father, take him altogether, was a man of weak resolves, and not to be much depended upon in what he had to do; but then Mr. Deal had upon this occasion spoken out with much more than his usual firmness.

It was therefore just possible that he might act with more than his usual firmness, and if so, Adolphus might make the unwelcome discovery too late, that the governor, as he called him, had the power to turn him completely off the estate, and send him, with a small allowance, elsewhere.

This was a contingency which, although not very probable, unless it was violently provoked by him, Adolphus, was yet a matter of possibility, so he resolved to see first what stratagem would accomplish for him, before he tried to satisfy his revenge by more forcible means.

There can be no doubt, however, but that the murder of Cesar Bobb was a thing agreed upon by the three villains, namely, John Grubson, Adolphus Deal, and the pious Mr. Tobias Slankey. The signal failure of that most atrocious attempt we are already well aware of, as well as the rather mournful consequences which ensued to the chosen vessel who had rashly undertaken the somewhat hellish job.

When night came, Adolphus did not join the family, but went out, declaring his intention of taking a walk to some of the neighbouring estates, but he did not go far from the house before he turned again, and, under cover of the trees, got back to that wing of it which was in the occupation of John Grubson, the overseer, who was waiting his coming with evident expectation.

They sat down together to drink some spirits and water, for the Scotch slave-driver was fond of his glass, and it would have been odd indeed if Adolphus had been destitute of any moral or social vice whatever.

"Do you think we shall succeed?" said Adolphus. "Mr. Slankey seemed to be very positive that he should be able to shoot him as he passed through Snake Hollow."

"Faith he did, Mr. Adolphus, and perhaps he has his own reasons for being so positive. I dare say he will succeed. He has a good double-barrelled gun with him, and I saw him put three slugs into each barrel. I know, too, that he is a good shot."

"In that case, then, the only doubt is, whether Cesar will pass by the Snake Hollow at all to-night?"

"I have little doubt of that. Slankey says that he will be sure to do so, on his route back to his own hut, after having a meeting at an appointed spot with Lucy Neal."

"Confound the fellow's impudence. The idea of a black fellow like that having the impudence to stand between me and—who is that? Some one is knocking at the gate."

The overseer rose, and found that the knocking proceeded from old Pompey, who, nearly bent double with years, and apparently extremely infirm, walked within the place, as he said,—

"Oh, Massa Grubson, me bery much beg you pardons for disturb you, but will you be good enough to let Cesar Bobb go wid me to Massa Samson's hut to see old friend ob mine? hi! hi! hi! Old friend going to get emancipated all along ob dying. Hi! hi!"

"Cesar Bobb, do you say? Where is Cesar Bobb just now?"

"At my hut, massa, and been the last hour; I spose we may go. Hi! hi! hi! I too dam ole to go alone, you see, massa."

"Yes, be off with you," said Grubson; and then turning to Adolphus he said, "It's of no use, you see, to-night. Tobias's information is not correct. Cesar is with old Pompey, and has no appointment with Lucy Neal to-night, so he will miss him, and only have the pleasure perhaps of catching an ague in Snake Hollow for his pains."

"Hi! hi! hi!" laughed old Pompey to himself, as he walked away, "you bery clever fellow, and bery great rogue, Massa Grubson; but old Pompey git de better of you dis time, me think for all dat. I shall one day, Massa Grubson, let you know what is like to happen to you. Hi! hi! hi!"

CHAPTER IX.

THE SEARCH IN SNAKE HOLLOW.—THE STORM.—THE COMPLAINT, AND ITS CONSEQUENCES.

AFTER this kind of proof of an alibi, which had been adduced by Pompey concerning the whereabouts of Cesar Bobb, the confederates could hardly expect Mr. Tobias Slankey to be at all successful in his expedition.

Probably at some future time in the course of this history we shall become aware of the reasons which influenced old Pompey in coming thus gratuitously to the aid of Cesar. It certainly seemed as if he either knew that the Rev. Tobias Slankey was to receive some injury at the hands of Cæsar, or that he actually had received it, and consequently that Cæsar's safety would be to that extent at all events compromised.

"Well, Grubson," said Adolphus, "shall we leave the preacher to wait on his fruitless expedition, or shall we go and warn him that he may come away."

"It don't much matter either way," remarked John Grubson, "only perhaps it aint worth while exactly to let him see that we are altogether unmindful of his comforts; so perhaps it will be as well, Master Adolphus, to walk down to Snake Hollow and relieve him: will you do so, or shall I?"

"Let us both go—I feel inclined to get out into the open air; and at all events I would not go alone, for Snake Hollow is about as uncomfortable a spot as one could very well imagine."

" Well, Master Adolphus, I must confess it's not a choice place, nor altogether one I should go to on a pleasure excursion: so I don't care if I leave your company."

They each put on their hats, and likewise a kind of wrapper not for the purpose of producing heat ; but to keep out the disagreeable chilling damps that arise at night from the hollow place into which they were about to go.

There was such a stillness in the air as is seldom met with—a stillness quite amounting to solemnity.   And it certainly had all its effects on the imagination of Adolphus Deal, for he crept closer to his companion, and the few remarks he did make were made in a whisper.

Upon John Grubson the stilly night had no such effect, and he certainly seemed rather surprised that his companion should allow it to have such power over him.

" It is very dark," said Adolphus ; "don't you think, there is something strange and heavy in the air ?"

" There may be a storm brewing," replied John Grubson, as he glanced up at the night sky, "that is possible enough ; there may be a storm brewing ; and if so, I can tell you, Master Adolphus, that I shan't care to be anywhere but at home."

" Oh, if it's only a storm, we shall easily get some shelter."

" Shelter—perhaps you've never seen a storm on this property or any of the contiguous ones."

" I certainly have not."

" Ah, I thought as much, or you'd never have talked of getting shelter ; it's quite out of the question ; where are you to get shelter except amongst the trees ; and a storm here makes little of pulling up half a dozen of them by the roots."

John Grubson went on further to illustrate by several anecdotes the immense power of storms in that locality ; until by the time they had arrived at Snake Hollow, Adolphus was in a very tolerable state of fright, and wished himself back again with all his heart.

As they neared] the margin of the strange and desolate spot which it had been fully intended that night should be the scene of a cold-blooded and deliberate murder, Grubson partially raised his voice, with the expectation that the preacher would recognise it, calling out,—

" Hilloa ! no game in Snake Hollow to-night ?"

There was no answer, but almost at the same moment there came a slow rumbling noise, as if some waggon, with iron wheels, was careering along the earth, and at the same moment a very light wind which had been playing around the branches of the trees, entirely ceased, and a calm ensued that was perfectly death-like in its character.

" Did you hear that," cried Adolphus, " did you hear that?"

" I did," replied John Grubson," and the sooner we warn our friend the parson to seek shelter, and then get it ourselves, the better ; for, if I am not tremendously mistaken, there is really a storm brewing which will commence with a squall that will sweep all before it."

" You think so ?   Let us be off at once—yet no, wait a minute. I must have my gun ; don't you recollect Tobias Slankey has got my double-barrelled gun ? Hilloa, Slankey—Slankey, why the devil don't you answer ? "

Adolphus ran impetuously forward for the sake of recovering his gun, perhaps not so much for its value as on account of his anxiety to get into his own hands again what might perhaps seriously implicate him in a very troublesome transaction.

" Slankey—Slankey, where the deuce are you ? Confound it, what's that ?"

" A groan," said Grubson, as he darted forward, and dashing aside the thickets that stood in his way, he came upon what seemed to be the lifeless form of the preacher, and which was just discernible by a strange yellowish kind of light that was creeping over the sky.

" Something has happened to him."

" Is he dead ?"

" I think not dead, but seriously hurt. Speak, Tobias, speak, if you can, and if you don't want to be left here as a prey to the wild beasts that prowl about in the night."

It would appear as if the preacher were just sufficiently sensible to hear that some words were addressed to him, for he uttered another low groan, but he did not move hand or foot.

"Here's a pretty affair!" continued Grubson, "somebody has fallen foul of him or else he has hurt himself in some way, and, by Heaven, here comes the squall!"

There was a strange rushing, wailing sound in the air, quickly followed by the crashing of the boughs of the trees, and in another instant Adolphus found himself dashed to the earth, and held firmly down by some great arm of one of the leafy denizens of the forest that had either wholly fallen, or had parted thus with one of its chief members.

The squall, for such it was, only lasted while any one with tolerable quickness might have counted twenty, and then the wind assumed the appearance of a more regular gale, while now and then there came a rattling peal of thunder on their ears, and at intervals the scene was lit up by a lurid flash of lightning, which, for a brief period, lent its brilliancy to every object.

"Help, help! oh, help!" cried Adolphus, as soon as he found he was not hurt so seriously but that he could cry out for assistance. "Help, help! John Grubson, I'm smothered; my mouth's full of sand, and there's a tree on top of me."

It so happened that Grubson, who had more experience in these affairs, had remarked growing close at hand a particular species of tree, which he knew usually, by its pliant nature, resisted the sudden squalls, which were incidental to the climate, and accordingly when he heard the rushing sound of the coming tempest, he had taken good care to provide against its fury, by clinging to this tree, so that it had really passed him uninjured, with the exception of a tolerable amount of fright, for if the tree to which he clung had given way, his destruction would have been inevitable.

"Well," he cried, "I suppose you're not much hurt, as you can call out so lustily."

"I don't know, oh, I don't know," said Adolphus. "I think I must be crushed to death, for I'm held down in such a way, that I can't move hand or foot. Is that thunder?"

"To be sure, it is. There'll be a storm now that will last an hour or two. Where are you? Oh, I can see you now—how that flash has lit up the scene! upon, my word, this will be a pleasant night."

Grubson was, at all events, sufficiently free to be able to lend something like efficient assistance to his companion. He saw, by the repeated flashes of lightning, that a tree had fallen within a few feet of Adolphus, and that a massive bough from it had caught him in its descent, and struck him to the earth, without inflicting upon him any very serious injury—that is to say, he had nothing more than bruises to complain of, and of them he certainly had a plentiful assortment, as well as of scratches about his face, so that it was quite clear Adolphus's lucky star was not in its ascendant, and that his evening's amusement certainly did not provide anything satisfactory for his morning's reflection.

A vigorous pull at his heels, however, sufficed to rescue him, at the cost of a great many more scratches, from the perilous situation in which he had been placed; and then, to their great surprise, for it was certainly more than probable that Mr. Slankey had been killed, they heard that gentleman's voice calling for succour.

"I'm a miserable sinner! the Lord have mercy upon me! Will nobody show me the way out of this damnable place?"

"This way, this way," cried Grubson, "come out from among the trees; I can hear the branches cracking and giving way above our heads; we shall run a chance all of us of having our brains knocked out now, if we don't get out of this, tolerably quick—this way, this way—there was a flash!"

John Grubson led the way, and both Adolphus and the pious Mr. Slankey blundered after him, as best they could, until they got clear of the intricate vegetation of Snake Hollow and into the open fields, where, at all events, there was less danger than among the fallen trees, which they could hear cracking and splitting behind them, as the squall occasionally came on like a moving wall, dashing down everything in its progress.

And now that the Rev. Tobias Slankey had fairly recovered the use of his speech, he became furious at the treatment he had received. He wept, cursed, swore, and raged; one moment vowing revenge, and at another shedding abundance of tears, as he declared he believed himself battered and bruised past all human aid.

"I'm a dead man," he said. "I'm a slaughtered vessel of grace. I was knocked down in a stagnant pool, and shall die with the stench in my nostrils, instead of in the odour of sanctity. I'm murdered—I'm a mass of bruises from top to toe—I'm undone, and it's all through being good-natured, and undertaking little odd jobs for other people; but I'll make my complaint—I'll raise the whole estate—I'll raise the whole country—I won't be slaughtered for nothing."

As the rev. gentleman uttered these words, he started off towards the house at a pace which quite defied Adolphus and John Grubson to keep up with; but as the storm raged still in great fury, they ran on as fast as they could, keeping as near as possible in the wake of the flying preacher.

CHAPTER X.

THE MEETING AT MR. DEAL'S.—THE OFFERED REWARD.—CESAR'S TRIUMPH.

THE Rev. Tobias Slankey did not stop until he had found his way to Mr. Deal's house, and then, something to the consternation of Adolphus and Grubson, instead of going into that portion in the occupation of the latter, he darted in at the principal doorway; and, little heedful of the alarm he might occasion, made his appearance in Mr. Deal's own parlour.

That gentleman was seated with his family, certainly not in a quiet and composed state of mind, for he could not but be cognisant of the fact that a storm was raging upon his estate.

The whistling of the wind without, and the crackling noise made by the boughs of some of the trees which were torn off in the immediate vicinity of the mansion, brought that circumstance with too painful an exactness to their ears.

Mr. Deal had before experienced these visitations of the elements upon his property, and he knew that nothing could be done, but patiently, and as calmly as possible, to wait until the tempest had done its worst, and then see what amount of mischief had occurred.

Still, however, it was with the most painful anxiety that he listened to the howling blast which was making war upon his property. Mrs. Deal's rather rubicund countenance was likewise blanched with fear, and Miss Deal sat trembling, for she had not had all the experience upon the property that her father and mother had.

It was just at this juncture of affairs that a rapid footstep was heard in the passage, for the door of the house was always merely upon the latch, so that any one might open it who pleased, and then, to the astonishment, not unmixed with terror, of the little family party, in dashed Mr. Tobias Slankey.

We can just fancy what the appearance of this pious individual must have been at this juncture. His clothes were torn and dirty; his face was covered over with a sort of greenish slime, which was almost of the consistency of paint, that had lain among the marshes and festering vegetation into which Cesar had dabbed his physiognomy; added to this, too, were streaks of blood which had started from the gaping wound in the form of a cross, that was in his forehead.

But we shall remember that the pious gentleman was an assassin, and shall not pity him.

Mr. Deal sprang to his feet, Miss Deal fainted, and Mrs. Deal screamed.

"Vengeance—I want vengeance!" said Slankey, waving his great arms about like the sails of a windmill. "I want vengeance, and I must and will have it."

"Good God!" said Mr. Deal, "what's the meaning of this?"

"D—n everything and everybody! I want and must have a general slaughter among the blacks. Just look at me, Mr. Deal—look at me, and say what you think."

"I don't know what to think, except that your intrusion here is most unaccountable."

"That's nothing, that's nothing," said the Rev. Tobias, weeping again, as a sense of his misfortunes came strong upon him. "I'm a poor chosen vessel—I'm a cracked vessel—a vessel without a spout or a handle. Look at my face, and there's a lump upon the back of my head which will prevent my ever wearing a hat again. Oh, these are horrid times. I was a different man when I belonged to the Little Bethel, in Camden Town, but, as I say, I'm a cracked vessel—it's enough to make anybody cry—I'm a vessel without a bottom."

By this time, Grubson and Adolphus had arrived at the door of the apartment, and were peeping in to see how the rev. gentleman was getting on with his complaints.

Mr. Deal saw them, and beckoned them in, saying in a voice of inquiry,—

"Have you any possible idea what's the matter with this man? He seems to me to be half out of his senses—what on earth is the meaning of all this?"

"I don't know, sir," said Mr. Grubson, "except that he's been caught in the storm, and knocked down by some of the boughs of the trees. We saw him running along by the side of one of the cotton-fields, and merely came after him to see what was the matter."

John Grubson gave Mr. Tobias a kick on the shin, to signify that that was the story he was to stick to.

"Of course," said Mr. Deal, "I'm sorry that any one should be so injured by the storm; but that sorrow, in this case, is a good deal tempered by the reflection, that I gave this man notice to quit my estate this morning, and I want to know what business he had running along one of my cotton fields?"

"It's nothing of the sort," cried Mr. Slankey; "it's all along of some devil they call the Mangoni. I was walkin galong like a peaceable Christian, and offering up a prayer for the blessing of everybody, when something jumped upon my back, about as heavy and as strong as an elephant; and, of course, down I went —it was in Snake's Hollow—then I was kicked, and buffeted, and punched, and thumped, until I became what you see me now."

"But that frightful, ghastly cross upon your forehead, how came that?"

The rev. gentleman gave a great howl, for at that moment he certainly had forgotten the mark that had been put upon him, painful as it was, for he was in such a general pain, that he could scarcely refer that feeling to any any particular part of him.

"Yes, yes," he blubbered, "I shall no longer be a shining light; I feel like a candle that has just gone out—like a pitcher that went for water, and slipped into the well."

"You certainly are in a doleful condition; but you have mentioned a name that gives something like credence to a superstition current among all the Africans on my estate, which is, that there is some being called the Mangoni, who will aid and assist them in their difficulties. I have made every effort to discourage such a superstition, not so much for my own sake, but that I wish not any foolish ideas of that sort to take possession of those persons who are committed to my care."

"I don't know, father," said Adolphus, "how it can be called a superstition, when we see Mr. Slankey knocked about in such a mysterious manner."

"You cannot be so absurd, Adolphus, as to fancy that Mr. Slankey owes his injuries to a supernatural being?"

"I don't know; but of this I'm certain, that if we don't think so, everybody else upon the estate will."

"I can scarcely imagine it ; but still, as it may be so for I well know how prone people are to take the most mysterious view of any case, I shall certainly, more forcibly than before, renew my interdict against Mr. Slankey remaining on my property. There is quite enough superstition, and quite sufficient fancies among the slaves without Mr. Slankey affording anything like a practical illustration of such matters."

"But is that all the justice I am to get?" exclaimed Mr. Slankey. "Am I to be half murdered, and maimed for life, and then just told to go away, for fear I should set a bad example. I was leaving your estate, Mr. Deal, when this happened ; but being a chosen vessel among your slaves, some of them had books and tracts, which it behoved me to get before I took my departure, and it was as I was going away, in obedience to your command, that I met with this injury."

"I admit," said Mr. Deal, "that there is a show of justness and fairness in what you say. I'm averse to deeds and violence of all sorts and descriptions, and therefore, without at all entering too nicely into the question, whether you might not have gone long before this time, and in safety, and without at all prejudging the case, as to whether or not you were the aggressor in the daring action in which you have come off so badly, I will offer fifty dollars' reward for the party who has so treated you."

"That'll do," said the rev. gentleman, "that'll do. I have been so long in this country as to know that, for fifty dollars, a man would eat his own father. Be assured that the culprit shall be found, and I only hope that he will be so quickly, before this cut that I have on my forehead is healed and has disappeared, in order that I may produce it in judgment against him."

"You need be under no obligations," said John Grubson. "Heal it may, but disappear it won't, for I perceive it is well rubbed over with gunpowder ; so that as long as you live, Master Slankey, you'll go about with a blue cross stamped upon your brow."

The preacher did not appear to have been aware till this moment of the exten of his misfortunes, and when he found that, upon competent authority, the cross was declared to be indelible, he commenced such a fresh supply of groans, that even Mrs. Deal was alarmed, although indignation had quickly recovered her from her first accession of terror.

We say indignation, because that lady was well aware, although she did not know the circumstances, that the rev. gentleman had in all human likelihood got his hurt while in the pursuit of some infamous transaction, in which her darling Adolphus had some interest. Hence she looked upon the Rev. Tobias Slankey as, in a manner of speaking, belonging to her party in family politics.

"I beg that you will leave the house," cried Mr. Deal, rising ; "I have done all that I can do, and in fact more than, if I were merely to trust to my inclination, I should at all have dreamt of doing. There is nothing in what has happened to reconcile me, Mr. Slankey, to your presence, and still as before I have to request you'll leave my property."

There was no withstanding ; and it was evident that both John Grubson and Adolphus thought it was high time to retire ; they took the reverend gentleman between them, and got him to the door, when their progress out was interrupted by a negro, who came to say that Cesar Bobb begged an interview with his master, as he had something to say to him of importance.

The conscience-stricken trio shrunk back, for they made sure that Cesar Bobb had found out, by some means, the projected assassination, and had come to lodge his complaint with Mr. Deal. It would not do, however, suddenly to show any great curiosity to know what it was Cesar had to say, and Adolphus hurried the preacher through the doorway, for he knew well that whatever passed would be communicated in due time by his mother.

"Come away at once," he whispered ; "come away!"

"Goramighty, Massa Slankey ! what eber hab been de matter wid you?"

The preacher did not condescend to make any reply to Cesar, but cast upon him a scowling glance, and then passed on—such a glance that, if looks would have killed, would certainly have very soon placed Cesar beyond all earthly troubles.

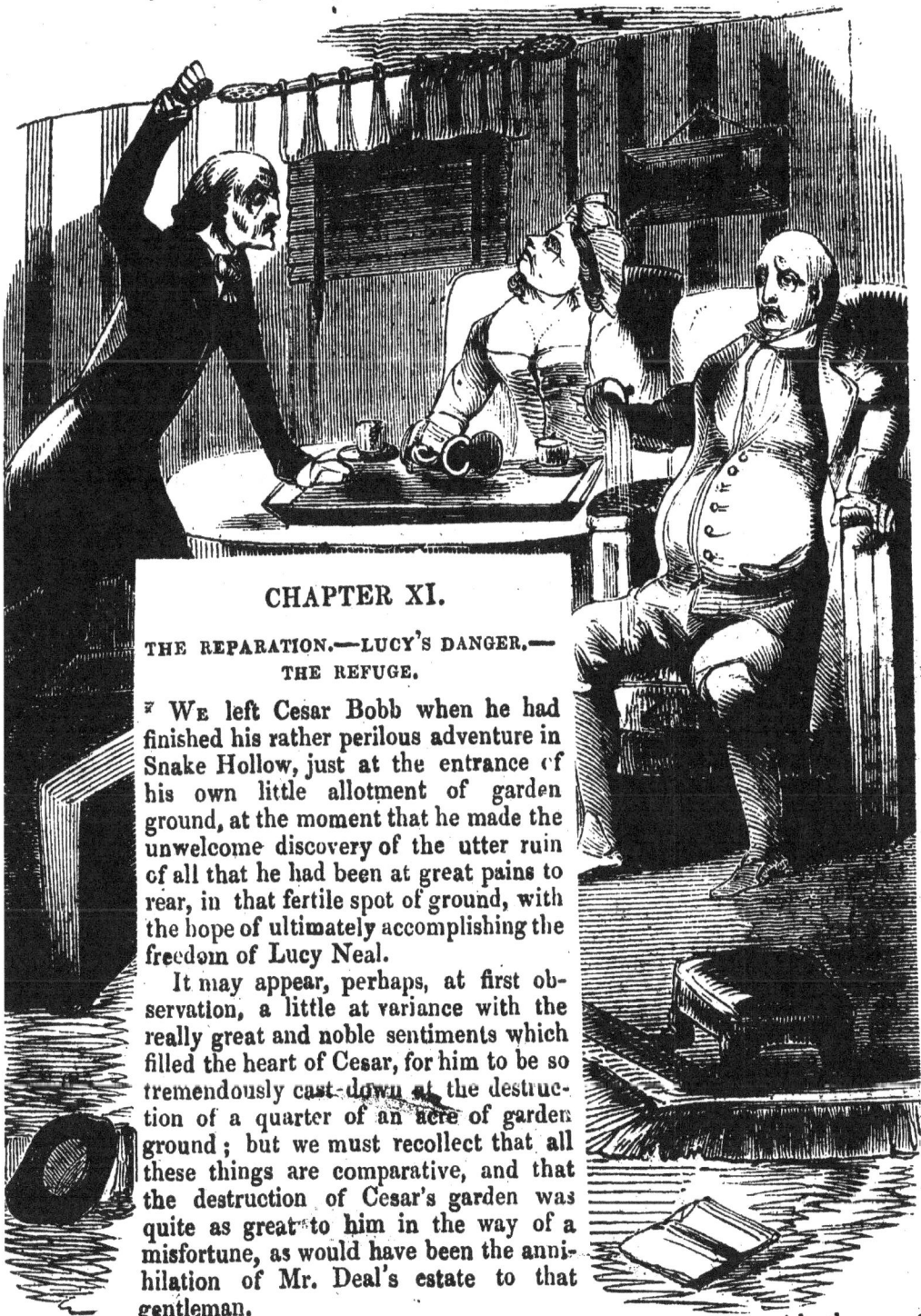

CHAPTER XI.

THE REPARATION.—LUCY'S DANGER.— THE REFUGE.

We left Cesar Bobb when he had finished his rather perilous adventure in Snake Hollow, just at the entrance of his own little allotment of garden ground, at the moment that he made the unwelcome discovery of the utter ruin of all that he had been at great pains to rear, in that fertile spot of ground, with the hope of ultimately accomplishing the freedom of Lucy Neal.

It may appear, perhaps, at first observation, a little at variance with the really great and noble sentiments which filled the heart of Cesar, for him to be so tremendously cast down at the destruction of a quarter of an acre of garden ground; but we must recollect that all these things are comparative, and that the destruction of Cesar's garden was quite as great to him in the way of a misfortune, as would have been the annihilation of Mr. Deal's estate to that gentleman.

For a few moments he surveyed the ruins of his little property with the most agonised feelings. It seemed to him as if fate had determined, on that evening, to do its worst; for not only had his life been attempted, and that, too, under such circumstances, which made the success of the attempt very nearly certain, but all that vestige of his industry appeared to have been rudely attacked, for the purpose of being swept from the face of the earth.

No. 5.

It was no stain to Cesar's manhood, that even a tear should roll upon his cheek, as he looked upon the scene of devastation before him, and contrasted it mentally with the appearance that pleasant little spot had borne on the preceding evening.

"Alas! alas!" he said, "my Lucy Neal—for anoder year dis will put an end to de opes of 'mancipation for you; and when de harvest time shall come for fruitage in dis garden, dere will be no fruit, no gay flowers—noting to sell."

It certainly was a melancholy prospect, and never with such lagging steps and downcast eyes, had Cesar walked up the little pathway that led to his hut.

But the state of dejection that had come over him was the worst at its commencement, and every moment he got better and more able to withstand with fortitude the evils that had assailed him.

He began to look about, to see the nature of the injuries which his little plantation had received, and upon an accurate examination, it appeared to him as if some one had rushed in, and in the course of a few minutes only, done as much mischief as he could, for the roots were trampled about; the taller plants being broken down, and the smaller ones crushed and trodden into the ground, so that a great amount of mischief had been done, no doubt, in an inconceivably short space of time.

It might be just possible to restore some of the plants to their original condition, and by care to render them again prolific, but what confidence could Cesar now have in his little garden, after it had once been subject to such an outrage? Might not the same enemy again appear when his back was turned, and again in a few moments destroy the labour of months? Certainly he might, and where then would be the recompense of poor Cesar?

He was indulging in these mournful reflections, when he heard something fall a short distance from him on the path; and dashing forward impetuously to see what it was, he found, lying at his feet, a stone, which again, as in the open plantation, was made a medium of giving to him a written communication, but unhappily not one that Cesar could read.

It was rather a large-sized piece of paper that was rolled round the stone, and the characters upon it were clearly traced; but that afforded Cesar no assistance, who gazed upon the, to him, unintelligible scrawl with feelings of surprise, mingled with deep curiosity.

"I must go to some one," he said, "to ascertain what dis means. Oh, Lucy Neal, if I had you now by my side, you could tell me what dis writing aims at. Let me see—who had got so much learning, as to be able to read it? Ole Pompey is de man; yes, ole Pompey is de man; he hab amazing edikation, hab ole Pompey."

Cesar was not all joking, and he ran as fast as he could from his own hut towards the one occupied by his old friend whom he found at home, and leaning over the hatch of his doorway, as was oft his custom after nightfall.

"Hilloa, Pompey, bery fine night; hab you lost a dollar, in consequence of tossing wid somebody, and looking up to the sky to see him come down again? Hi! hi! hi!"

"No, Cesar; I look up at dat star."

"What star, Pompey?"

"Dat star—it be your star, Cesar, and just come out of a bery dam black cloud—dere was, or dere will be, Cesar, for you danger this night."

"Goramighty, Pompey, you strike de right nail on de top ob de head, but before I tell you what hab happened, read dat, Pompey, and tell me what he says. I know you hab power ob learning, Pompey; dey say you hab swallowed de dictionary in early life."

Old Pompey took the paper with great seriousness, and read as follows:—

"Cesar Bobb will go to Mr. Deal, and tell him that his garden is destroyed, and if questioned he will say it was done while he went with old Pompey to see a friend at Mr. Samson's plantation. Cesar Bobb did not meet Lucy Neal to-night. Cesar Bobb did not come through Snake Hollow. So says the Mangoni, for the happiness and welfare of his people."

Cesar heard these words with breathless attention, and in a moment comprehended that they contained advice and laid down a rule of action for him to proceed upon. Turning to Pompey, he said,—

"De Mangoni is de friend ob de poor slave. My life hab been attempted to-night by Slankey, de preachy-preachy man; and I do understand dat de Mangoni advise me what to do."

"Yes, yes," said old Pompey, "it be plain: de Mangoni is your friend, Cesar; obey what he do tell you, and go to Mr. Deal at once. What is dat you hab with you, Cesar, like a great long stick?"

"Goramighty, I hab forgot—it is a double-barrelled gun I hab brought from Snake Hollow; both of the barrels were fired at me by dat dam rascal I left there."

"Did you kill him?" cried Pompey; "did you hab his blood?" and he suddenly rose up tall and erect.

"Lord bless us, Pompey, what a dam big fellow you are! I don't think him quite dead, but not far off."

Pompey sank down again to his usual half-crouched-up position.

"Hi! hi! hi!" he said; "ole Pompey dam ole—a bery little ting give Pompey a pain in de back, bery bad cough too, and rheumatic all ober de left shoulder. Poor ole Pompey weak as eber such a little cat—smallest piccaninny knock ole Pompey down. Hi! hi! hi! Go, Cesar, go; do what de Mangoni says: all is right, all is right."

Cesar had far more faith in the good advice of Pompey than in all the mysterious injunctions of the Mangoni, and accordingly he proceeded at once towards the house to lay his complaint with Mr. Deal.

It was then that he encountered Adolphus Deal, John Grubson, and the Rev. Tobias Slankey, all of whom were so anxious to know what was really Cesar's errand.

When he was introduced to Mr. Deal, who made a practice of seeing any of his slaves when they thought proper to request an audience of him, he merely stated that, while he was otherwise engaged, his garden had been utterly destroyed.

"Indeed, Cesar," said Mr. Deal, who, of course, had no means of establishing the remotest connexion between his present visitor and the hurts which the Rev. Tobias Slankey had received; "indeed, Cesar, that is a serious outrage, and such as you know I would discountenance to the utmost. I suppose it must have happened whilst you went with old Pompey to see somebody on Mr. Samson's estate."

If a bombshell had been thrown at Cesar's feet, he could not have given a greater jump of surprise than to hear Mr. Deal thus echo, as it were, the advice which the Mangoni had given him; for Pompey had not at all communicated to Cesar, in the hurry of the brief dialogue they had had, that he had been to Mr. Deal, to ask leave for both of them to go on that errand.

Probably Pompey, in due time, will explain that he meant to take Cesar with him on that visit and missed finding him; so that he either gave it up altogether, or paid it by himself, at all events, it was with considerable confusion that Cesar stammered out an affirmative to Mr. Deal's remark.

"Well, Cesar," added that gentleman, "everything seems to be going wrong to-night; first of all there is the storm upon the estate, which does me I don't know how many pounds worth of damage; then somebody comes to me, half murdered, to ask for redress; and, finally, your garden is destroyed; so that, what with one thing and another, I have not much peace."

"Bery sorry, massa," said Cesar, "only I thought I'd come and tell you."

"Yes, yes, Cesar, that's right enough; and, as you are concerned, the matter, I hope, can be easily put to rights. I offer a reward of twenty dollars, or say fifty, for I don't like these outrages upon my estate—I offer a reward of fifty dollars to whoever will bring me the culprit who has destroyed your garden, Cesar."

"Fifty tanks, massa!"

"And as, of course, the matter's of importance to you, you can get the ground put to right as soon as possible, and I will give you all your time until it is done;

but you must work diligently, Cesar; and when you have got all the things ready, you can take from my garden such plants as will replace your stock in as profitable a condition as it was before the damage happened to it."

Cesar thanked Mr. Deal for this liberality; and it is no deterioration from the merits of that gentleman to say, that he behaved in this way more as a matter of principle than from any peculiar sympathy in this individual case; and, at all events, Cesar went away satisfied.

We must now turn attention for a brief space to Lucy Neal, who was not entirely without her share of adventures on that eventful night.

The mysterious warning which had been given to Cesar, concerning the Snake Hollow, made a deep impression upon her mind; and knowing, as she did, that he was far more inclined to be adventurous than careful, she, after parting with him, was troubled with all sorts of apprehensions.

She took her way towards the huts where the female slaves lodged, endeavouring to persuade herself that all would be well; but when she did, the reason held a very successful war with the imagination.

Over and over again she told herself that the same mysterious power that had given him the warning had, in all probability, both the will and the capacity to protect him; but, despite all that, she felt that that night, to her, would be a sleepless one, and replete with terrors.

She shared her hut with a negress, who had but recently come upon the estate, and who was deeply attached to Lucy Neal for the advice and kindness she had experienced from her; but Lucy felt that the society of any one would be irksome to her; and, when she reached the enclosure belonging to the little hut, she leaned upon the little wooden palings, and gave way to a full tide of recollections of the past.

How hopeless did her position seem to be; it was certainly true that Mr. Deal had said, he would protect her; but to what a world of oppressions and indignities might she be subjected, which he could not save her from.

It was while she thus gave way to sad and gloomy thoughts, that she heard the first murmurings of the storm; and a new dread took possession of her, namely, that Cesar was in the open plantation, and exposed to its violence.

Before, however, she could take a second thought on the matter, the squall came which had been so disastrous in its consequences all over the property, and which had, certainly, given some sort of retribution to those whom we call the three conspirators, who had endeavoured to do so much mischief to innocent persons.

The slave who resided in Lucy Neal's hut was so alarmed at the sound of the tempest, that she rushed out screaming, and not taking the slightest heed of Lucy, she flew past her; and the last our heroine saw of her, just then, was her half-clothed figure rushing, with frantic speed, towards Mr. Deal's house.

Lucy Neal had seen such storms before, and consequently she was not so frightened as she would, certainly, otherwise have been. She knew that if the first squall passed over without doing material damage to her hut, she might consider it comparatively safe, and accordingly, such being the case, she made her way at once within it, to avoid the dashing shower of dust and other matters which were carried upon the face of the wind.

There she waited upon her knees, with her head resting upon her hands, praying, not for her own safety, but for the safety of him whom she knew loved her, and who, she was well aware, would, at any time, have cheerfully sacrificed his existence for her sake.

She felt the hut rock now and then as the gale swept over it, and likewise, with a rushing sound, there went off portions of the thatched roof, which gave way before the impetuous blast; and 'twas well they did so, or otherwise much more serious injury might have ensued.

And yet, notwithstanding all the noise and riot without, a sense of great loneliness began to creep over Lucy Neal; and, fancying she heard the wind abating somewhat in its violence, she made her way from her own hut into the open air, and intent upon making an endeavour to ascertain if Cesar were safe, she rapidly took her way across one of the cotton fields towards his habitation.

Lucy was unfortunate, for at the moment she reached it, Cesar was holding his brief conversation with old Pompey, and the hut was vacant.

She saw the devastation which had taken place in the garden, and great fear took possession of her; she entered the hut, calling upon Cesar by name, but there was no response, and only the sad echo of her own voice came back upon her ears.

Alarmed at the silence, and thinking that a presage of misfortune, she crossed the garden, and re-entered the habitation. Her thoughts as she did so painfully reverted to the possibility of finding that, in some hopeless defence of his property, Cesar was seriously injured.

The possibility of finding him dead or hurt past all recovery made her feel sick and faint as she paused upon the threshold; it was certainly only a possibility, but yet of its kind a dreadful one; and if it should be true, she felt that all hope for her in this world was at an end.

The very death-like stillness of the place, which ought to have tended to convince her that there was as strong a probability of the mere absence of Cesar as of any mischief having befallen him, came upon her senses most oppressively.

"Cesar! Cesar!" she cried, "speak to me if you are here; let me know the worst, if you have a word to say to me."

All was profoundly still, and now she stood in the lower apartment of the little building; and it was a great relief to sink upon a rude couch that was there, and wait a little until her eyes became accustomed to the semi-darkness of the place, and she could perceive that it was untenanted by any one but herself.

There was only one other little room besides this to search, and anxious as she felt to do so, because it would bring her the assurance that at all events, Cesar was not murdered in his own home, she shrank from the task, lest it should convince her of a much more frightful alternative.

The minutes, however, were lagging fast, and Lucy Neal had a suspicion that she had been a long while upon her errand, for what with the violence of the storm, and the conflict which her own emotions made in her bosom, she could scarcely be expected to have any right notions respecting chronology on that evening.

She only had a confused feeling that it was getting late, and that she might be liable to much misconstruction if she remained long where she was.

Animated then, with fresh hope, for the continued silence in the place, and likewise the undisturbed appearance of its few little articles of furniture, brought proof almost to a demonstration, that nothing had occurred within the house of a character, she made her way into the other apartment, and satisfied herself at a glance, for it was not much larger than a cupboard, that there was no appearance of any struggle having taken place, or that Cesar had come to any mischief.

"Thank Heaven!" she exclaimed, "thank Heaven, that as yet I have no knowledge of evil having befallen him, and so I have a right to conclude that he may be safe.

She felt now much revived in spirits, and began to think of taking her way back again to her own hut, when the distant sound of a footstep in the garden without came upon her ears.

Lucy Neal could have no distinct reason or argument for asserting to herself that this was an unfriendly footstep; she only knew it was not Cesar's; and, at the same time, there came a presentiment across her mind that it was that of an enemy.

She shrunk back into the farthest corner of the hut to listen.

CHAPTER XII.

THE ANGRY INTERVIEW.—JOHN GRUBSON'S THREAT.—ADOLPHUS'S FRIGHT.

THE footstep sounded again, and then there was a pause of several minutes, during which Lucy listened with the most painful attention, but could hear nothing; so that she almost began to think it was possible she had deceived herself, and that really no such sound as that which she considered to indicate a human footstep, had met her ears.

But still there was the apprehension remaining, and she lingered yet awhile longer, in order to muster up courage sufficient to face the uncomfortable emergency, if there should be any one within hearing.

She was just about to emerge from what might be called her hiding-place when, without the shadow of a doubt, she heard distinctly a voice, and felt confident that some one was speaking in a low tone, in the little garden. By straining her attention likewise, and advancing a few paces, she, in a few moments, contrived to hear actually what was said, and certainly what came to her ears, was by no means of a pleasant or reassuring character.

"Make haste, make haste," said some one, in a low voice, "come in at once, and we'll soon manage it."

"Manage it, Master Adolphus?" said another, whom she at once recognised as Grubson, "manage it, sir? I should think we shall. I believe there's very little doubt about that. If we don't have him one way, you see, we can another."

"Yes, yes, that's all very well; but come along quick," said Adolphus Deal, for it was no other than he, who, with his partner in iniquity, John Grubson, had come to Cesar's cottage upon some desperate and unholy errand.

"Quick—quick! will you, Grubson? You dawdle as if there were half a dozen days to do the thing in, that is better by half done in half a dozen minutes. What if we should be observed? You know that would be far from pleasant."

"I don't see what odds that'll make," said Grubson. "Surely, if anybody has a right to go about the slave huts at any time of night, or day either, it's you and I, Mr. Adolphus."

"Yes, yes—that's all very well, but still there's no occasion to create suspicion."

"Not in the least, nor do I wish to do so."

"Have you got the cup?"

"Oh, yes, that's all right enough—I've got the cup. You needn't be under any apprehension, Mr. Adolphus; and as for your father, I expect he'll be in as nice a rage as ever anybody was in. Why he won't know how to contain himself, seeing that he sets such great store by that cup, and thinks it worth so much money, he'll be thoroughly frantic. Look here—here's a nice article I've made of it—hammered it flat."

"Well, well, that's all the better."

"It is all the better, for it looks more natural."

At this period in their dialogue they entered the hut, and Lucy, who was in the inner room, felt that her discovery was a matter of absolute certainty if they should come into that apartment.

There was a chance that whatever they came to do might be done in the outer room—but it was only a chance, and whether a good one or not she could not tell, considering that she could form no opinion with regard to their object.

Perhaps a more worldly-minded person than Lucy Neal, and one more accustomed to view society in all its different phases, and under its different aspects, would have come to something like a prompt the conclusion; but so pure a spirit as Lucy Neal's could scarcely conceive the amount of wickedness that might lurk in the minds of such men as Adolphus Deal and John Grubson.

To her it was a complete enigma what they could be at, and she waited in breathless impatience for some more intelligence concerning their thoughts and feelings.

She had shrunk so far back in her anxiety to hide herself as effectually as possible from observation, that she now heard more indistinctly than before what was being said, and could make out but very little of a consecutive dialogue. The principal impression that their words brought to her mind was, that something was to be concealed; but what the something was, or what was the object of concealing it, she could not by any means discover.

It soon, however, appeared to be a matter of certainty that she must be discovered, for in about another moment, as if in pursuance of a sudden determination they had both come to, John Grubson and Adolphus Deal walked into the adjoining room; and scarcely had they been a minute within it when, by the flash of a light they carried, they saw Lucy Neal crouched in a corner, showing every symptom of alarm and agitation.

"By Heaven! she's here," cried Adolphus.

"Who—who?" said Grubson, hurriedly.

"Lucy Neal."

"Mercy!" she cried, "do not kill me!" for the looks of Grubson were of a most threatening character, and fully warranted the supposition that he intended committing some deed which would at once put an end to Lucy's capacity of giving evidence of anything she might have overheard.

"What do you do here?" he cried, with brutal ferocity.

"Hush! Grubson, hush!" said Adolphus, and then he took him aside for a moment and whispered to him, after which Grubson advanced, saying,—

"Well, Lucy, it aint of much matter, but the fact is, we were going to get up a sort of entertainment upon the estate, and finding nobody in this hut, and the fields being in a bad state from the storm, we came in here to speak about it. I dare say you overheard us : it's no matter if you did."

The natural intellect and acuteness of Lucy Neal was quite a match for what John Grubson thought his wonderful cunning, and she said, with an appearance of the most heartless simplicity,—

"I overheard nothing, but shall be glad to hear."

"Oh, pooh! come, come; you thought we would be angry, and so you won't admit you heard us say about the—the——"

"The what," said Lucy, to John Grubson's great disappointment, for he had fully expected her to fill up the sentence.

"She knows nothing," whispered Adolphus. "Lucy Neal, you may save yourself from the consequences of an indiscretion, by being a little more civil to me."

"Au indiscretion! what indiscretion?"

"You know that it is contrary to the rules of the estate for any of the female slaves to be seen near the men's huts after nightfall."

"Yes," cried Grubson, "and always punished."

"My purpose was innocent," said Lucy.

"Indeed! and what might that purpose have been?"

"There was a storm, and I came to see if one in whom I have an interest had suffered from its violence."

"Cesar Bobb, you came to see that impertinent scoundrel—who dares to interrupt me in my fancies," cried Adolphus; "but hark you, Lucy Neal, I will succeed you will find yourself in a most uncomfortable position, in consequence of this infringement of the rules of the estate ; and the only way in which you can procure your own safety, as well as the future safety of Cesar Bobb, will be, by being more kind and civil to me."

"Never, never; I have already experienced kind words and kind treatment from Mr. Deal, and to him will I again proceed, and explain to him the true causes of my appearance here."

"Curses!" said John Grubson, "I must cure you of this propensity you have of running to Mr. Deal about everything. I won't suffer it—look to it, I say, Lucy Neal, and in the morning, perhaps, you'll find that an overseer can be more troublesome than he has ever been yet."

"And, by Heaven!" added Adolphus, "as I may not have another opportunity of saying my mind to you, I'll say it now, Lucy Neal. I love you, there's not a black girl in the plantation can come near you. You shall be a lady if you like and do no more work. You shall have slaves of your own to wait upon you. I'll take you away somewhere, where you'll never be heard of again, and it may be easily supposed you have run away, while Mr. Grubson and I taking the management of the pursuit, can easily arrange so that you will be never troubled."

"Never," cried Lucy, "never will I stoop to such baseness. Adolphus Deal, take my answer at once, and for ever. I despise you, as much as I do your offer."

"The girl's out of her senses," he cried, and as he spoke he advanced, and taking her by the arm, adding, "if you won't be mine by fair means, you shall by foul. Do you think I'm going to be defied and disappointed by a slave?"

Lucy Neal uttered a shriek of alarm, and then, in an instant, before another remark could be made by any of the parties, the window of the hut was dashed in from without, and a loud voice cried, in strange, unearthly accents,—

"The Mangoni! the Mangoni!—kill, kill, kill!"

Such an accession of terror came over Adolphus Deal, that he made a frantic effort to reach the door of the hut, dashed aside John Grubson as he did so, while that individual was himself so paralysed that he seemed to lose all self-possession.

"The Mangoni! the Mangoni!" shouted the voice again, and then there came the sound of strange unearthly laughter, which filled the place with countless echoes.

It was not in Adolphus Deal's nature to stand this, and, consequently, he scampered off at the top of his speed, leaving John Grubson to follow as best he could, and that valorous individual, finding himself completely unsupported, made his escape likewise, with an amount of precipitation that in a very few moments got him far beyond the precincts of the slave's hut.

Lucy Neal sank upon her knees, for she was terrified, as well she might be, at the manner even of her deliverance. A death-like stillness ensued, and it seemed to her as if the mysterious being who had now twice interposed at such critical junctures upon Mr. Deal's estate, had disappeared again the moment it had performed its mission.

"Speak, oh, speak!" she cried, "be you whom you may; be you a being of earth or of heaven, I implore you to speak. Let me at least be conscious that, in returning thanks for this deliverance, I am heard by Him to whom my words are addressed. Speak to me, oh, speak, I beg, I implore."

All was still; not the slightest sound came to disturb the repose of the place, and Lucy Neal felt convinced that the mysterious being, be he whom he might, had gone off with as much celerity as he had appeared, and seemed to be alike as indifferent to praise as to censure, and to be only intent upon preserving the inviolability of his *incognito*.

She trembled, as well she might, to find herself alone, after what had occurred. She almost dreaded to pass through the deserted garden, and yet she must do so to reach her own habitation. She certainly did for a moment think of waiting until Cesar Bobb returned; but, after what had been already said by John Grubson about a rule of the estate, which she certainly knew, but had for a time forgotten, she dreaded to give occasion for further reprehension by remaining.

"Hush, hush!" she cried, suddenly, "there's another footstep upon the green sward! when will the trial of this night be over?"

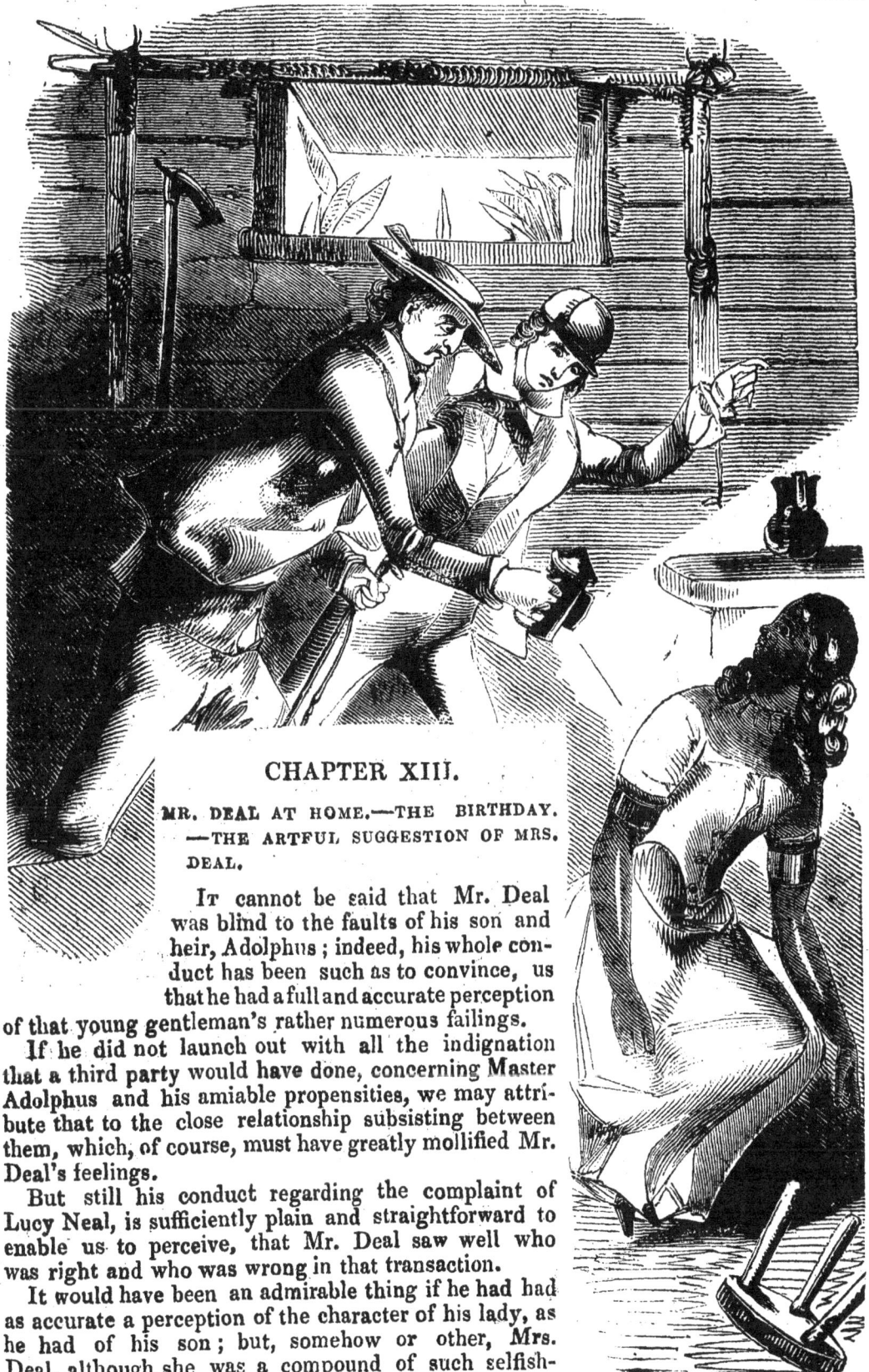

CHAPTER XIII.

MR. DEAL AT HOME.——THE BIRTHDAY.
——THE ARTFUL SUGGESTION OF MRS.
DEAL.

IT cannot be said that Mr. Deal
was blind to the faults of his son and
heir, Adolphus ; indeed, his whole conduct has been such as to convince, us
that he had a full and accurate perception
of that young gentleman's rather numerous failings.

If he did not launch out with all the indignation
that a third party would have done, concerning Master
Adolphus and his amiable propensities, we may attri-
bute that to the close relationship subsisting between
them, which, of course, must have greatly mollified Mr.
Deal's feelings.

But still his conduct regarding the complaint of
Lucy Neal, is sufficiently plain and straightforward to
enable us to perceive, that Mr. Deal saw well who
was right and who was wrong in that transaction.

It would have been an admirable thing if he had had
as accurate a perception of the character of his lady, as
he had of his son ; but, somehow or other, Mrs.
Deal, although she was a compound of such selfishness and arrogance as, in any other person, would have

No. 6.

awakened a large amount of his indignation, contrived to make him believe that
she was something of a wonderful woman, and that her failings were only those
of temper, and quite incidental to the possession of great talents.

Perhaps one of the most surprising things in domestic economy, and in the social
intercourse of human beings, consists in the fact, of how many clever men suffer
themselves year after year, as it were, to exist at the will of some ignorant and
capricious woman, elevating her in their own imaginations to some fancied height,
to the attainment of which she has herself no pretensions, and allowing their own
better judgment to be completely stupified and led astray by her vicious counsels
and insinuations.

This was most decidedly the case between Mr. and Mrs. Deal; from long habit
he allowed her to say things and to do things which those who knew him out of
his own house would hardly have deemed it possible he would succomb to.

He certainly did sometimes resist—it would be decidedly incorrect of us to say
he did not; but then the resistance never got further than mere words, and if Mrs.
Deal chose to be persevering, she got her own way at last.

But one of the most vicious systems which this cold selfish woman indulged in,
consisted in the fact that, from their very earliest infancy, she had contrived to
make two parties in the house—on consisting of herself and children, and the
other of her husband.

She never would allow Mr. Deal the merit of doing or saying anything pleasurable to his children; the merit of such transactions were all to come through her; and
Mr. Deal was either to be coaxed or badgered into the affair by some peculiar process known only to his lady, and which the children were called upon to give her a
vast amount of credit for conducting.

The effect of this pernicious example was that Mr. Deal never had the confidence of his children, and they always considered that he was somebody that stood
in the way of enjoyments; and when he granted anything, it was the cleverness of
their mother they were called upon to admire, and not by any means the good
feeling of their father.

This grew up with both children and mother, and, like all weak, ignorant
women, Mrs. Deal was quite as much enamoured of the vices of her son as she
was of his virtues, if indeed he had any of the latter with which to establish such a
distinction.

We have seen in the transactions connected with Lucy Neal, as far as they have
gone, the full carrying out of all these failings and habits; and in the consultation
which ensued between Adolphus and his mother, we are led to believe that the
morality of the transaction did not at all shock that good lady in her considerations
concerning it.

On the following morning she commenced operations in a manner which ought
to have awakened any one's suspicious that some plot of a very serious nature was
in progress.

Indeed, under any other circumstances than those of his wife being the principa
minister of the affair, Mr. Deal would not have had a moment's doubt about it; but
there he was oblivious and blind.

"Mr. Deal," she said, as they sat at breakfast together, "you must be aware
that Julia's birthday is next week—of course I don't know what you intend to do
now, but you always used to give an entertainment on the children's birthdays to
all our friends."

"They are no longer children now," said Mr. Deal, thoughtfully.

"Surely they are as much children now as they were last year, or nearly so,
and then you know you had a very magnificent ball."

"I regret," said Mr. Deal, as though he were revolving something in his mind, "I
regret very much that the conduct of one of our children, at all events, is not such
as to meet with my approbation."

"And pray, Mr. Deal," said his wife, with all the audacity in the world, "pray,
Mr. Deal, which one of your children may that be?"

"Can you think of asking when you know it was Adolphus to whom I alluded?"

"Oh, indeed, Mr. Deal, you were young yourself once, and I really don't see any occasion to make such a rout about poor Adolphus."

"I remember being young," said Mr. Deal, "but I certainly do not remember being vicious."

"Vicious, indeed, that's a very bad term to apply to your own child. I'm quite surprised at you, Mr. Deal, quite surprised; but, at all events, whatever Adolphus may have done to make you angry, I cannot see what effect that ought to have upon Julia's birthday."

"Certainly not, I'm not so illogical to say that it ought, but you must bear in mind that you spoke of Adolphus yourself, and that of course he must be present at Julia's *fete*, if she have one."

"Certainly, certainly; and I should say, Mr. Deal, you would be the last man, or ought to be the last man, to think of excluding your son from anything in the shape of an entertainment—that, Mr. Deal, would not be the way to reform him."

"I don't say it would, but I'm very much afraid Adolphus is past all reformation."

"I don't; I should be sorry to say such a thing. You and I, at all events, ought to be the last persons to insinuate it."

"Well, well, do as you please, do as you please. I don't know exactly how I have been led into this argument; but if you want a *fete* on the occasion of Julia's birthday, in Heaven's name have it."

This was just all that Mrs. Deal wanted, she had gained her point; the *fete* was to be had, and that was all she cared for—that is to say as a preliminary to other matters of much more serious moment, and which she considered, if they all turned out as she anticipated, would materially assist her Adolphus in the accomplishment of his purposes.

We shall perceive, as we proceed, that Mrs. Deal must have been one of that unholy confederacy which seemed to have been leagued together for the absolute destruction of those who were in every way most worthy to be preserved.

We have been loath to think that a woman and a mother could lend herself for one moment to such transactions; but facts are stubborn things, very stubborn things, and may not be gainsayed, although all our wishes and all our feelings rebel and rise up in arms against them.

Having once, then, gained the consent of Mr. Deal for the birthday *fete*, Mrs. Deal left the room, but she returned in a few minutes with just the plausible hurried air of somebody who has forgotten something, and said,—

"Oh, by-the-by, we shall want further assistance in the house, and as I never like to take any of the slaves off the estate without your knowledge, I thought I'd just tell you."

'Well, well, take what assistance you require. Mr. Grubson will settle the matter for you."

"Of course, it's a great advantage for a slave to come off the plantation into the house."

"Well, I suppose it is."

"Most certainly; and, therefore, to show you, Mr. Deal, that I have really no animosity against that black fellow Cesar Bobb, we'll have him, and if we should want any assistance of female slaves, Lucy Neal shall be one of them."

"Well, I'm glad of that, for, as regards poor Cesar, he has met with a very severe blow in the destruction of his little garden; and although I have told him I will do all I can to make matters square again for him, yet I know that he has suffered severely from the disappointment the failure of his garden crop has given him; so that if he can be made to feel any little advantage by being brought into the house for a time, let him have it."

"He shall—he shall—he shall have all the advantages that I intend for him by being brought into the house."

"But, mark me, mind," said Mr. Deal, "I will not have him oppressed by Adolphus, for although you, of course, have no unworthy feeling towards the black, I don't know but what Adolphus may; and, once for all, I will not have it. I have governed my estates hitherto, I hope, with temperance and moderation, and I will certainly continue to do so."

" Certainly—certainly—oh, of course."

" Then you quite understand me ?"

"I do ; and I'm sure what will happen will turn out to be quite satisfactory."

Mrs. Deal gave a short, dry cough as she left the room, which Mr. Deal certainly did not understand the meaning of; it sounded rather suspiciously, as if the lady had something on her mind, in the background, with which she did not wish him exactly to become acquainted. But, then, Mr. Deal did not know so well as the reader does the sort of woman he had to do with, and after a few moments' wonder and thought upon the subject, he gave no further heed to it, and forgot it.

A matter of business likewise pressed very close upon his mind at the same time, for there was a large sale of slaves at about twenty or thirty miles distant from his property, and he intended to become a purchaser of some of them, in consequence of having for some time rather felt the want of additional hands on his property.

It sounds strange indeed to European ears, " a sale of slaves," and it is sincerely to be hoped that America, while she is making efforts, or pretending to make them, to remove various blots from her escutcheon, in the shape of swindling and other little peculiarities, will not be deaf to the voice of Europe, but will cast aside that most inglorious and iniquitous traffic which. if it exist in one portion, although that may be the smallest of the Union, is one of the bitterest stains and disgraces to the whole.

And so, hoping that in time to come, Brother Jonathan will make some effort to be just a little respectable, we close this chapter, which is really a more important one than at first sight it would appear to be.

CHAPTER XIV.

LUCY'S AGREEABLE SURPRISE.—THE SEARCH IN THE HUT.—THE STRANGE COMMUNICATION.

WE left Lucy at a moment when, for a second time, she heard the sound of a footstep in the dilapidated garden belonging to Cesar, and when for the second time she shrank back, appalled, at the idea that her persecutors might have returned, more full of wicked intentions than they were before they had been scared away from the hut by the Mangoni.

A feeling of desparation came over her, and she looked eagerly about for some weapon, by the aid of which she should be able to protect herself, in case it should be necessary to do so.

There was nothing in the hut that would have answered the purpose of a defence, or, at all events, nothing that was easily observable, and the footsteps came on so quickly that there was no time for a more accurate examination.

But what was her joy in another minute to hear the voice of Cesar pronouncing her own name to himself in accents of affection?

For a few moments she was so overwhelmed with pleasurable feelings, to find that it was indeed he, and not her enemies, that she could not speak, but let him fairly advance into the hut and take a seat, while she remained silent in its extreme corner.

Cesar seemed weary as he threw himself upon one of the little wicker-work stools, manufactured by himself, and which formed the only seats in the place. He drew a long breath, and then he spoke ; need we say that the words that came from his lips were highly satisfactory indeed to Lucy Neal?

" Well," he remarked, " Massa Deal is not a bad massa ; he gib me enough to put my garden to rights, so dat de money I hab saved up for Lucy will not be wasted, and all will be well. I do much fear, though, dat my lub for Lucy Neal, which is part of my heart's existence, will make dat rascal, Adolphus, do what mischief he can ; well, well, let him beware ; de spirit of an ancient race is in de heart of de poor slave, and Massa 'Dolphus and Massa Grubson may both take warning by de fate of Slankey. Hi! hi! I hab marked Slankey for life—de Mangoni could not hab done it better."

Lucy made a slight movement, and Cesar sprang to his feet; but all was still again ; although he seemed to have some notion that there was danger, for he spoke in a lower tone, as he said,—

" I hab heard a noise ; what can it be !"

He listened attentively for a considerable time, and until Lucy said,—

" Cesar Bobb, it is the Mangoni."

" No, no," he said, springing forward, " it is de voice ob Lucy Neal."

In another moment he clasped her in his arms, exclaiming,—

> " Oh, how happy I do feel
>   Now I hab you by my side,
> My own sweet Lucy Neal."

" Cesar, Cesar, I must go at once. I have done wrong by coming here at all— very wrong ; but it was the storm that made me think some mischief had come to you."

" You are quite right, Lucy ; you are not wrong—you cannot be wrong. Oh, Lucy Neal, I did not tink I would hab de joy of seeing you again to-night."

" My visit, Cesar, has been a much longer one than it ought to have been already. I must go at once, only pausing to tell you that Adolphus Deal and John Grubson have been here."

" Adolphus Deal and John Grubson !" exclaimed Cesar, starting, as well he might, at this intelligence.

" Yes, Cesar, and what they came for I do not know and cannot even guess."

" Did dey see you, Lucy ?"

" They did, Cesar, they did ; but that is no matter: the Mangoni was here, and stood between me and all harm."

" Den dey did dare to insult you ?"

" Think nothing of it, think nothing of it, but endeavour, Cesar, to ascertain what their errand was to the hut ; it was not in search of me, for they could not know that I was here. What they have been about I cannot guess, but as you know the place better than I, search it well, and see if you can discover in anything they have left behind them any indication of their purpose."

Cesar made a rapid survey of his little premises, but certainly could discover nothing at all of a suspicious character ; in fact, it appeared perfectly inexplicable why Adolphus and the overseer had at all visited the place.

But the obscurity in which the cause of that visit was involved by no means robbed it of its alarming circumstances. It was quite clear that John Grubson and Adolphus would not visit the hut for nothing, and therefore there naturally arose the question, of what was the something which induced their domiciliary visit, and to that hung a corollary certainly to the effect that the something was not of a pleasant nor of a favourable character.

Probably Cesar Bobb made less of the matter, on account of the presence of Lucy Neal, than he would have done had he been quite alone; for, far from wishing to alarm her more than was necessary, he rather strove to make light of the matter, and to induce her to think that it was of much less consequence than it really presented itself to him.

She asked him for an explanation of what he had hinted concerning Tobias Slankey, and then Cesar gave her an account of his dangers in Snake Hollow, and of the manner and amount of revenge he had taken of the preacher, inducing her, as he spoke, to tremble, for two reasons—first, for the danger that had assailed him ; and, secondly, for the consequences of the just retribution he had inflicted upon Tobias Slankey.

" Oh, Cesar," she said, " can you expect for one moment that this man will not thirst after revenge until he has obtained it? You will not be safe now, night or day, from his machinations.

"I am at least prepared," said Cesar; "it is someting to know what a dam rascal anybody is, and I rather tink I hab frighten him."

"Doubtless; but, at the same time, Cesar, you have aroused all his feelings of hatred and revenge, whereas before he was only acting as the partizan of another, and could have no personal ill-will towards you."

"Goramighty," said Cesar, "I don't know what you mean. I bery much doubt if anybody could do more dan shoot one wid double-barrel gun. What you tink of dat, Lucy?"

"You are right, Cesar, so far, but still I tremble. Hush, Cesar, hush! I hear something. This night is full of dangers, mysteries, and surprises. Oh, that the morning were come again!"

Cesar rushed from the hut, and standing in the centre of the little garden, to his surprise, by the dim light, he saw a tall and powerful negro.

This man stood perfectly still, so that Cesar had full opportunity of seeing his dress and appointments. He wore a yellow shirt, and around his arm was tied a great bundle of straw, the ragged ends of which hung about him in all directions.

Cesar advanced a step, for he seemed to understand something of his visitor's motive and object; and then the stranger spoke in a deep, hollow voice, saying,—

"When de moon shrink away in de heavens, and den when de first glimpse ob de small crescent show himself in de night sky, de time will hab come."

He then plucked one of the straws which formed a portion of his curious head-gear, from amongst the general mass, and cast it at Cesar's feet.

In another moment he vaulted over the low paling of the garden, and disappeared in the night air. Cesar rushed forward, and, in an excited tone of voice, cried,—

"When de time shall come, I am ready. Stop, Jack Straw, stop! I am ready— I am ready!"

The call was in vain, for the strange visitor was lost to his sight amid the darkness that reigned around, before he had well finished those words, and Cesar stood for a moment or two irresolute whether to follow him or not.

Probably the impulse in the affirmative might have triumphed, for in the excitement of that moment he forgot even the presence of Lucy Neal, until she seized him by the arm, and cried, in imploring accents,—

"Oh, Cesar, Cesar, what is all this? what is the meaning of all this? There is, I am confident, some fearful secret, that may concern your very life. Let me know it, Cesar. I charge you to let me know it. Keep nothing from me, or else I shall begin to doubt the reality of that affection which you say you entertain for me. Why do you fix your eyes so strangely upon that retreating figure? Speak, Cesar, speak! What mean you by it?"

"Hush, Lucy, hush! You shall know all dat I know—all—all. That is Jack Straw."

"Jack who?"

"Jack Straw; but you neber heard ob him."

"No, Cesar, the name brings no information to me. What did he want with you, and why did he so mysteriously throw that straw at your feet?"

"You shall know all dat I know, Lucy Neal. There will be a rising among de coloured people."

"A slave insurrection? Oh, horror!"

"Yes, horror to those who make a property of deir fellor-men! De day of retribution must come, and Jack Straw hab announced it."

"I understand now, Cesar, I understand too well. There will be one of those frightful general risings among the coloured people, by which they will be enabled for a time to shed much blood, and to fancy themselves free, but which will end, as those risings have before ended, in terror and defeat. Cesar, Cesar, keep out of it."

"No; dere will be danger, and in de day of danger Cesar must be wid his people."

"But Mr. Deal is kind and good to us."

" Lucy, dat de slave master be kind to de slave is noting in favour of slabery; if Massa Deal traffic in flesh and blood, he must take de consequences, if he was an angel from heaben."

"But, Cesar, what will be done, even if the slaves should be for a time triumphant?"

" Why, de first ting will be to look out for strong tall trees and pieces ob hemp."

"What for, Cesar? what for?"

" To hang up all de oberseers, and arter dat we hang up all de massas, and arter dat we hang up all de missusses, and leab em all to dry in de sun of their own plantations."

" Yes, and then comes the war of extermination and most frightful reprisals. Cesar, I must leave you now, but we will talk of this again. It will be many days yet before there is a new moon. Heaven send that some change may take place between this and then."

Cesar escorted Lucy Neal a considerable distance on her way; in fact he did not lose sight of her until he saw her enter her own hut, and then with slow steps he walked back to his own little habitation, pondering upon what had happened.

It was evident that the sudden appearance of Jack Straw had given a complete change to Cesar's ideas—his thoughts were no longer intent upon his own personal safety, and the notion of a general rising among the slaves seemed to divide the empire of his thoughts with even Lucy Neal herself.

CHAPTER XV.

MR. DEAL'S PURCHASES AT THE SLAVE AUCTION.—THE APPROACHING BIRTHDAY.

MR. DEAL has already announced his intention of purchasing some slaves at an auction which was to take place at some short distance from his own estate.

At about the middle of the day—that same day on which his lady had been so very solicitous to get his consent to the birthday entertainment—he began to make preparations for his journey.

He did not at all intend to start at that hour, for no horse could have withstood the mid-day heat of that latitude, and it was not until the sun began to decline in the west, that Mr. Deal mounted a surefooted steed, and turned its head in the direction of the property which was to be parted with.

It was customary to travel at night for the sake of coolness, and as these sales of human beings frequently took place at torchlight, which was the case with the one at present, he calculated that if he took three hours on his journey he would be there just about in time to make the purchases he wished.

His route lay through a very desolate country, a great portion of which was much uncultivated, while here and there upon fertile spots of about thirty to forty acres each, there were thriving plantations. A community of interests had made an apparent community of feeling among the planters and slaveowners, so that in any case where Mr. Deal's road would be shortened by going through any person's property, he knew he could do so with the greatest ease by merely presenting himself at any of the inclosures—an accommodation which in more than one instance, he knew he should be glad to avail himself of.

On shorter journeys Mr. Deal, in common with most of the planters, generally took with him an attendant, but upon this occasion he did not do so, preferring to ride alone, knowing that when he arrived at his journey's end, there would be ample accommodation for his horse.

He was well known as rather an indulgent slaveowner, so that except in very troublesome times indeed, there was very little likelihood that he would meet with any interruption.

Thus, although he kept nearly three hundred human beings in bondage, he did not anticipate any personal danger in riding unattended through so large a tract of country.

It wanted about half an hour of what might positively be called actual sunset; and a most delightful evening it was. There was a soft, balmy air, which carried upon its wings the incense of thousands of plants; birds of gay plumage fluttered about among the trees; and altogether a more pleasant looking evening for a ride, admitting the inevitable disadvantages of such a climate, could not have been imagined.

But let not the inhabitants of more northern and chilly regions envy the soft luxuries of tropical lands. It is true that the former have not the richness of vegetation, the gaily plumaged birds, and the glorious sunshine of the latter, but it seems to be an universal law of nature—at least so far as regards our earth—that, while there is no bane without its antidote, there shall, likewise, be no pleasure without its bane.

Those who would seek the deep blue skies and sunny aspects of more southerly regions must be prepared to encounter serious evils.

The animal kingdom and every species of the reptile tribe grow into as rank luxuriance as vegetation. It is not pleasant to go to bed with a rattle-snake. It is a disagreeable surprise to plunge into a cold stream and find yourself in the jaws of an alligator.

Under such circumstances one would be apt to envy those even in the torrid zone, who find so much difficulty in keeping themselves alive that they may be quite sure nothing of inferior vital powers or less ingenuity than the *genus homo* can have an existence.

Habit, however, is in truth a second nature, and people get used to finding snakes in their gardens, centipedes in their coat sleeves, and alligators in their fish ponds.

Mr. Deal rode on rather thoughtfully, for the late events upon his estate had given him more uneasiness than they really seemed to warrant.

He well knew the ungovernable overbearing character of his son, and he likewise well knew that nothing was more culculated to goad the African race to desperation than any rough interferance with their women. Indeed, by pursuing a different line of policy, he knew well he had got up for himself a strong moral power on his estate, and it certainly was not pleasant to lose that merely because Master Adolphus happened to be vicious.

"No," said Mr. Deal to himself, "I must nip this sort of thing in the bud; it must not be—I cannot, and will not endure it. He is tampering with and undermining all that I have been endeavouring to accomplish for many a year past."

We have before hinted at the rapidity with which, in these southern climes, day changes to night; and now, by the time Mr. Deal had got four miles on his journey, the sky was as dark as it could be.

But there was an unusual freshness and coolness in the air which was pleasant and invigorating, and which he rightly attributed to the agency of the storm of the preceding evening.

In such regions, unless some very heavy floods take place at the period of a storm, the most favourable period for undertaking a journey is immediately after one of these convulsions of the elements has taken place.

This, probably, was one reason why Mr. Deal felt anxious to go himself, instead of making his purchases by commission, which he might most certainly have done.

The only disagreeable part of the journey he had to take consisted in the crossing of a swamp, through which there was a wide, open, and firm road, to those who knew it, and as he was among that number, he did not anticipate any difficulty in his progress.

It was a strange, shifting sort of morass, and evidently took its origin from somewhere considerably below the earth's crust; for in all seasons it was equally soft and saturated with moisture, which would not have been the case had it derived its origin from land drainage.

It was well known, too, that when any alteration or shifting took place in this morass, there were always persons ready to point out to any chance traveller where such changes had taken place; so that Mr. Deal rode on, never doubting but that he should have ample assistance if it happened to be requisite.

An unusual gloom had spread over the sky, or he fancied so, as he entered the confines of the morass, and he had not gone far before he began to think that, unless his ears deceived him very much, some person was going on in front of him, mounted, and riding at very much the same pace that he was.

He concluded, of course, that it was either one of the owners of one of the neighbouring plantations, going, like himself, to the slave auction; or, possibly, some overseer sent upon a similar errand, and in either case Mr. Deal felt that he should not object to his company; so he increased his speed towards the central roadway of the morass, with the hope of overtaking the party, be he whom he might.

Strangely, however, it appeared to him; the faster he rode, the faster rode the man that was in advance, and what was more strange still, he heard the footsteps with as much distinctness when he rode slowly, as when he put his horse to a sharp canter.

Mr. Deal could not help feeling a little vexed at this apparently tricky conduct of the person he was pursuing, and he was just revolving in his mind what he could do to put an end to it, when the sound of the horse's hoofs ceased entirely, and in a a few moments he saw before him a dusky figure, sitting perfectly motionless upon an equally motionless steed.

He naturally checked his horse and advanced gently, so that getting quite near to the strange horseman, he saw that he had upon his head a great quantity of straw, and was otherwise strangely habited.

"Hilloa!" cried Mr. Deal, "who are you, I should like to know?"

"A coloured man," was the reply, "and yet nobody's slave. You is Mr. Deal, turn back and go by de path, by de black cedar."

Mr. Deal knew there was such a path, but it was a round about one, and he had passed the end of it purposely.

"Why should I retrace my steps?" he said.

"Know why," replied the stranger, "I do advise you :—You are not de worst of de coloured man's persecutors, and if you was de bery worst, your time hab not yet come. Cast your hat in advance and see it sink in the morass.

"If it be true," said Mr. Deal, "that the reason you warn me against proceeding, is because the morass road has deviated, I am much beholden to you. You know my name, and therefore no doubt know my plantation ; you can come when you like for your reward."

"Indeed! Massa Deal."

"Yes, and that reward shall be ample."

"When I come it shall, but I shall take it widout de ceremony of asking ;—turn back—turn back."

Mr. Deal felt rather hurt at the uncourteous manner in which his observations were received, and he said,—

"I don't know that I've any reason exactly to believe what you say ; I do not like to cast my hat before me to make the experiment, but I perceive a log of wood close at hand, which seems as if it had been dropped by a negro carried across the track, and with that I will try the experiment you suggest. If you are right, I can easily forgive the discourtesy of your manner, on account of the importance of your matter."

Mr. Deal knew that he could depend perfectly upon his horse standing quiet, and he, accordingly, at once alighted, and picking up the log of wood, which was by no means a considerable one, he flung it past the strange horseman, and as far in advance as he could, upon what appeared to be a good, hard, solid roadway.

He watched it eagerly by the dim night light, and he saw that it disappeared in a moment, being swallowed up as if by magic.

A shudder came over him ; for he felt certain that if he had not been stopped, his destruction would have been inevitable. He remounted, and turned his horse's head away from the treacherous morass, and as he did so, he said,—

"Mark me—I know not who you are, or what you are, but you have saved my life ; and come to me whenever you will—with whatever request you may that it is in my power to grant, it is yours."

"Agreed," said the stranger. "I am satisfied."

"Well," said Mr. Deal to himself as he rode on "there was very near being one guest less at Julia's birthday *fete*."

CHAPTER XVI.

MR. DEAL'S PURCHASES.—A SUDDEN SURPRISE TO CESAR BOBB.

MR. DEAL went the remainder of his way in perfect safety, and reached the plantation at which the auction was to take place, of those unhappy beings who could not but feel acutely the horrors of their situation.

If it happened by good fortune that a slave fell into humane hands, the dread of a change must be very great indeed, and must produce the most poignant feelings of alarm; and then, again, if the master who has already possessed them be severe and exacting, there must be always some ties of relationship or friendship to rend asunder when a change of owners takes place.

A glare of light, caused by a number of lamps and torches, brought Mr. Deal to the spot where the auction was to take place, and there he found a strange motley assemblage of persons, surrounding a man who stood upon a chair, and who had already disposed of a number of lots to the highest bidders.

To a really humane, gentlemanly, and educated man, like Mr. Deal, one must suppose such a scene to be peculiarly revolting; but that it was not so, proves what habit will accustom some to, and how all the better feelings of human nature may be smothered by a constant association with what is of a brutalising tendency.

He surrendered his horse into the charge of a slave who advanced to take it, and who walked it off to some rich pasture land in the immediate vicinity.

Mr. Deal then watched the progress of the sale for some time, until he bought a lot to his liking, which consisted—according to the catalogue—of

"A lively young negro, born in Georgia, capable and willing to work, and warranted sound; answers to the name of Alexander Blackblossom."

This lot Mr. Deal bought; nor did the young negro seem at all put out of his way by the change of masters.

"Hi! hi! hi!" he said. "Goramighty! me taught me'd fetch ten dollar more dan dat—hi! hi! hi!"

It was near the end of the sale, and some of the indifferent old lots were beginning to be put up, which went remarkably cheap. There was one in particular of an elderly negro, who was vaunted by the auctioneer as being a remarkably smart hand at feeding poultry, and as Mr. Deal happened to want such a person at his establishment, and only twenty-five dollars was the purchasing price, he became the master of this old slave, who, he was told, answered to the name of Brutus Golightly.

He certainly did not come all that distance to make only two purchases, but still he was tolerably satisfied with those he did make; and, after accepting the hospitality for the remainder of the night, and announcing his intention of departing at early dawn with his new purchases, before the heat of the day should have commenced, Mr. Deal saw his horse carefully disposed of, and then retired to rest.

He had ordered that he should be aroused an hour after sunrise, and this was punctually done. Perhaps the reader will be curious to know how Mr. Deal got his purchases home, and in our answer we shall again prove that custom supersedes humanity. They were made to trot the whole distance after his horse. He certainly did not go at a quick pace; but it was so customary for a single horseman to bring home slaves in that manner, that it certainly never occurred to Mr. Deal that he was doing anything extraordinary in giving them a journey of between twenty and thirty miles over what was in some places a very troublesome bit of country, and as little did they think of uttering a complaint.

The sun had got a considerable height in the heavens before the Deal estate was again reached, and then Mr. Deal was met by John Grubson, to whom he handed over both the negroes, his duty being to show them the limits of Mr.

Deal's property, to appoint them sleeping places, and to take a full and accurate
description of their persons.

If a slave had any peculiarity or mark upon him from birth, it generally saved
him some pain and inconvenience afterwards, for if he had no such distinguishing
symbol, and the overseer felt that there might be a difficulty in swearing to him,
it was usual enough to stamp a small initial letter upon him somewhere with a hot
iron, or to give one of his ears a snip.

It happened, however, in this instance that John Grubson was satisfied, and
consequently Mr. Deal's two purchases escaped the performance of any such uncomfortable operation. They were appointed to a hut that was vacant, close to
old Pompey's, and, as was always the case upon the occasion of any new arrivals
coming, when the slaves had done work for the day, they congregated round the
strangers, asking as many questions as any genuine Yankee could have done for
the life of him.

"Dey call me Blackblossom," said the old slave, "but my real name be Cesar
Bobb, and I would be sold to twenty massas, Goramighty, yes, if I could find out
my son Cesar, who was took from me."

The moment these words were uttered, our friend Cesar rushed forward, and
threw himself into the arms of the old negro, exclaiming,—

"Fader, fader, you hab found your son Cesar! I am dat piccaninny as was took
away by dam tief. Here is affecting scene! I hab found my ole fader. Jolly ole
pimp he is. Hi! hi! hi!"

———

CHAPTER XVII.

THE MEETING AT OLD POMPEY'S.—OLD CESAR'S NARRATION.

BLACKS are terrible gossip-mongers and famous story-tellers. It was noised in
the course of a quarter of an hour all over the estate that Mr. Deal had bought
Cesar's father, and an extemporaneous jollification was got up upon the occasion,
in the midst of which the old man was seated, and made quite a great character of,
as he deserved to be.

Lucy Neal was duly introduced as, should circumstances be favourable, the bride
elect of Cesar Bobb, junior; and, to listen to the hilarity, the songs, and the world
of gossiping that ensued, one would not have supposed there was such a thing as
a heavy heart upon the estate.

Cesar for the time quite forgot that there were such people in existence as
Tobias Slankey, Adolphus Deal, or John Grubson, and much of the apprehension
which had taken so firm a hold of the imagination of poor Lucy, vanished before
the general hilarity of that evening.

"It's a bery extraordinary ting," said Cesar, "dat de ole man should come into
Mr. Deal's estate, more special just now, when some people don't care a *straw*
about some people."

It was evident that this allusion to the visit of Jack Straw to the estate was
generally understood, for significant glances passed from one to the other of those
who were assembled, although not another word was spoken upon the subject.

Cesar, however, in his own mind, was quite satisfied that not a hut had been
left unvisited by the singular man who had made so strange a speech to him in his
own garden.

"Yes," my piccaninny, "said old Cesar, "it is bery sing'lar, and shows what
a bery fine ting it is to know how to feed fowls. Hi! hi! hi! If I hadn't known
how to feed fowls, Massa Deal would not hab bought me."

"No," said old Pompey, "but it's easy to see you'b been among geese all your
life—hi! hi! hi!—and dat's what makes you look so like one."

" What you say dat for, you black fellow?"

" Black fellow ? You're a nigger, quite a nigger !"

" What you say ?   Nigger ?"

" Don't make a row," cried Cesar.   " I tell you what it is, all ob you—de ole man is de greatest story-teller and dam ole liar in all ob de world : he'll tell you all ob his adventures—all what did happen and all what didn't."

" Oh ! Hi ! hi ! hi !" cried old Cesar.   " I understand you.   Now, I am going to knock you down flat, you bad boy, Cesar."

There was now an urgently-expressed desire on the part of all present that old Cesar should relate his adventures, and as the old man seemed rather pleased to be made the centre of so much attraction, he, after a few preliminary hems, commenced.

We need not follow Cesar's peculiarity of dialect in this narrative, so take the liberty of translating for him :—

I was not a slave in my own country ; oh no ! there I did not labour with an overseer at my back ; I knew not what slavery was ; I was free—ay, as any of your white people, perhaps a great deal more, for I could have gone out to hunt or to fish in any of the wild forests, thirsty plains, or the deep and rapid rivers that joined the sea on the Guinea coast.

Those were days that I knew before I felt the horrors of slavery. We had slaves too ; but they were the slaves of our own prowess—the booty of our warlike expeditions—those whom we had taken in fair war.   I can't say but what it was bad enough—too bad—much too bad ; but then it was sanctioned among our own people, the usage of ages, and among people of our own kind ; but, at the same time, it was not for money, we had nobler and better objects in view ; we did not steal and sell one another.

My wife was young and fair ; my family were young, there were many of us, and we were in happy ignorance of the fate that awaited us.   Certainly, we were not Christians ; we knew nothing, then, of the missionaries, nor of what they taught.   I was then contented, and I may say happy.   My hut contained all I loved, and all I valued on earth, when I was suddenly awoke from my slumbers by loud cries and shouts.

I knew, in an instant, my hut was surrounded by an enemy ; but we were not then at war with any other tribe, and I could not understand how or why I was thus attacked.   My wife trembled violently, and even the cries of my children were stilled.

I arose to seize my arms, but at that moment the hut was forced open, and instantly filled with armed men, who seized me, and flinging me down, bound me hand and foot ; and my wife and all who were in the same place with us were all bound together, their hands behind them, and then chained together in gangs.

I was dreadfully cut up when I saw this, for I well knew for what fate we were all seized thus ; and, if any doubt had existed, the fact of the men who had thus suddenly captured us having many ornaments and articles that were the produce of white men's hands, would have convinced me that we were for the slave market.

The truth shot through my brain when I first saw the chief among them put a bottle to his lips which I knew contained brandy.

" My God ! my God !" I exclaimed ; " we are slaves ! We have been captured to be sold to the white men, to be sent to far countries."

My wife sobbed, my children looked up in our faces and cried too for sympathy, for they knew not what they would have to suffer—they knew nothing of slavery— nor I, but I had heard of what others had endured from one or two who had escaped from the slave-dealers', and what they told me was enough to make one's heart sicken at the very thought of becoming one of those, who are forcibly sent to different parts of the earth to spend the best years of their life—to become old and decrepit in other men's services, and finally to die without once casting a single glance upon those scenes which make home and childhood so dear to all.

It was a sorry night to us. It was the last of our freedom, and the first of our captivity, and such a night I never wish to pass again.

We were all driven off by our savage captors. Had I been aware of their coming, or had I known or apprehended such an attack, I should have been able to beat them off; and it only showed me how much surprise could get the master. We were all seized and bound by a few men, whom we could have seized and bound.

But it mattered not. I was quite unable to remedy what had happened. As it often happens to those who are thus seized, we were all silent—not a word was spoken. Our tears, for the most part, were the only marks of grief we exhibited; we knew very well that we could not help ourselves. We were too much stunned to have the full use of our faculties, and yet if we had, what would they have done for us?

It may be we might have increased our evils by adding bodily pain in addition to what we already suffered.

We were hurried along by our captors, being bound together in twos, a rope or chain passing from each couple to that which followed it.

Thus we were forced along at a pace, and for a time that even we should have been unable to have kept up but for the goad and lash.

Then for the first time in my life did I become acquainted with the lash. That was the first time my shoulders felt the smart of brutality. My very heart sickened at the sound of it swinging through the air; and when I saw my wife subject to the same degrading brutality, my soul would no longer submit, and I rushed on the wretch who had tortured her.

I might as well have remained inactive, and submitted without any appearance of resentment: it served but to anger our captors.

I had been secured to another and bound strongly; but, upon the sudden energy of the moment, my bonds gave way, and I had nearly reached the man who had inflicted the blow, when the chain by which I was attached to the couple before and behind, checked me, and the ruffian who had precipitately enough got out of my way, now he saw me secured, came forward, and struck me repeatedly.

Nor was that all I suffered—quite the reverse. My poor wife was struck repeatedly without any provocation upon her part, the only motive being, the poor one that it appeared to give me exquisite anguish. I saw the barbarous brute strike her, and then turn menacingly to me, and, when he saw my agony, laugh at my pain, my tears, and my attempts to free myself of my bonds.

"Ah! ah!" he laughed, with ferocious glee, "rive as you will, you are sure never more to get back to your own country. Your wife will be some one else's before a month is over your head, you black rascal."

"Villain," I exclaimed, "may you die the death of a dog, and——"

Before I could finish the sentence, I was struck across the head with a bamboo cane; so hard was the blow that I fell, stunned; however, I was soon aroused from my stupor, and compelled to pursue my route.

We were compelled to travel the whole of the night at a rapid pace, and near morning we crossed the ford of a rapid river. We got over safe enough—not so all of those who accompanied us by force; two of my unfortunate companions were drowned, and I believe that they but hastened their own end; at all events, they refused to aid themselves, which is not a very unusual thing among those whom others take from their homes, and from their own native land, and all they hold dear.

There were also some others—children and females, but I cannot now remember well; but we got over, and then we went into a wood, and here it was we, for the first time, halted to rest and to take food.

Here we were permitted to throw ourselves upon the ground, but we were placed in small bodies at certain distances apart, with some armed men to guard us. In one of those parties I was placed, and my wife in another.

This was to me a piteous spectacle. I could just see her fall, almost insensible, to the earth; and I was unable to fly to her assistance. I was forced to lie down too, and only a little water was served round to us; at the same time, we received a little solid food—and but little—especially when the distance and exertion we had been compelled to make, was considered; but by some of us even that was refused, who chose rather to perish of hunger, than to submit to the fate that awaited them.

I do not know, but I think, that I should have done the same, but for the leaving behind my poor wife—she would have been no worse off then if I had perished; perhaps her grief at my loss might have caused her death.

That, of course, would have made little difference; they would have made no allowance for her grief; and I did hope, that some lucky moment would come when we might yet get back to our own country. No state of misery is so low that hope is shut out altogether, and I even hoped, though I can't tell why—I had no reason to hope then.

I fell asleep in the midst of my woes; the fact was, I was completely fatigued, almost amounting to insensibility.

I will not tell you all the horrors we suffered on the road, while under the charge of our captors; indignities and blows were inflicted, without any regard to our powers of endurance, or even provocation. They were often given us, if it were only for the sake of keeping up our terror, and their hands in action.

Thus we went on till the heat of the day grew excessive, and we were compelled to penetrate deeper into the woods, in order to escape the scorching rays of a tropical sun.

There we were met by a party who appeared to have been waiting for us. These were indeed our enemies—they were the white men who had invited one tribe of black men to war on another tribe, and kidnap their people at the same time, to make articles of commerce of them—to make them mere objects of barter.

I found that we were not far from the sea. We were permitted to lie down while the chief who had conducted this assault upon an unoffending people, who were at peace with all, and who dreamed not of harm, was enjoying himself.

There was a carousal then among our captors and those who came to buy us; and after some hours the bargains were concluded—we were exchanged for the most trifling matters—things that were of no value, but which in their eyes, especially with the aid of spirits, they believed them to be of great worth; but they were ignorant, and knew not how they were defrauded.

It was for the sake of such things that we were torn away from our homes, and all that was held dear. We were soon forced away from this spot, and we exchanged our coloured tyrants for white ones.

We were now regularly chained and put in pairs, with strong iron chains, and made to walk in gangs. Men and women and children; all were compelled to tramp in measured tread, while our white drivers walked along before us, armed with cutlasses and guns; and they would hardly have any use for them, considering how we were secured; not but what we would have made a desperate, though an unavailing resistance—death, fighting, would have been far preferable to the anticipated horrors of a slave-ship.

We were, however, too firmly shackled to think of anything of the kind; our hearts were too much oppressed by terror, pain, and the impossibility of making an attempt of the kind.

In a few moments we were quite out of the reach of our late masters, who had returned with their booty to their own homes, and we pursued our way towards the seashore, which was yet a couple of hours' journey from where we then were.

There was a deep gloom spread over us when we saw the ship that was to convey us away. It was with deep sorrow that we were convinced of the melancholy truth—we were to be slaves to the white men.

A slave-ship, we had all heard, was a place of far greater torment than could be conceived; for all who had ever escaped such a period of suffering, declared that no earthly hardship and torture could equal it.

I threw myself down on the sands and refused to move. I thought I had better die than experience what we dreaded most—the horrors of a slave-ship. I was ordered to get up, but I would not move.

"You won't get up, won't you, lad? then I'll try and make you," said one of the drivers, who had the charge of me and of that gang to which I was attached.

Accordingly, he took from his pocket a sharp spike, which he fixed on the end of a stick, and then goaded us with it in the same manner that I have seen bullocks goaded.

This for some time failed to move me; but, at length, the pain was so intolerable, and I was bleeding from more than one wound, I was compelled to get up.

"Oh, I thought I could cure an obstinate nigger," said the man; and more dead than alive, I was hurried into a boat, then pushed off from shore.

Once on board a black-looking vessel, we were ordered down below, between very low decks, where none of us could stand up in. Here was a scene of horror and misery that can hardly be imagined.

The voyage from the Guinea Coast to Alabama took many weeks, and the sufferings that we endured I can hardly describe.

In the first place we had barely room to sit and lie down in; we saw nothing, save the wants of our fellow sufferers. There were few or no means of ventilation, and many died on the passage, and were thrown overboard like so much offal.

One man who had been a chief in our country had made a desperate resistance when he was first surprised, and was sorely wounded, yet he had been forced along and kept, notwithstanding his gaping wounds.

He was a fine man, so, therefore, it was hoped he would live, and realise a handsome sum on the safe arrival of the ship in Alabama.

But the poor fellow was never destined to reach that port, for his ugly wounds were festering for want of care and attention—the want of care and proper air and food no doubt helped towards the same end.

"I shall never reach land again," he said.

"We know not where we are going," I said, "and cannot tell."

"I shall not live long; my wounds will not let me, and the smell of this horrid hole will kill me before many hours more are past. I am almost suffocated as it is now, but a short time hence it will be worse."

I endeavoured to comfort him, but it was of no use; he had been used to command, and knew not how to be a slave. He died that night, and was thrown overboard, a prey to the sharks that followed the ship.

Somehow I think it must have been instinct that caused the sharks to follow us, but whatever the cause, a number of sharks followed us through the whole voyage—a strange and unnatural occurrence—but then they were well fed on the flesh of the negro.

My unfortunate countrymen died off very rapidly; man after man fell ill, and I could hardly stand when I had been at sea three weeks. The number of slaves on board would exceed belief, when you come to consider and to examine the space allotted to the numbers that were crowded below."

To add to our misfortunes, we suffered dreadfully from a storm that occurred, and which caused us a loss of some of our water-casks, so that in a few days we were compelled to put up with short allowance of that necessary article.

During the storm, all the portholes were secured, and the whole of the air that had been supplied by those means was cut off. This produced the greatest misery that could be inflicted. We were sick, and stifled.

In the morning it was found that thirty-three men were dead.

My wife was very ill, and my children but little better. I was unable to stand; there we were for many weeks, and about one half of our numbers had been carried off by disease and ill-usage.

This gave us an increase of space, and more air and water, in consequence of which, those who survived got a little better. But still the place was dreadful to endure. We could sooner have lain on deck night and day, than have gone below; but there was enough of power to make us.

"The captain and his officers abused us, because we fell away and became

miserable, lean, gaunt wretches, unfit for any work, and apparently on the brink of the grave, instead of the muscular, active-looking men we were when first seized and carried away.''

"The tarnal critters," said the captain to the purser, one day, " will die in spite of all I can do. What on earth can they be arter.''

"It's just like them thar niggers," said the purser.

"Tarnation seize 'em. What's to pay for the voyage I don't know, I'm sure, if many more of them black critters are going to give us the slip by coming the dead dodge. We shan't be able to pay wages.''

"They are as obstinate, captain," said the purser, " as a pig, which you want to drive in at one gate, and he will persist in going in at another.''

"Exactly," said the captain. " Cuss 'em, I'll have it out on 'em. The next time I sees one on 'em going off in that way, I'll be level with him: I'll put him overboard alive, and see if I can't frighten life into them,''

"If he die," said the purser, " which is very likely, considering how obstinate they are, they will die off just the same.''

"Shouldn't wonder if they did," said the captain, who used to walk up and down the decks whenever the slaves were brought upon the deck, counting up in his own mind how many dollars each one would bring.

He used to thrust his hands into his pockets, and look at some one from head to heel, as he turned over the coin in his fingers.

"There's that big rascal," he would say, "he ought to bring, let me see— seventy, aye, seventy-five dollars—say eighty; I'm sure he ought to fetch eighty Why, darn the feller, whatever is he about?"

This sudden exclamation in the midst of his calculations was caused by the negro he was looking at being suddenly seized with symptoms of a distressing and dangerous illness.

"Cuss his black hide, he's ten dollars worse than what he was five minutes ago— why, the brute won't be worth anything in five minutes more; he'll only be fit for food for the fishes, and very ugly eating, too, it strikes me."

The unfortunate man reeled and fell; and as his disorder was evidently mortal he was ordered to be thrown overboard.

This piece of inhumanity was committed because he was vexed at losing a man, worth, according to his own computation, near eighty dollars.

However, I survived; my wife and family all continued to hold out, though they were very ill, and I had more than once expected that they would have been thrown overboard, and I only saved among them, to endure the horrors of slavery; but it isnot so, they recovered, and we all came to Alabama.

When in port, we waited a few hours before we were landed. We were not allowed to stand or to come upon deck; we were all confined below until the order was given for us to do so.

This precaution was, I suppose, to prevent our being taken by any vessel which might be cruising about, not that there was any such fear, I believe, but they always take precautions in port.

After some hours had passed, we were not to be landed during the day. This was a moment of great anxiety and sorrow to me and my wife, for we did not know but what we should be separated for ever, and never more see each other; but a long and lasting severance might, and most probably would, be the result.

"We are to be sold, I dare say—indeed, it must be so. My God! my God! what a life is a slave! compared to which this is but an introduction," I could not help exclaiming: I could not help thinking and believing death was preferable.

My wife sobbed, and lay on the bare boards some few yards from the spot to which I was secured; and though she was fainting from agony of mind at the hought that we should be both separated—the idea of being separated from each other!

But I was chained, and I could not move from where I was. I raved and cursed, but at length utterly exhausted, I sank into a kind of insensibility, more ike death than sleep; but from this I was awakened by the sounds of locks and chains, and a rough voice crying aloud,—

"Rouse up here, you black varmint, rouse up here; we are in glorious Alabama, and if ye were kings instead of black niggers, you couldn't see a more beautiful sight; get up, you black rascals, or, darn me, but you'll have a taste of the cow-hide, which is no easy matter to digest."

At the same time he accompanied his word with a crashing made by smacking a cow-hide whip—a fearful engine of torture in the hands of a strong man who knows how to use it skilfully.

We all got up. We were surprised and terrified. I can hardly tell how or why. It was pitchy dark; there was no sign of light, not a stray ray, and we knew it was night, and hardly knew what was the object of this nocturnal visit. Indeed more than one of us thought of refusing to go above, lest we were about to meet with wholesale destruction in some dreadful shape or other

However, some went up, and I was dragged up among others, and got upon deck, when we found that other slaves were on board, and descending the sides of the vessel and entering some boats that were alongside, and some were leaving the vessel.

I was forced towards one of the boats to be rowed ashore. I turned towards the deck, and was about to speak.

"Get on, you black nigger;" said the captain, "now you get over—do you think I am going to keep the boat waiting for you?"

"My wife—my wife and children!" said I. I could say no more.

"Now, cuss your black hide," said the captain, "what have I to do with your female black, and your ugly young imps? Now, darn your carcass, get over. Here, big Jem, bring that cow-hide here."

In a moment more a stripe across my back, that cut the flesh deep and brought the blood briskly down, was inflicted on me. I rushed at the captain, and with one blow felled the dastardly hound who ordered the blow.

"Over with you, unless you want a bowie-knife in your ribs, for I'm etarnally bumped if the captain's dander won't be riz."

The man who spoke, thrust me over the side, and I fell like a log into the boat, incapable of doing anything, or hardly being conscious of what was going on. In a short while after, my wife and children (there were two of them), were forced over in another boat, in the same manner, while the one which I had been forced into was rowed off from the ship.

We landed, and were hurried along from place to place, when we were finally secured in a place that was dimly lighted; but we were unable to discern anything of the place, the lights being inadequate for that purpose.

But here we were all huddled together until the morning, when day came upon us, and to my great joy I found I was placed close beside my wife, a circumstance that had not happened to me before; and I then for the first time embraced her, and endeavoured to console her in her affliction, for she was much depressed, and deep grief appeared to have settled upon her.

"Hold up some little while longer," I said; "a few more hours may tell us our future lot, and then grief, or comparative——"

"We may be parted," she said, dolefully.

"We may," I returned.

My wife sobbed, and I was too much affected at our misfortune to be able to comfort her, but fell into as sad a state as she; but at length I felt it my place to cheer her up if it were possible, and whispered to her there might yet be hope, and that there would be a time, even in slavery, when we could regain our liberty. We could live or die together yet. "Let us hope the best," I said, "nor fear the worst."

This had in some measure the effect of subduing her more violent emotions, but still her tears fell fast, and my features bore no joy.

Soon after, at an early hour, the place was opened, and a number of strangers, with loose cloaks and large hats, knotty sticks, and cow-hide whips, entered the slave-market—for such was the place where we were placed, under a cover, and in a secure place, for the weather was hardly clement enough to permit the buyers to walk about with comfort to themselves.

Among them was the captain of the ship who had brought us over; he looked at me; but, as he was speaking to another person, he did not say anything to me, though I could see very well he would not let an opportunity slip away of giving me some return for the trouble which I had given him.

At length I heard the person he was speaking to, say,—

"Well, captain, what have you brought with you this voyage?"

"Much of the old sort, governor," said the captain; "you see them, good, bad, and indifferent, black as well as white, though I can tell you this, that when you come to buy slaves, you buy at a disadvantage for their seller; though him as buys gains, I reckon."

"I can't see that, captain."

"I'll tell you then, governor. You see them black cattle, as I calls them niggers, always gets sulky—they will die, cuss 'em, like sheep, and we are obliged to throw them overboard like smoke; and them as lives, you see, grow mopish and skinny, cuss them. I say a man don't get his bread at this kind of work; he don't indeed, governor. I'll be etarnally chewed up into a quid of true Virginny if I do."

"Well, you must take the good with the bad, you know, captain. We always put a good season agin a bad, and strike the difference."

"Tarnal good! but I never thought of that," said the captain. "I'll raise the price of them there slaves, and as it's a bad voyage, why, it will be a little consolation for me to know that I am not entirely out of pocket."

"Which are your slaves?"

"These are them. These critters you will observe, governor, are real niggers—they are all fresh, and full of fire and spirit for work, only, you see, the voyage has been a bad one, and they do look a little skinny."

"They do look considerably so, I think—that man yonder is old."

"Not he, governor—it's only his looks—he is a young feller, that critter. I can tell you it's the voyage—nothing but the voyage. You've no idea of how soon these fellers get plumped out, and look well when you've once taken them to your estate."

"I have bought them before," said the planter.

"You have, governor, and know what I have told you is true; but what description of article is it that you want, governor? I can suit you."

"I hardly know," said the governor, as he was called, being merely a planter, as he cast his eyes over the whole lot of us.

There was something humane in this man's countenance. He was a stout, big man, and one who lived easily, and who appeared to be one who would not unnecessarily use harshly any animal whatever, much less a human being.

"Poor things," he muttered, "poor things; it is a hard lot after all is said and done.

"Why, them blacks, you see," said the captain, "are tarnal critters, and no more ike a Christian than I am a river-horse."

"Is that a family?" he said, pointing to myself, wife, and two children.

"Yes, governor, and a real bargain; for, suppose anything happens to the old crows, why you have the young 'uns to fall back upon. If them two were to die, the young 'uns would grow up in the ways you wanted them."

"It would be long before they were of any use. Poor things, they don't seem to understand this way of life."

"No, governor; now if you wanted such a family—you are a kind man, and would use 'em well—they would do you rial service, I'll warrant—I'll say this for that nigger, he's an out-an-outer—as kind as a young kitten, and as docile."

As he spoke he grinned at me with a smothered feeling of revenge, for the injury I had inflicted on him, which showed itself in his face.

"What do you ask for them?"

"Two hundred dollars, and remarkably cheap at that."

"Two hundred dollars! too much—too much," said the stranger.

"Well, they'll fetch me that before the market is closed," said the captain.

"Now, captain, I'll tell you what I'll do—you shall give them to me for one hundred and fifty dollars down."

"You have been a customer afore, governor, and I would not refuse a good offer; but I'll make you an allowance—one hundred and ninety."

"No."

"Well then, eighty."

"No! seventy-five, and here's your money."

"You are hard, governor; but I'll take your money—this is the first I have had to-day—and the niggers are yours, stock and branch."

Thus were we summarily disposed of, and were sent under the charge of a man to the estate of this gentleman, who lived at no very great distance from the slave-market—about half a day's journey.

Here we were put in gangs, and compelled to work under the superintendence of overseers, who could use the cow-hide. I was grateful that we had been purchased all together; and I had a cottage given me in which myself and wife and my children lived. We were very well treated, and found ourselves comparatively happy, though slaves in a foreign land.

The labour was hard, and such as white men couldn't endure; but we wer used to a hot climate, though not to hard work.

From other slaves we learned the difference between our usage and that of others on the neighbouring estates; indeed, we saw a very great deal of this on all sides of us, but here we were contented.

To say that I never entertained hopes of getting away, and returning to our own country, would be to speak falsely—it was our grand wish; but in time this wish was lessened, as we became contented and satisfied. We were used well, and had an abundance of all things that constituted the necessaries of life.

Our children had grown up in the ways of the place, and we had added to their numbers, which rendered our condition more in accordance with the views of those who were our masters; we were unable and disinclined to return to the state in which we formerly were, for the sake of our children.

After some years our master's affairs became deranged; he could not obtain from his estate the means of supporting himself and the burdens imposed upon him; his crops, too, failed upon several occasions, and he had other losses besides. The merchants to whom he sold his goods were bankrupts, and he could get no money from them.

Evils appeared to accumulate faster that can well be imagined, and he himself was unable to meet all, so that he himself became a bankrupt.

Once more, our misfortunes became heavy and immediate.

We knew that the estate would be sold, that all upon it would be likewise sold and the slaves among the rest.

Should we be all together, or separated, and carried off to different estates?—this was the question that naturally arose in our minds, and which caused more than one negro family to run away from the estate.

This was a serious matter, and we were compelled to keep within doors for several days prior to the sale, which would prevent our running away. We all expected that we should be separated from each other, and the thought nearly drove us to distraction.

This was a state of things we did not wish—we did not like, but we were the children of circumstances, and had to wait the will of others.

The day of sale came round, and we were compelled to stand or sit in different rows and places where we were all looked over, and pulled about like so many pieces of lumber, and our purchasers were apparently calculating what use they could put us to if they purchased us.

Some of them even struck us with the cow-hides, but only to see how we were willing to obey the whip.

This sale was a long and tedious affair, for several days we were thus drilled, and kept standing about. True it was we did not work, but that to me, and many more was no alteration, for we were most acutely harassed with fears for the future; we did not know what our lot might be—we all wished to live on the same estate—to work together, and to live with each other; but that was uncertain; and it was even more probable that we should not have the good fortune that we so much desired—to be bought by one master.

The time came for our turn, and we were at length purchased; but, alas! we were all bought separately. Families were severed to please the wants and wishes of purchasers, and the negro's afflictions were of no consideration in this matter.

Now commenced some of the worst scenes in my life, except, perhaps, the slave-ship. We were all taken from each other, and carried miles apart: the father and mother—parents and children,—were all sent different ways.

My wife was very ill for some time, and she was treated with great brutality by the overseers where she was carried to.

As for myself I have passed through some scenes that would make a man's heartache; but no matter now, I have passed through all that, and past misfortunes are easier to be borne than the present or future."

       *   *   *   *   *   *   *

Old Cesar's narrative was over; and Lucy Neal's tears fell fast, as she looked in the old man's face.

CHAPTER XVIII.

THE BIRTHDAY FEAST.—THE LOST CUP.—THE SEARCH.

HAVING brought our *dramatis personæ* thus far in this veritable record of their actions, we will suppose that a few days have elapsed, and that the evening before the birthday *fete* is gradually drawing to a close on the Deal estate.

Some few changes have taken place, not of a very startling character, but still of sufficient importance to merit mention; notwithstanding, they are such as may be, by our readers, almost inferred from what has preceded them.

In the first place, Cesar has availed himself of Mr. Deal's kindness, and got his garden put all to rights; so that it is in a more profitable condition than ever, because Mr. Deal allowed him to take some rather rare plants, of which there was abundance, from his private pleasure garden, immediately around his own house.

In the second place, Cesar had had due notice that he was required, for a few days, to leave his work on the plantation, and come into the house, for the purpose of assisting in the arrangements for the birthday entertainment; and the assistance of Lucy Neal had, likewise, been required by Mrs. Deal.

There was nothing unusual in this state of things; nothing that could create the least alarm or suspicion of any foul play being intended; so that Cesar felt rather glad than otherwise, for he knew that Mr. Deal was liberal, and expected to add a few dollars to his store by the transaction.

The only dislike that either he or Lucy had to the arrangement was, that it involved the necessity of encountering Adolphus and Mrs. Deal occasionally; but then it was just the same, for if they avoided Mrs. Deal and Adolphus by being upon the plantation instead of the house, they encountered John Grubson, and by being brought into the house instead of the plantation they avoided him; so that the affair was as broad as it was long, as far as regarded disagreeables.

The arrangements for this entertainment were entirely left to Mrs. Deal and her daughter, and neither of those ladies were at all inclined to be saving on the occasion. They knew very well that Mr. Deal could afford to have his money spent, and when they had a *carte blanche* to spend it, they took amazingly good care to make the most of it.

Adolphus, too, came in for his share of what was going on; and, although he had an ample allowance from his father for all necessary expenses, Mrs. Deal gave him more money whenever she could put it down to some other account.

The neighbouring planters, within a circle of twenty-five miles, were invited, along with their families, to grace the festivities.

"It's quite necessary," said Mrs. Deal, "to ask everybody we know much of, as well as every respectable person we know little of; for there is no saying exactly who Julia may marry, although, of course, she'll marry a planter."

By some mysterious means the Rev. Tobias Slankey appeared to have pocketed the affront that had been put upon him, and to have taken himself off; indeed, the whole affair connected with the squabbling between Lucy Neal and Adolphus, Cesar and Tobias Slankey appeared to have lapsed into a kind of peaceable oblivion.

Perchance, though, this is the calm that is to precede the storm.

Our readers may fancy what a delightful thing it was to Cesar to be even for so brief a space, domiciliated under the same roof with Lucy Neal ; and, although for various considerations, he would not seem unduly to seek her presence, yet opportunities would occur in the course of the festal arrangements which enabled him now and then to say a few words to her.

"Lucy Neal," he said, on one of these occasions, " I hall hab more dollars to put in de hole in de hut, to'ards de 'mancipation of somebody, you know. Hi ! hi ! hi !"

"Cesar," replied Lucy, "you seem pleased, but I must say for my own part, I am not without apprehensions; a something seems to come over me at times, to the effect that all will not be well."

" All not well ?—What you mean, Lucy ?"

" Perhaps I may be too apprehensive, Cesar, and unjust even towards our enemies ; but does it not strike you that Mrs. Deal's sudden kindness towards us has really something suspicious in it: do you not think so, Cesar ?"

This was certainly presenting the affair in a new light to Cesar Bobb, and giving him more uneasiness than he cared to own ; but he tried to laugh it off, by telling Lucy that he thought there was no danger, although, in reality, he was far from feeling quite clear upon that point himself.

If what she had said was not sufficient exactly to make him entirely agree with her in opinion, it certainly was sufficient very considerably to damp his ardour, and he certainly wore a more clouded brow than he had done before.

And Mrs. Deal was so truly urbane and gentle, that any one would have suspected that she was overshooting the mark a little ; it certainly was something too wonderful to suppose that that lady, with such admirable skill, should have discovered that kindness was superior to power, and that if she wished to obtain the truest service, she must achieve it through affection, and not through fear.

Adolphus, too, seemed to have repented him of his bad behaviour, for when he came into a room in which was Lucy Neal, laying out some fruits and preserves upon a table, he merely turned and left it again, without making the least remark to her.

On such a large scale were the preparations for the entertainment, that most of the household remained up during the night, feeling convinced that unless everything was done in proper time and order by a very early hour, they would have failed in giving satisfaction to their very imperious mistress.

Among those who so stayed up were both Cesar and Lucy, but at all events when the morning did dawn, they all had the satisfaction of knowing that everything had been done which the fastidious Miss Dea or her mother could desire.

And that morning was, in the opinion of young and old, one of the most delightful ones that had ever shone upon the estate ; it seemed, indeed, as if nature were quite willing to aid and assist in that public demonstration of joy, at Julia Deal reaching another year.

By times, horses and carriages, and in one or two cases parties on foot began to arrive at the estate ; it was a general holiday with all the working slaves, and they, with their usual aptitude at extemporaneous entertainments, had got up, in an incredibly short space of time, a ball, at which they figured in their best attire ; and at which with their natural love of dancing they did not think it at all unreasonable to commence the first thing in the morning.

John Grubson dared not, in so marked a manner, contravene the orders of Mr. Deal, or he would gladly have placed some impediment in the way of the enjoyments of the slaves.

It was rankling to his heart to see that they were so happy, while he, notwithstanding all his power and all his money—for John Grubson was very tolerably off—found it impossible even to taste a moment's enjoyment, and his very sleep was haunted by uncomfortable reminiscences.

His mind, however, was soon now occupied with other matters, and the slaves and their fancy ball became secondary considerations to the more important events in which he was mixed up, and had pledged himself to take a part in.

Need we say that those events pointed to the destruction of Cesar Bobb?

And let it not appear strange that such men as Adolphus Deal, Grubson, and Tobias Slankey took so much pains for the ruin of a poor negro slave ; for it must be remembered, that despised as Cesar might be in consequence of his position, he was still a piece of property, and that, too, of sufficient value, that Mr. Deal was more than likely, apart from motives of humanity altogether, to make a considerable riot, should he come by his death by unfair means.

Hence it became necessary to ruin their victim, whom they dared not kill, and Cesar Bobb, inefficient and beneath contempt as he was in the eyes of Adolphus Deal, was intended to be made the victim of as diabolical a plot as ever entered into the mind of man to subject his fellow mortals to the consequence of.

But we must not anticipate—facts shortly will speak trumpet-tongued for themselves.

There was a quantity of rare old plate in the Deal family, and it was only upon occasions like the present that the bulk of it was produced.

Some of this plate had been presented to Mr. Deal for different public services he had rendered, so that he valued it very highly, and far beyond its intrinsic worth, which probably was the principal reason why he did not like to see it exposed to the changes and vicissitudes of ordinary every-day use.

This plate was to be displayed in the dining-room ; but before it was so laid out, Mrs. Deal suggested to her husband the propriety of going through it, and making an accurate list, to guard against the possibility of any of it being missing after the entertainment, without his knowing it.

Now, Mrs. Deal knew perfectly well, that not only was Mr. Deal rather indolent, and not likely on that account to make the inventory she suggested, but she knew that he was not suspicious, so she was not at all surprised when he replied,—

" Oh, it will be all right !   We have had it out on other occasions, without any being missed.   The negroes are not dishonest as a race, although, of course, there are bad specimens among them ; but, at all events, I don't think we have one in the house who would touch a thing."

" It's all very well to be so confident," said Mrs. Deal ; " but you know what a quantity of flowers and ribands were stolen from me by a young girl from Barbadoes, we had a good while ago."

" Yes," said Mr. Deal, " there I grant you're right.   If they take anything, it will be finery ; but you may depend upon it, that my silver plate will be much safer than your ribands and artificial flowers."

" Well," said Mrs. Deal, " if you're satisfied, I am, and we will say no more about it."

There was a good deal of desultory eating and drinking before the dinner was served, but when that king meal did make its appearance, about eighty guests sat down to partake of it.

There was rather more clamour than is usually to be met with at entertainments among people of wealth ; but we must remember that, although there was scarcely a man among the assemblage who could not have commanded his thousands at a moment's notice, they certainly did not belong to the aristocracy of human nature, and some of them were really grossly ignorant men.

So yoked together, however, were the planters in a common interest, that Mr. Deal did not dream of drawing any invidious comparisons, but sat down at his board with men whom he could not but despise, and whose sole quality consisted in the possession of so many head of slaves.

Mrs. Deal presided at the head of the table, looking like some immense horticultural specimen, for she was attired in a gaudy dress of satin, on which were embroidered immense roses, while on her head she wore a kind of wreath, which certainly made her look like the goddess of quantity if not of quality.

Miss Deal was dressed in white, certainly in more becoming taste than her mother, although that colour, or rather no colour, certainly made look darker a complexion which had not escaped entirely free from the influence of the scorching sun of that climate.

The other guests were very gaily attired, with the exception of some few who professed some sectarian principles of religion, the principal elements of which seemed to be moitifi cation.

The dinner went off boisterously, and what Mrs. Deal thought very well indeed; a few healths were drunk, and then, as was the custom, the male guests rose to adjourn to a cool room, there to enjoy the wine and fruit which they knew would be laid out in abundance for them.

This was a spacious apartment, and one of the coolest in the house, being always kept in the shadow, and closed up; the guests all entered it; excert

Adolphus Deal and John Grubson. These two lingered behind, and exchanged significant glances with Mrs. Deal, who, as she passed them, whispered,—

"It will be done soon."

"In a quarter of an hour, or I'll wager my head," said Grubson.

"A failure is impossible, I suppose ?"

"Quite out of all question; be at hand to put in a word if necessary."

"I will—I will."

There was a flurried look upon the countenance of Mrs. Deal, which, perhaps, she would have despised herself for exhibiting; and yet, somehow or another, there must have been some touch of shame in the heart of that woman, or she would not have worn such an aspect.

She repaired to her own room, and swallowed a stimulant; after which, chewing the leaves of a sweet herb, to take any odour from her breath of the spirituous compound she had indulged herself with, she went again to meet her lady guests.

* * * * *

"Well, shall we enjoy ourselves?" cried Mr. Deal, when he and his guests were seated in the cool apartment, where he had caused to be provided every material which could contribute to their comfort.

"Enjoy ourselves," cried one, "to be sure, we shall. Giv

me a full bottle, a chair for my feet as well as the one I'm sitting on, a handful of
cigars, and I'll show you what a man can do in the way of enjoying himself."

This was a movement very much applauded by many, and in a short time a
number of the guests were similarly disposed.

"Come here, Caractacus," said Mr. Deal to a negro ; "go and fetch me my
silver mug—I like to sip my claret out of it.   It holds a pint, gentlemen, so I know
exactly what I'm about."

"Yes, massa."

The negro knew the mug well enough ; it had been placed upon the sideboard
on all such occasions, although it was not in general use, but was put aside along
with the plate.   However, it was fully expected to be found in its usual place, and
Caractacus was not a little surprised to find it missing.

"Goramighty!" he said, "me cannot find massa's mug ; "here, Cesar, hab
you seen a mug about here ?"

"Oh, yes," said Cesar. "Hi! hi! hi! a dam ugly mug—you hab him just under
your nose."

"What you say ? Me thought you sensible fellow, Cesar, and now me find you
is outrageous fool."

"What do you mean by keeping me waiting for my mug?" cried Mr. Deal,
angrily, for although he was tolerably kind to his negroes, he certainly liked to
be obeyed.

"Bery sorry, massa, but I can't see him."

"Not see it—look again.   I would not lose the mug willingly."

Caractacus did look again, but certainly with no better result than before ; and
Cesar looked, and several others looked, but all to no purpose—the mug was not
to be found.

This disagreeable fact was reported to Mr. Deal, who rose from his seat with an
air of vexation upon his face, and went himself to take a hasty look, among the
plate that was laid out, for the rather-important, missing article.

The guests began to see that something was amiss ; the animated conversation
drooped a little, and all eyes were directed upon Mr. Deal, who looked from Cesar
to Caractacus, and from Caractacus to Cesar, with, perhaps, a pardonable amount
of suspicion in his manner.

CHAPTER XIX.

THE ACCUSATION.—THE FATAL DISCOVERY, AND THE ARREST.

The silence that ensued had certainly a very ominous character about it, and then
Mr. Deal would have resumed his seat, and said nothing about the thing at that
juncture, had not one of his guests cried,—

"Don't mind us, Mr. Deal, we are all friends ; if anything is lost, have a hunt
for it at once."

"Oh, never mind it just now," said Mr. Deal ; "it need not interrupt our merriment ; it's only my silver claret cup, by some unaccountable means, has become
mislaid."

"Only a silver claret cup !" said another ; "you take these things easy.   Why,
it was only two years ago I flogged a nigger to death for stealing a silver spoon."

"Ah !" remarked a third, "that was rather a singular circumstance, I think.
I've heard you say you found out afterwards that the nigger you punished
didn't do it."

"Yes, I did ; but you know the example was all the same, and the neighbouring
planters all subscribed as usual, so that the loss of making an example of a nigger
very properly don't fall on one individual."

"True, true; but what can have become of your silver mug, Mr. Deal?"

"I don't know," he said, growing more vexed each moment. "It certainly is not small enough to be overlooked—it's provoking too, because it was a present."

"Have it found, have it found," cried a number of voices.

"Well, my friends, I must confess I should be uneasy if I thought it was altogether lost. So, with your kind permission, I will endeavour to recover it Have you seen anything of it, Caractacus, or have you, Cesar?"

They both declared with perfect truth that they had not.

"Then go," said Mr. Deal, "one of you, and tell Mrs. Deal I wish to speak to her."

Caractacus, as being more familiar with the house, went, and when in answer to her husband's summons, that lady made her appearance, no one could fail to see how death-like pale she looked.

"Oh," said Mr. Deal, "my silver claret-cup is mislaid—have you seen it?"

"Yes, certainly."

"Then, that's all right. Where did you see it?"

"Last night I placed it myself upon this sideboard, and told Cesar Bobb to polish it, as it was dim in consequence of having been laid by for a length of time."

"Told me, missus!" cried Cesar. "I bery much beg you pardon. You neber told me noting about claret jug. Me neber saw him in all my life."

Quite a shout of indignation arose from Mr. Deal's guests at this piece of most awful effrontery, as it was considered, which Cesar was guilty of, in denying a statement made by his mistress. Probably such a frightful instance of insubordination had never before taken place, and an old planter, who was present, cried out in a loud voice,—

"There, Mr. Deal, that comes of indulgences to niggers, and all your new-fangled notions about their being human beings, and so on. You see what you get by it: Mrs. Deal is actually contradicted before your very face."

There was certainly no gainsaying the dreadful fact Mrs. Deal was contradicted by a slave, and there stood the lady with not a particle of colour in her cheeks, and there stood Cesar Bobb looking at least six inches taller than usual, and gazing steadfastly at her. Who was then the real slave? He who was in bondage, or she who was the slave of her own bad heart?

The silence that now ensued had something strange and ominous about it.

At length Mr. Deal spoke, and it was quite evident from the tone of his voice that he was much disturbed, and under the influence of a variety of contending emotions. Probably the presence of his brother planters made his pride revolt at being placed in such a position as he was by a slave, and then again from old and long acquaintance with the little peculiarities of his lady, he knew that she was liable to make little mistakes in the way of evidence.

"Let this affair," he said, "drop for the present; I do not wish the festivities of such a day as this to be disturbed by anything of this sort. The matter shall be fairly inquired into, by-and-by."

"Indeed, Mr. Deal," said Mrs. Deal, "since a slave has thought proper to tell me to my face that I have uttered a falsehood, it is, I humbly conceive, quite necessary that the matter should be investigated at once. There is not one gentleman present who would suffer his wife to remain under such an imputation a moment. It ought and must be at once investigated, and I am certain that there is no gentleman present who will hesitate to excuse the trouble and annoyance which such an affair occurring in the midst of gaiety will produce."

This was a speech which had been well conned beforehand, in case the necessity for uttering it should arise. It was as certain of its effect as any vulgar, claptrap sentiment to the audience of a minor theatre; and a clamorous approbation of the sentiment uttered by Mrs. Deal immediately rose from the guests. They one and all approved of the noble principle, as they called it, upon which she acted, so that Mr. Deal found himself in a minority of one.

And if anything was at all wanting to make up the necessity of an immediate and searching investigation into the affair, surely that was now to be found in the singularly audacious conduct of Cesar Bobb, who, seizing the opportunity of a temporary lull in the perfect tempest of approbation which the words of Mrs. Deal produced among the guests, spoke manfully.

"Dis be de case," he said . "Mrs. Deal may wait bery well if she likes, I cannot. De consequences to Mrs. Deal ob making a mistake, or ob telling a lie, be noting ; but de consequence ob poor Cesar Bobb doing any such ting be ob a bery different character; so, I say, make de 'vestigation at once. I am innocent, and declare dat I hab not seen massa's silver mug, and did not know massa had one at all."

"Be it so, then," said Mr. Deal, with an air of vexation. "I will see justice done on my estate. Justice to all, from the highest to the lowest. I will not have a poor slave oppressed; but if indeed this slave be guilty, I need not say that he has greatly aggravated the consequences of that guilt by his conduct to-day."

"Let him have the whip at once," said one. "I warrant that will make him confess."

"Or kill him," said Cesar.

"How dare you speak to me, you scoundrel? I am sure things have come to a pretty pass, indeed, when a slave takes up what one says in this sort of way. If any one upon my plantation was to do such a] thing, I wouldn't leave a whole bone in his skin—no, not if he had cost me five hundred dollars."

"Peace, peace," said Mr. Deal. "There shall be justice done to all ; Cesar Bobb, let me advise you to say nothing more. You cannot better your condition if you are innocent, and you may make it frightfully worse if guilty. Be quiet, and you shall have even-handed justice done to you."

"Dat is all dat I do ask," said Cesar.

"And you shall have it, so you need say no more at present. You stand suspected of stealing my silver claret cup, and you deny in full the imputation, so that your accuser is called upon to substantiate the charge."

As Mr. Deal uttered these words, he looked at his wife, as much as to say, you have commenced this disturbance, and it is for you now to get out of it the best way you can. But the guests by no means approved of this really just mode of putting the matter, and thought Mrs. Deal wonderfully ill-used, that her husband did not at once, upon the mere utterance of a suspicion on her part, of the guilt of a slave, have Cesar subjected to some severe punishment.

"I tell you what it is, Mr. Deal," said an old planter, taking him aside ; "what you are doing now is really calculated, let me assure you, to be very mischievous. If you get up an opinion in the minds of the slaves that they are to defend themselves against anything said of them by whites, they will go from bad to worse, and we shall have them asking for other privileges, so that at last there will be no slaves at all."

"Well, well," said Mr. Deal, who was much vexed at the whole affair, " I wish there really were none. You surely would not have me punish the poor devil innocent or guilty."

"Certainly, I would."

"Indeed, and pray upon what doctrine of common justice do you assert such an opinion ?"

"Simply that it is dangerous to let the slaves see that there can be any hesitation about believing the word of a white person against theirs. You may depend that if once the idea gets among them, that they are permitted to make any defence, we shall have no ending such matters ; and, as I say, the time will come when they will tell us they are as good as ourselves, and then, as they, of course, outnumber us considerably, there is no knowing what might happen."

Mr. Deal certainly was a slaveowner, and, of course, had some of the prejudices of his class—prejudices which, always in his mind, had kept up a kind of warfare with his original views of right and wrong. He could not deny the expediency of what the old planter said to him, but he certainly did revolt against the idea that he should punish Cesar Bobb upon the mere suspicion of Mrs. Deal, especially when he knew that she had a dislike to him, Cesar.

"No, no," he said to himself, "justice shall be done, or else I shall be covered with odium and contempt." Then turning from the old planter, who had taken him aside to give him such abominable and cold-hearted advice, he said, aloud,—

"Cesar Bobb, are you guilty or not guilty?"

"Not guilty," said Cesar, in a loud voice, which was thought quite an offence of itself by Mr. Deal's guests, for what an atrocious, daring thing it was of a slave to speak otherwise than in respectful and low tones in the presence of slave-owners.

"Then you must abide the consequences of an accurate investigation into the whole affair. Mr. Grubson, I shall feel obliged if you will undertake this piece of business.

"I will, sir," said John Grubson.

"And I will assist him," said Adolphus Deal; "so that there can be no suspicion of anything but the greatest fairness in the whole matter."

"I am innocent," said Cesar, "and so I have noting to fear, if I had—I—I——"

"Why do you hesitate?" said Mr. Deal. "Hesitation is a sign of guilt."

"No," said Cesar, "I was only going to say that Massa John Grubson and Massa 'Dolphus were no friends ob mine, as I well know, on account ob Lucy Neal."

"There," said Mrs. Deal, "you hear him; he would actually insinuate that my son would do what's wrong. Oh, is it not a dreadful thing for me to be obliged to hear such things from a slave, and my own friends and family all by to see me so insulted?"

The lady, partly because she thought it would produce a good effect, and partly because she was really so irritated that she could hardly contain herself, now gave symptoms of going into hysterics; and probably, but for Mr. Deal's presence, poor Cesar would have come off but badly at the hands of the company, who thought it certainly one of the most dreadful things they had ever heard of, that a planter's wife should actually be forced into hysterics by a nigger.

"You had better," said Mr. Deal to his wife, "retire to your own apartment; I will take care that no time be lost in this transaction, now that it has already gone as far as it has, which I freely say I am sorry for, considering the occasion on which we have met."

Mrs. Deal had sense enough to feel that she had accomplished all she could just then, so she took her husband's advice, and did walk away. She had aroused suspicion, forced inquiry—which she well knew the end of—and she had, by her conduct, got up a strong feeling against poor Cesar, so that he was not at all likely, under any circumstances, to escape some very serious consequences.

But Cesar felt tolerably secure; he knew that he had not touched the claret cup; he knew perfectly well that he had never seen such an article since he had been in the house, and so he felt certain that the accusation must fall to the ground, and that he would be defended by Mr. Deal in obtaining an honourable acquittal. Alas! poor Cesar little really knew the demoniac spirit of the woman he had to deal with—he little knew to what lengths she was likely to go to compass her dastardly ends.

Cesar felt some one gently touch his arm. He turned, and saw Lucy Neal.

Tears stood in her eyes, as she said to him, in a whisper,—

"Oh, Cesar, they will sacrifice you."

"No, Lucy, no, I am innocent."

"But do you think, Cesar, that innocence will protect you from those who would be your destruction? I do not know the nature of the fearful plot that is got up against you, but that there is one, and that this accusation is the commencement of it, I can well perceive."

Before Cesar could make any reply to this new view of the subject, which was certainly alarming, John Grubson stepped up to him, and said,—

"Come, you will be so good, my fine fellow, until this affair is settled, as to con-sider yourself a prisoner, and, in order that you should be in no sort of mistake about that, I shall lock you up."

Mr. Deal had given Grubson authority to do this, and, in another minute, Cesar Bobb was hurried from the house, and conducted to a sort of shed adjoining it, in which he was locked up.

CHAPTER XX.

THE FINDING OF THE SILVER CUP IN CESAR'S HUT.—THE TRIUMPH OF MRS. DEAL.

It was not likely that John Grubson nor Adolphus now would be backward in consummating their villany; and when Cesar was safely stowed away in confinement, they went to the private counting-house of the latter, where no less a personage than the Rev. Tobias Slankey was concealed, to enjoy a laugh over the success of the first move made for the destruction of poor Cesar, they now looking upon such destruction as quite certain.

"I think we have him now," said Adolphus.

"Safe," added Grubson, "nobody can save him, and I mean to say that Mrs. Deal managed the matter amazingly well."

"Yes, tolerably, and if my father don't hang him, it shan't be from want of evidence to make him do so, nor from want of urging in the matter."

"Ah!" remarked the Rev. Tobias, "it would be to my eyes a goodly sight to see him hung. Look what a state all through him I have been reduced to ; I shall have all my life now to wear a piece of sticking-plaster on my forehead."

"Oh, I don't see that you need care about the cross that's marked on your head," said Grubson, with a laugh ; "you can say you were born with it, you know, and then you will be all the more of a saint in consequence."

"Don't talk to me about it, I groan whenever I think of it—I absolutely groan."

"No doubt of that, but now, Mr. Adolphus, I think that the sooner we set about this matter the better."

"Agreed—come on at once."

"Hold, do you go back to the house, and say that, after considering over the affair, we have made up our minds to go at once and search the hut of Cesar, because we have found out that he has been once there, since he was sent for to assist in the house."

"Good."

"But likewise say that, as we have been accused of unfairness towards the prisoner by himself, it so far hurts us, that we are inclined to take some one else with us in the search, and see if you can get a couple of your father guests to accompany us on a search, the end of which we know well enough."

"I understand ; of course, it's much better to have other evidence besides ours."

"Yes, evidence that cannot be suspected. I will wait for you here, and take a glass of wine with Mr. Slankey till you come back, and be as quick as you can."

"I will, I will."

Adolphus, in pursuance of this advice, went at once back to the room in which his father's guest were assembled, and with great apparent fairness stated his errand, and the determination they had come to, of searching the hut of poor Cesar.

When he had finished speaking, he heard at least a dozen voices declaring the willingness of themselves to make part and parcel of the expedition, and at length he went back to John Grubson, accompanied by four of the guests.

He did not wish that prematurely the Rev. Tobias Slankey should be seen to be still upon the estate; so he called to Grubson to come out of the counting-house, which that worthy did; and the party of six proceeded to walk across the plantation, towards the long range of huts belonging to the negroes, and in one of which Cesar Bobb resided.

The day was now clear and beautiful, but these six men had but little appreciation of the beauties of nature, occupied as their whole souls now were in a strong desire to prove Cesar guilty.

The four planters felt that, after what had taken place, it would really be quite dreadful for Cesar Bobb to escape some very severe punishment; and soon finding that Adolphus was not at all hurt at any strictures upon his father, they commented, in very severe terms, upon the bad example he was setting to all slaves, by allowing them such a liberty and licence of tongue as had been exercised by Cesar.

As this was a subject upon which they all agreed, it was quite wonderful to see upon what excellent terms they were; and one of the planters was so pleased with John Grubson, that he told him he was quite a man after his own heart, and that if he chose at any time to leave Mr. Deal, he would take him at once as overseer.

In such like conversation as this, they passed the time as they walked, until they arrived at the range of tents, where all was still and serene, for the slaves had availed themselves of the privilege which had been accorded to them that day, of having a little recreation, and were enjoying themselves by singing and dancing in the large barn-like building, where the Coloured Ball took place, to which we introduced the reader at the commencement of this narration.

It was not deemed expedient, or necessary to impart to the four planters the treacherous trick which was about to be played Cesar, although if they had known it, as possibly they did suspect it, they were not men who would have shrunk with any very great horror from the destruction of an innocent man, who was "only a nigger."

The silence of the huts, and the doors all upon the mere latch, ought, by the sort of confidence in the absence of any evil, to have struck forcibly upon the consciences of Adolphus Deal and John Grubson; but really it would seem as if, with some people, that necessary portion of the human mind had been entirely omitted in the making up of such individuals.

Certain it is that those of whom we speak showed no sort of disposition to forego the accomplishment of their purpose, but went on towards it rather exultingly than otherwise.

It was gall and wormwood to both Adolphus and Grubson to see what a rich and trim condition the garden of Cesar's hut was in, owing to the kindness of Mr. Deal towards him; but a moment's reflection satisfied them that what they were about to do was of a nature fully to compensate them for any disagreeable thing they might feel, in the contemplation of the temporary prosperity of the person they hated.

The reader will not forget, as a key to all, the exultation on the part of Grubson and Adolphus, nor the visit that was made to Cesar's hut, while Lucy Neal was concealed in it; and from that we may very well gather that there can be but little doubt of the fact of Mr. Deal's silver cup being there, although that Cesar knew anything about it is quite another proposition.

"Here we are, gentlemen," said Grubson; "you see how comfortable and well off the rascals are."

"A great deal too comfortable," said one of the planters.

"Yes, but that's Mr. Deal's, in my opinion, injudicious management. You may depend, gentlemen, that the more comfortable you make them, the less they feel inclined to work."

"Oh, of course."

"But Mr. Deal thinks otherwise, and a man must have his own way, you know, with his own."

" He will find out his mistake."

" I hope so.   Walk in, gentlemen: here we are.   This is the rascal's hut, and although it don't, of course, matter a straw to me, whether the cup be found here or not, I must say I have a very strong suspicion upon my mind, that I cannot at all banish, that it will be."

" And I, too," said Adolphus.

" Well," said one of the planters, " if it be so, and Mr. Deal don't hang the fellow, I shall say he may as well give all the slaves on his estate their freedom at once.

" Yes," said another, "and be off with him as quick as he can, for we don't want such examples here, I'm sure.   There's no knowing the amount of mischief that an injudicious proprietor may do to the general great cause of slavery. Upon my word, this is a comfortable hut.   I should not sleep quietly in my bed at night, if I thought any of my niggers were half so well lodged as this ; I really should not."

" It's abominable," said another.

" Atrocious," said a third.

The fourth lifted up his hands as much as to say, " Only see, now, the folly of some people, who actually seem to think slaves ought to be comfortable."

The search commenced by a general kicking about and breaking of the few articles of furniture which poor Cesar possessed—an act of wanton malice which evidently gave the greatest possible amusement to the party.   Then they commenced a more deliberate search, and some time elapsed without anything at all suspicious being found.   At length John Grubson paused, and said,—

" Well, gentlemen, we don't seem to get on very quick."

" No," said Adolphus, " but I have thought of a plan."

" Indeed !   What is it ?"

" Let us stand at the door of the hut and look round it, asking ourselves, supposing we wanted to hide something within it, where we in our judgments would do so."

" Good—capital.   Come on ; I warrant that among us we shall find out all the hiding-places.   What do you say, Mr. Warren ?" addressing one of the planters.

" Why," said Mr. Warren, looking around him with as critical an eye as possible, " I should say that taking one thing into consideration with another, I should hide anything in a bit of that thatched roof."

" Bravo, bravo !" cried Grubson.

" Capital ! capital," remarked Adolphus.

Mr. Warren looked amazingly well pleased at this circumstance, which put him quite on good terms with himself, so that he simpered like a young lady who was just asked to dance.   At all events, the conspirators knew well that in him they would now have a fast and firm ally.

" I propose," said Grubson, " that we search the roof at once, before thinking any further about it.   The suggestion is such a remarkably good one, that it may save us completely from any further cudgelling our brains upon what really, after all, is such a thankless subject."

This was generally agreed to, and the mode of searching the roof consisted in striking it severe blows with a heavy stick that John Grubson had with him, blows which certainly would soon cause anything heavy that might be there concealed to fall out of it.

And, of course, he well knew what would fall out of it.   There was a jingling sound, suddenly, as if the stick had struck something metallic, and then down came Mr. Deal's silver claret cup.

*   *   *   *   *   *

" Yes," muttered Mrs. Deal to herself, as she sat alone in her room, and heard the sound of voices below, and now and then the rather uproarious manner in which a toast was proposed and responded to. " Yes, I rather think that we have got the better of that black fellow now, who had the unparalleled impertinence to place himself in my son's way."

Poor Mrs. Deal, you may enjoy your triumph for a short period, but it would have a little dashed that triumph if any one could have whispered in your ear that a day of frightful retribution was at hand.

*   *   *   *   *   *   *

And thus was consummated one of the most diabolical acts of treachery and baseness of which human nature could be guilty—an act which, under all

the circumstances was doubly and trebly bad; bad, because the motives for seeking revenge against Cesar Bobb arose from his protection of innocence and virtue; bad, because of his dependent and helpless position, and, worse than all, because coming from a woman and a mother.

But how true it is, that the more we dive into the secrets of human nature we discover how much of an angel woman can be, and how much of a devil.

No. 10.

CHAPTER XXI.

CESAR BROUGHT UP FOR JUDGMENT IN THE MORNING.—THE APPEAL OF LUC   Y

WE left Mr. Warren and John Grubson at rather a critical moment in the hut of poor Cesar, who was so hideously and so wrongfully accused of the robbery of Mr. Deal's silver cup.

It was, indeed, a most critical moment, and surely as critical a moment for the villain, John Grubson, as for poor Cesar Bobb; for if shame and conscience could do anything with the overseer, it ought to have been done then, when the silver cup which he had himself hidden came rattling down upon the floor at his feet.

But the man who could conceive so diabolical a plan of ruining any one, and commence its execution, was not likely to turn back at the time that it was being successful; and although John Grubson's voice was strangely altered as he spoke, he cried,—

" There it is—there it is, as sure as fate. Well, this is evidence with a vengeance. What do you think of that, Mr. Warren?"

" Oh, it's just what I expected of course—oh, quite of course. The black fellow who would dare to contradict his mistress is sure to be a thief, and indeed Mr. Deal is so foolishly indulgent to the slaves, that I should not at all wonder if he got murdered in his bed some night, and it would really serve him right in some respects."

Mr. Warren gave free utterance to this sentiment, but he did not condescend to explain why such an anomaly in human nature was to occur, as Mr. Deal having his throat cut because he was kind.

" Well, if that black fellow aint hung for this," exclaimed John Grubson, " it's an odd thing to me.''

" An odd thing," cried Mr. Warren, " I say it will be a criminal thing, and nobody will be safe if Mr. Deal don't act with severity. The idea of allowing a slave to contradict his mistress! Why, whether she was right or wrong made no matter."

" None in the least, Mr. Warren, none in the least; and you may depend, sir, that if this sort of thing aint nipped in the bud, we shall have the slaves taking up their rights in a short time."

" Yes, and an insurrection."

As Mr. Warren uttered these words, he turned sharply round, for he thought he heard a sound behind him, and there sure enough stood old Pompey looking more bent down by years and infirmities than ever, and trembling like an autumn leaf.

" Well, you black rascal, what do you want here?" said Warren.

" Noting, noting," said Pompey, " what hab you found, Massa Grubson?"

" The silver cup that Cesar Bobb stole from Mr. Deal, and hid in the thatch," replied Grubson.

" Hi! hi! hi!" said old Pompey, as he walked away, "hab it come to dat, bery good joke indeed. Hi! hi! hi! bery good."

John Grubson felt an uncomfortable sensation, as old Pompey walked slowly away, and yet he scarcely knew why, for even if, as it flashed across his mind, it might be possible old Pompey had seen the cup hidden by him, Grubson, such testimony would be of no avail, for the evidence of a black is not received against a white.

Even Mr. Warren looked after the old negro for a few moments in silence, and then he said,—

" Is he mad?"

" I suppose so, sir, he is old and superannuated nearly past work, and I dare say his mind not quite right."

"Oh, Mr. Grubson," said Warren, "it's one of the most troublesome things in the world to know what to do with old niggers that can't do a fair day's work. I've tried all sorts of plans."

"Have you, sir?"

"Yes, but somehow there they stick on hand, and won't come by any accident, even if you put them ever so much in the way of it, and that only shows the obstinacy of niggers, Mr. Grubson. They are continually complaining of being slaves, and yet when you give them an opportunity of going out of the world, they won't."

"Oh dear no, sir, you will never get them to do anything they ought."

"No, I've often noticed that; and if you, Mr. Grubson, can think of any good mode of getting rid of old niggers without, you know, making any disturbance about it, I shall be obliged if you will tell me; and I can only say, if ever you like to leave Mr. Deal, my plantation is open to you."

"I thank you, sir, I shall bear your kind offer in mind."

"Do so—do so; and now I think we may as well go back with this most damning proof of the guilt of that Cesar Bobb, as they call him."

It was certainly a most damning proof of the charge brought against Cesar—the production of the very article he was suspected of stealing from the thatch of his own hut; and neither Mr. Warren nor John Grubson could now entertain the smallest doubt of the success of the prosecution against the unhappy Cesar, whom they considered must either be hanged outright, or subjected to such an amount of corporal punishment as would destroy life more painfully still.

And little did he suspect, while confined in the outhouse to which he had been conveyed, that any such frightful evidence would be adduced against him on the morrow, as the finding of Mr. Deal's cup where he, Cesar, no more imagined it to be than in heaven; and yet knowing the enemies he had, and their malevolence, he might well expect some result of a harsh character.

Oh, how devoutly he now wished that he had the opportunity of escaping, and running off to the woods, where, after the visit of Jack Straw to his hut, he felt quite certain he should find a number of runaway slaves in a state of revolt against their cruel, unfeeling, and most sanguinary taskmasters.

In vain, however, did he try to escape from the place in which he was confined. It resisted all his efforts, and he was completely without weapons or tools of any kind with which to force the fastnesses that confined him.

"Oh, Lucy Neal! oh, Lucy Neal!" he exclaimed, "if I could but take you with me to some land ob freedom, where de black man is not considered a stick or a stone because God made him de colour dat he is, I should be happy."

But Cesar was not one to waste what might be valuable time in idle lamentations, and he made every possible effort to escape from the place he was confined in—efforts, which cost him some bruises and cuts about his hands, but which, for all that, were utterly fruitless, and not such as advanced him on the road to liberty in the least.

And so he passed some uneasy hours until, murmuring blessings upon the head of her whom he loved, he lay down and fell into a deep and dreamless slumber—a slumber far more refreshing and satisfactory than any of his enemies enjoyed, although they had about them all the means and appliances to court repose.

And now came the morning with its soft dawning light brightening up in the heavens, and casting its beautiful and cheering glow upon all things—a morning alike beautiful to the oppressed as to the oppressor. But there was one who wept sadly, and looked with lustreless eyes upon that coming day of dread—that one was Lucy Neal.

She possibly had much less hope even than Cesar of a satisfactory termination to the frightful train of circumstances which had commenced, for she, with a woman's tact, knew better than he how frightfully vicious such a man as Adolphus Deal might and could be when crossed in his passions; and much she dreaded that some dreadful scheme was in progress, of which she and Cesar only as yet knew the commencement.

She did sleep, but her slumbers were visited by sad mirrors representing Cesar suffering punishments invented by the ingenuity of different barbarous overseers, and of which she had read from time to time, and heard accounts of.

It wanted a little of sunrise when she rose, with her head and heart throbbing with excitement, to endeavour in the cool morning air to procure some ease from the fever which apprehension for the fate of him whom she loved had awakened in her young blood during that night of painful thoughts.

At one time she thought of making an appeal to Miss Deal, but she knew the weakness of her character; and, after all, what could she ask for—mercy to the guilty, or justice for the innocent? If for the latter, the answer would of course be at once—prove that innocence; and so would she be defeated.

Alas! poor Lucy Neal, never before had you felt such agony of mind, and never had there been a truer illustration of the fact that,—

'The course of true love runs not smooth.'

Thus she was, with every disposition to be of service to Cesar Bobb, utterly at a loss to know how she could be so; and, like many a wiser person than herself, she found she was compelled to wait, with what patience she could exert, until circumstances should throw in her way some mode of proving her affection.

Lucy wandered from the house into the trim and beautiful garden in which Mr. Deal took so much pride, and sitting down upon the seat of a summer-house, she wept bitterly.

Not for long, however, was she allowed the unmolested company of her own tears. She heard a hasty footstep—there was a rustling among the branches of a creeping plant of great beauty, which entwined its leaves and flowers amid the trellis-work of the summer-house, and in another moment Adolphus Deal stood before her.

A slight shriek of terror came from Lucy's lips, but Adolphus, fancying she was intent upon escape, suddenly seized her forcibly by the wrist, saying,—

"Hold! You shall hear me, by Heaven! for I don't know when I may have another opportunity of saying what I must—I will say to you. I tell you what it is, Lucy, I——"

"My cries shall alarm the house," she said; "unhand me, Adolphus Deal, you are a villain!"

"Indeed! That's a hard word, and a foolish one, to come from the lips of a slave."

"'Tis you who are the slave, for you are the slave of your own bad passions, Adolphus Deal. Let me go directly—I will not remain here."

"Then you should not have come here, Lucy Neal. If, when first I let you know that I loved you, you had been complying, I should have thought nothing you. But it is your opposition which has done all the mischief, and I tell you now} that whatever befals Cesar Bobb, he will have to thank you for, for you will be his executioner."

"What baseness!"

"Pshaw! Lucy Neal, you are an educated girl, and one can talk to you. Come, now, listen to reason, will you, for once in a way. You know what Cesar Bobb is accused of, and you know, or, at all events, you can guess, that there's a tolerable chance of his being found guilty. You, and you only, can save him."

"I save him?"

"Yes; be a little civil to me, and he shall be saved. Be mine, Lucy, and I will even now suppress the fact of the silver claret cup being, as it has been actually, found in the straw thatch of the roof of his hut."

"Now, great Heaven protect the innocent!" said Lucy; "I see it all. The frightful plot is full and clear before my eyes. John Grubson and the preacher hid that cup in the thatch."

"What?"

"I say they hid it there, and you know it, Adolphus Deal. How the coward colour forsakes your lips—how you tremble! Oh, Adolphus Deal, it is not yet too late for you to repent, and endeavour to pause in your frightful career. Be just—save the innocent, and I will pray for you. You know that the silver cup has been hidden for the purpose of giving life and semblance of truth to this frightful charge; and now, for your own sake, I say, retract it, and repent while you yet have time."

"Well," said Adolphus, as he tried to hide his trembling by holding to the side of the summer-house, "well, this is cool, at all events—why, you must be mad, girl, thoroughly mad; but I tell you that one way or another you shall yet be mine. Beware!"

"Yourself beware, there is a God above us."

As she spoke, Lucy Neal seized an unguarded moment, and, rushing past Adolphus Deal, soon got clear of the garden, for she was as fleet as the antelope, and it was in vain for him to follow.

CHAPTER XXII.

THE CHARGE, AND ITS WITNESSES.—GUILTY!

No doubt this interview between Lucy Neal and Adolphus Deal had the effect of largely increasing the bad feelings of the latter against poor Cesar, and induced him to stop at nothing for the purpose of insuring, if possible, the absolute conviction of that most innocent man, who, in comparison with his persecutors, was as light to darkness.

There is nothing in all the world so diabolical, nor so capable of urging human nature to violent extremes, as the disappointed passion of a bad man; and so frightfully angry now was Adolphus Deal, that he made a vow to himself to stake his very life for the attainment of his vicious and desperate objects, so maddened was he at being foiled.

"She shall be mine yet," he cried, as he ground his teeth together, "she shall be mine yet. I will wade through anything to obtain her, and this delay does but have the effect of increasing my passion."

While he uttered these words, he was not aware that John Grubson had come close to the summer-house; but that individual, who had nothing at all to gain by listening to the raving of Adolphus Deal, thought that he had better announce his presence, which he did, by affecting to have a violent cough.

"Who is that?" cried Adolphus, fearful that some unfriendly one might have caught the words he had uttered.

"Oh, it's only me, Mr. Adolphus," said Grubson, "all's right!"

"Oh, you, Grubson, have—have you got the cup?"

"Oh dear yes; and you may make quite up your mind, sir, as to the fate of Cesar Bobb."

"That's well, that's well, confound him, he seems to have a charmed life; but, after all, the disgrace and the punishment of this affair is much better than killing him."

"A vast deal, sir, and as for Lucy Neal——"

"Hush! not a word; I am maddened at the sound of her very name—say no more to me of her—say no more—I cannot, will not, hear of her just now."

"Not hear of her, sir? Why, I thought——"

"Never mind what you thought; it is vengeance that just now fills my mind; let love come afterwards; of course my father must believe in the guilt of the slave, now."

"He cannot help it. Mr. Warren is a witness to the finding of the cup."

"Good, and what will be the result?'

" Cesar Bobb must have some very severe punishment; and if it is left to me to execute, you may depend, Mr. Adolphus, it shan't leave him life enough to swear by. But come into the counting-house, sir, we can talk of the affair much better there than here, where we don't know what spying eyes may be upon the look out."

Adolphus Deal and John Grubson walked to the private counting-house of the former in deep conversation as they went ; but no sooner had they left the summer-house, than there was a rustling among the leaves of the creeping plants that half hid its entrance, and Mr Slankey made his appearance.

A handkerchief wound round his forehead concealed the cross, which was there indelibly marked, and he looked pale and wan.

" Very good," he said, " very good ; I begin to think that now there is an inclination to throw me overboard, but I'll stick to Adolphus Deal like a leech ; I will be paid, and paid well, too. Besides, that girl, Lucy Neal, comes between me and my wishes. I love her—yes, I actually love her better than ever I loved any of my female flock, at Little Bethel, in Camden-town where I used to preach, in London."

Suddenly Mr. Slankey gave a start, saying,—

" Hilloa ! What's that, eh ? I'm sure I heard somebody or something."

All was still again ; but just as he had made up his mind that he had been deceived by some accidental noise, he chanced to turn his head in the direction of the back part of the summer-house, and there he saw a sight which transfixed him, for a few moments, with terror and wonder.

It was one of the longest and most hideous faces which had ever greeted the eyes of the reverend gentleman, and resembled one of those strange, hideous masks which the South Sea Islanders wear during their wars for the purpose of intimidating their enemies. The great eyes were glaring upon Mr. Slankey, and he could see that the face was advancing towards him. It was a horrible apparition, and it seemed to possess the fearful, fascinating power of the serpent, for Mr. Slankey could not move, nor could he withdraw his gaze from the frightful face.

Nearer and nearer it came, until it almost touched him, and then a voice said,— " I am de Mangoni."

The Reverend Tobias had too wholesome a dread of that name to hear it with indifference, and he was about to utter a cry of dismay, when he was clutched by the throat by a hand that seemed to be of iron, and then his senses forsook him.

When Tobias Slankey recovered, he found himself alone in the summer-house, and he heard a clock from somewhere strike ten.

We must now leave this reverend sinner to his own cogitations, while we proceed to detail what took place on that eventful morning with regard to Cesar Bobb.

Theft was so rare a thing upon Mr. Deal's plantation that, now there was a distinct charge of that character, he made up his mind during the night, as he thought over the affair, that both for his own sake, and for the sake of the accused man, it should be fully investigated, and that, too, with every circumstance of ceremony which could add solemnity to the affair.

Mr. Deal was, in common with most of the large slaveholders, a magistrate, so that he could go into the inquiry himself and adjudicate upon it if he chose without any trouble, but even if he had any fear that in consequence of being himself the prosecutor, he positively ought not to act as a judge, he had guests actually in the house who were likewise magistrates.

There was a very large hall in the house, which was only sometimes used for extraordinary occasions; and when Mr. Deal rose in the morning, he determined to make that into a judicial court for the examination of the charge against Cesar Bobb. He gave orders to John Grubson that as many of the slaves as could be spared from labour were to be allowed to be present at the scene, for he intended to make as strong a moral effect as he could among them.

We have before remarked that Mr. Deal was not a bad man, although too apt to be led by those about him with worse dispositions than himself, and more sinister motives.

The domestic slaves, that is to say, those who resided in the house as domestic servants, soon had the hall we have mentioned in a state of readiness; and by nine o'clock Mr. Deal, rose from his breakfast-table, and announced to his guests that, before he did anything else, he would make an endeavour to set at rest the question of the guilt or innocence of the slave who stood accused of stealing his silver claret cup.

He was much applauded by the guests who remained, for they promised themselves what to them was an immense amusement, namely, the seeing a negro severely punished with any depreciation of their own property, which could not fail to be the case, if they indulged themselves in any such manner with one of their own slaves.

"Well, Mr. Deal," said one, " the good opinion you have expressed so often of all your slaves will be a little shaken now, I suppose ?"

"What about ?" said Mr. Deal. "Do not let us prejudge anybody. The accused is not yet declared guilty."

The hall in which the judicial examination was to take place had rather an imposing appearance when it was got completely ready for that purpose, and was well calculated to strike a proper kind of awe to the breast of any one who might be really guilty, but, as we well knew the innocence and the unconquerable spirit of Cesar Bobb, we expect no such effect to be made upon him.

It was exactly ten o'clock when Mr. Deal, who placed a Mr. Stanmore, likewise a magistrate, in the official chair, sent for the prisoner, who in a few minutes was conducted to the hall.

The appearance of Cesar Bobb was certainly not that of a guilty man, come to hear the evidence which was to convict him; for, on the contrary, he looked taller than usual, in consequence of the upright manner in which he stood, and his calm unflinching eye, as it roamed round the assembly, was such, that there were a few there who dared not meet it. At the lower end of the hall, stood about thirty of the slaves on the estate, while sitting upon chairs near to the magistrate were Adolphus, his father, Mr. Warren, John Grubson, and some other guests, who took an unfeigned delight in what was going on.

Mr. Deal commenced the proceedings, perhaps rather irregularly, by saying,—

" Cesar Bobb, you know you are accused of stealing my silver claret cup. If you are guilty and say so, perhaps by sparing any further trouble, you may entitle yourself to more mercy."

"Massa !" said Cesar, " me do not tink you a bad man—me tank you with all my heart and soul ; but me be innocent, and wild horses tearing me limb from limb, would not get me to say dat I was guilty."

"Bery good," cried a negro from the lower end of the hall.

"Peace—silence !" said Mr. Deal. " John Grubson, I think you said to me a short time since that you had something to say."

"Yes, sir," said Grubson, stepping forward, " and what I have to say, sir, I am very sorry for. The fact is, the estate has quite got a name for the honesty of the slaves upon it, and I'm very sorry to be able to come forward to prove a case just the contrary way ; but the fact is Mr. Warren and I went to the accused's hut, and thoroughly searched it."

" Finding noting," said Cesar.

"But this silver cup," added John Grubson, holding up the battered claret cup, which he had kept concealed.

There was a visible sensation in the hall, and the magistrate, looking at Cesar Bobb, said,—

" Well, you are about as unblushing a rascal as ever I came near, I think."

" I am sorry for this from my heart," said Mr. Deal. " Have you anything to say, Cesar Bobb ?"

" Yes," he cried, in a loud firm voice, " I hab someting to say, Massa Deal.

I hab to say that I am innocent, even if fifty cups were to be found in my hut. I did not place him there, perhaps John Grubson knows who did."

" Why, you scoundrel," cried Grubson, turning as white as a sheet, " I'll——"

" Do nothing," said Mr. Deal, "at present. Peace! justice shall be done. Cesar, you are doing yourself much injury. I am a kind master; but you shall find me a just one, and that I cannot and will not overlook a fault like this. Mr. Warren, what do you say?"

" Oh! just that the cup now produced by Mr. Grubson was found in Cesar Bobb's hut. I can swear to that if it was necessary; but I should think my word will do against a nigger."

" Cesar, Cesar," said Mr. Deal, " you will have no door open for mercy by pursuing, despite of such proofs, an obstinate declaration of innocence. Give me an opportunity of being merciful to you by confessing your crime and begging leniency."

" Stop!" said Lucy Neal, as she stepped suddenly forward from among the throng at the lower end of the hall—" stop! I have something to say about the finding, as well as the hiding, of the cup."

CHAPTER XLIII.

MR. DEAL'S DETERMINATION.—THE ATTEMPTED MURDER BY ADOLPHUS.

THE firmness of tone in which Lucy Neal uttered these words was such as to command attention even from those who were the least willing to accord it, and who, strange to say, considered that they were in some measure degrading themselves by listening to the words which came from the lips of any of a different colour to themselves.

Mr. Deal, in particular, leant eagerly forward to listen.

" Yes," she exclaimed, "I have something to say as to the finding and the hiding of the silver cup, Mr. Deal. It is contrary to a rule of the estate for the female slaves to visit the men's huts. I know I subject myself to censure by having done so; but I did visit the hut of Cesar Bobb during his absence, and while there I heard the sound of approaching footsteps. I hid myself; and then John Grubson and some one else came into the hut. I heard them doing something with the thatch roof. What it was at that time I did not know, but I do know now."

" What—what?" said Mr. Deal.

" They were hiding the silver cup."

" It's false," said Grubson; "it's false! You were not there. It's false, I say."

" Hold, hold!" cried Mr. Deal. " Drop all this passion. Who was the other person?"

" Tobias Slankey, the preacher."

" That I contradict," said Adolphus, stepping forward; "for Tobias Slankey was very ill, in consequence of some ill-usage he received on the estate, God knows from whom, and I let him remain in one of the huts, close to the cotton trees, whence I know he has not stirred since. I did so from a feeling of humanity towards him, although you had ordered him off the estate."

" And I authorised Adolphus to do so," said Mrs. Deal, advancing, "and promised to take the blame upon myself, if any should arise. So this girl's story being proved to be false in one instance, is not to be believed in another, I should say."

Mr. Deal looked bewildered, as thus evidence after evidence poured in upon him against Lucy Neal and Cesar Bobb. The magistrate was quite convinced of the guilt of the prisoner, and the planters who were present looked quite derisively at Mr. Deal, while some of them whispered to each other, that perhaps he had an eye himself to the good-looking Lucy, and so did not wish to convict one in whom she took such an evidently-strong interest.

"Well, Mr. Deal," said Mr. Warren, "what do you think of all that?"

"Cesar, have you anything else to say to me?"

"Noting, massa, but dat you may kill me, and yet I am innocent."

Mr. Deal was silent for a few moments, and then he said,—

"No, Cesar; I never took the life of any one on my estate, and severe punishments, endangering life, I have never sanctioned. I shall take you or send you a couple of hundred miles off, and have you sold, along with your character, as a thief. Let the responsibility of dealing with you, should you be again criminal,

No. 11.

lie upon some one else's head, not mine. That is my determination; and as for you, Lucy Neal, I am willing to think you have been mistaken, and nothing that has passed shall be remembered to your prejudice."

"Oh, sir," exclaimed Lucy, "spare him. He is innocent; he is indeed. It is I who am the cause of all these unhappy circumstances. There is one here who has pursued me with a dishonourable and a dishonouring passion. I rejected the overtures with scorn, and thus vengeance has fallen upon one whom it was known I loved."

Mr. Deal cast an anxious and a sharp glance at Adolphus as Lucy uttered these words, as if he too well knew to whom they might apply; but yet it did appear to him rather too monstrous that his son should lay such a deliberate plot for the destruction of an innocent person, and, like many men, he rejected from his mind what was really a positive fact, because he shuddered to think it might possibly be true.

"Let us have an end of this," he said; "I am satisfied, and until I have taken steps to carry out my determination as regards Cesar Bobb, you will see, Mr. Grubson, that he is kept securely. Do not allow him on any account to mingle with the other slaves."

"Or any one to see him," said Adolphus.

"You will allow me, Mr. Deal," said Lucy, "to have an interview with him before he goes. I do here avow that I do love him; but it was not that love which prompted me to say what I have said. Oh no! I would have said as much in the cause of truth for my bitterest enemy, even for John Grubson, but you will not, sir, refuse me a parting interview with one whom I may never see again, and who, were it with my dying breath spoken, I should still declare to be innocent."

Mr. Deal turned aside, as he said in a low tone, —

'Mr. Grubson, you will allow this girl to see your prisoner."

"And me, massa—oh, me," cried Cesar's father, pushing forward. "Oh, massa, massa, you hab not de heart to say no to me."

"Mr. Grubson, you will likewise allow this old slave to see the prisoner."

"Why, really, Mr. Deal," began Grubson, "with all the respect in the world to you, sir, I must say that——"

"There is no occasion to say anything, Mr. Grubson: let it be as I say, if you please. There is no occasion to be over rigorous. And now, my friends and guests, the sooner you forget all about this affair the better, for it is not of the pleasantest by any means. Remove the prisoner, Mr. Grubson, and I only hope I may never look upon his face again."

"No, massa, no!" said Cesar, "do not say dat; de time will come when I hope that de most welcome sight you can look upon is de face ob Cesar Bobb. I do not blame you, massa, you hab been misled by de wickedness ob which you hab no idea; but de day wi'' come when you will know all. God bless you, massa, you might hab, under de circumstances, done much worse by poor Cesar Bobb dan you hab done; so I say, God bless you; more partic'lar for let me see my dear Lucy Neal."

There was much sensibility and pathos in Cesar's manner, as he uttered these words. Mr. Deal made no answer, but Adolphus, who was a pretty good judge of the changes of his father's countenance, felt convinced, as he glanced at him, that he was not yet quite satisfied upon the subject of Cesar's guilt, although he was borne down by weight of evidence.

"Curses on him!" muttered Adolphus, "he shall die."

John Grubson caught the eye of Adolphus, and gave him a look which signified that all was not lost yet, although Cesar was saved in consequence of the moderation of Mr. Deal.

Adolphus understood that look, and as soon as he could, without exciting attention by abruptly leaving his father and the guests, he made his way to his office, where sure enough, as he had fully expected, he found Grubson waiting for him.

Then, when he knew he might do so without danger or censure, Adolphus gave vent to his passion, and cursed and swore to his heart's content over the proceedings that had just taken place.

"Why, what consequence is it to the black rascal," he cried, "whether he is one man's slave or another's? Sell him, indeed—sell him because he is a thief. What's the good of that to me?"

"Nothing," said Grubson. "I was in hopes that some punishment would have been decreed, which would have filled Lucy Neal with such terror that she would have yielded to you, for the purpose of saving the black rascal; and then we could have managed matters famously, but things have taken too easy a turn by far. What's to be done?"

"Cannot you answer such a question as that, Grubson? Where is all that devilish sagacity of which you have so often boasted? Is it to be found wanting at a time of all others when it is of most essential service?"

"No, Mr. Adolphus, no. I will think of something if you cannot, or will not; I make you a promise that you shall yet, by fair means or foul, succeed in all you wish; and as for that Cesar Bobb, I say don't let him live over to-night. What's so easy as to put him out of the way, so that there is no further trouble about him? If we don't, you or I may be sent a pretty journey to sell him."

"But can it be done safely?"

"It must be done safely, or not at all. Trust me for that, Mr. Adolphus; I have thought of a plan. Now listen to me, and make yourself quite easy as regards that part of the business; as to the girl, there may be more trouble yet."

"And the girl I must and will have."

"You shall. I did not say there was any impossibility—I only talked of trouble, Mr. Adolphus. Of course you must be aware that I risk much in these matters?"

"No, no, you risk nothing that I am aware of. I can give you money at once, Grubson, for, thank the fates, I am pretty well supplied by my mother with cash; and you know that, when the estate comes to me, you will only be the second man in power upon it, so I don't see that you will risk much."

"Well, well, Mr. Adolphus, I don't complain, far from it; you know, you are a person after my own heart, for you and I agree well upon the subject of the treatment of the slaves, who, confound them, are almost, what with one foolish indulgence and another from your father, beginning to think they are equal to us. There's no knowing where such matters may end."

"I'll let them know who is master some day. But your plan with regard to Cesar Bobb, what is that?"

"His death."

"Of course. Nothing else would satisfy me."

"Well, then, listen to me, and I will tell you how it may be managed, so as to seem as if, dreading the fate that awaited him, and conscious of his guilt, he had taken his own life. This way, Mr. Adolphus; I must go into the cotton field, and we can talk as we go on."

John Grubson and Adolphus Deal walked towards where the slaves were at their labour; and, by the earnest manner in which they conversed, and the number of times that Adolphus nodded his head, it was evident he was very well pleased with the plan propounded to him by Grubson, and considered that Cesar Bobb was as good as already sacrificed.

The Rev. Tobias Slankey shrunk from out of a corner, when they had left the spot where they had been conversing, and, shaking his head in a dubious manner, he said,—

"So it seems I am to be kept out of this. Well, well, we shall see, we shall see, we shall. I'll just pop after them, and try and dodge them among the trees, and hear what they say. They shall have me with them in the matter, whether they happen to like it or not. Oh dear no, Master Grubson, I am not going to be thrown overboard now."

As Slankey spoke, he, with great caution, followed the two scoundrels who were consulting together about so atrocious a deed; and he did get sufficiently close to them to overhear something of what they said. But that something was so indis·tinct that he could make nothing of it; and it was only at last, when they were just emerging from the trees, and paused a moment, and spoke a little louder than usual, that Tobias heard Adolphus say,—

"That's decided, then, Grubson; and, as it's now time I should show myself at the house, to do away with the remotest suspicion that we are plotting anything, we had better not meet again until night."

"Agreed. I will be in the summer-house at ten, and before eleven, I think, we may safely conclude that this business will be over. Hang the fellow, he's more trouble than he's worth. The idea of a slave giving people such a world of bother."

"Ah," snarled Adolphus, "but I'll be even with him yet; and, when I come into possession of the estate, Grubson, we will have a different state of things, I rather think."

CHAPTER XXIV.

CESAR'S ESCAPE, AND THE MISADVENTURE OF ADOLPHUS.

IT is night again upon the plantation. The lustrous and beautiful night of such a region where darkness is never total, and where the sun but for a very few hours sinks below a horizon, is always illuminated by reflected and refracted beams.

Cesar Bobb is in his prison. Towards the latter part of the day his father had visited him, and had brought him a message from Lucy Neal. That message was to take some sleep early in the evening, in case he should not have an opportunity of doing so later; and Cesar Bobb was not slow to comprehend from such a message that something was to be attempted for his rescue.

He soon found, however, that Lucy Neal had not thought proper to trust his father with any such secret, for the old slave said,—

"Goramighty, what she mean, Cesar, by devising you to sleep in de early part ob de ebening?"

"Oh, I don't know," replied Cesar, "except it be dat bird in de hand is better n two in de bush."

"Hi, hi, hi! Well, Cesar, you hab rare spirits; but after all, my boy, you hab good luck; you is to be sold to some one else, and as you is strong and young, you will always be took good care ob."

"Oh, I shall do bery well, and perhaps Mr. Deal may alter his mind, and keep me after all; for in his own mind, I think he hab bery great doubt still about de cup."

When Cesar had got the old man to leave him, which he soon did—for the old slave saw no great evil in being transferred from one master to another, and there-fore did not at all consider Cesar's position as a bad one—he set about carefully thinking over the possible contingencies of Lucy's message.

The more he considered it, the more certain in his own mind he became, that the message desiring him to sleep in the early part of the night had much more particular reference to his being awake at its latter portion; and why should he be wished wakeful, if nothing was to come of such a circumstance?

"Yes, yes," he said to himself. "My Lucy Neal will try to do something for me, and I do pray to all de heabenly powers dat no harm may come to her; I would rather die dis blessed minute."

"Hi, hi, hi! How you feel now?" said a voice. "Damn you."

Cesar looked towards the grated window of the place in which he had been stowed away, and he saw the face of a negro named Bashi, whom he knew very well as the worst upon the property, and one who was no friend of his.

"Hi, hi, hi!" again cried Bashi; "you look remarkable like bird in own trap. Hi, hi, hi! De oberseer, Massa Grubson, put me to keep guard ober you, and gib me a jolly long gun to shoot you, if so be you try to get yourself away, and won't Bashi! Hi, hi, hi! How you feel, Cesar Bobb; 'pon my soul, you look considerable melancholy. Why you not sing im song? Hi, hi, hi!"

Cesar knew that in his present circumstances, nothing would be so delightful to Bashi, as getting him into a wrangling conversation; because he, Cesar, was so situated that he could not personally resent anything; so he made up his mind to make no reply whatever, but to allow Bashi to go on talking until he was tired.

"Hi, hi, hi!" said Bashi. "I hab orders to gib you drop o' rum, for all dat, in dis bottle. Here it is. Hi, hi! Hope it will do you good, Cesar Bobb."

As he spoke, Bashi pushed through the bars of the window a half-pint bottle such as was usually used to carry that quantity of rum, which, when mixed with water, in the fields is a most refreshing drink in that climate. But Cesar could not help wondering at the kindness thus shown to him. His first thought was that he must surely be indebted to Lucy Neal for the present; but then again, if so, it would not have come through Bashi's hands, and when he thought that, he grew suspicious.

"Well, hab you drunk it up?" cried Bashi.

"Oh, yes—oh, yes," said Cesar, as he placed the bottle in a corner on the floor.

This information evidently gave Bashi great satisfaction; and he opened Cesar's eyes to the prudence of not drinking the rum by saying,—

"Hi, hi, hi! Don't you feel sleepy, Cesar Bobb?"

"Oh, bery bery," said Cesar, as he added to himself, "so dat was a sleeping draught, what they calls a damn lot ob opium. I shall pretend to fall bang asleep, I shall."

"Well, Cesar," said Bashi, "how you feel now?"

Cesar made no answer; and then he heard Bashi remark, "Hi—hi! Massa Grubson quite right, dat is send him fast asleep, sure enough. Well, all de better for me. He can't try noting now to 'scape away, and put me in bodily fear. Oh no!"

Cesar moved himself as far as he could, both from the door and from the window, and resolved to conform to Lucy's instructions, not to go to sleep at the latter part of the night, by not going to sleep at all, which was certainly, under the circumstances, the most prudent line of conduct he could possibly have adopted. Bashi now supposing that the opiate had done its work, did not attempt to say anything more to Cesar, but walked to and fro, with a musket upon his shoulder, keeping his solitary ground, and occasionally humming some of the melodies then popular among the slaves on the estate.

This state of things lasted until the night was considerably advanced; and then Cesar suddenly started, for he heard a voice speaking to Bashi, the tones of which thrilled upon his ears. He knew that voice well—it was Lucy Neal's.

"Well, Bashi," he heard Lucy say, "there can be no harm done by my bringing Cesar a little rum."

"Oh, he had enough rum."

"Enough? Have you given him any?"

"Oh yes. Ever so much, Miss Lucy Neal, and he gone bang off to sleep; it was so jolly good. Hab you got some rum wid you, Miss Lucy?"

"I have. Will you taste it, Bashi?"

"Well, don't care if I do. Ah, 'pon life, it bery strong, damn fine old rum. Ah—gib me anoder drop, Lucy—ah—bery good—damn fine rum. Oh, Miss Lucy, you be nice gal, Lucy Neal."

"Oh, Bashi, you are a flatterer. Take another drop; it will do you good, for you have a dull watch here, and this old rum, you know, never does anybody any harm. Drink, Bashi, don't be afraid."

"Afraid, Miss Lucy Neal—nobody can dare say as Bashi was afraid ob a rum bottle. Oh dear no, no—I—I—bery good—damn fine old rum."

"I'm glad you like it, Bashi. Let me hold your gun—ah, that is better, you will be more at your ease sitting down—and so you love me a little, Bashi. Take another drop."

"Lub you," said Bashi, who was fast getting into a state of maudlin intoxication,—"lub you—oh, bery, bery, and old rum too—I—I lub you best—no, I lub de old rum—no—I—I—how funny de trees are dancing ob a jig."

"That's the effect of the night air, Bashi. Take another drop, and you will be better."

Bashi did so, and then he smacked his lips, and tried to speak, but his voice failed him; and after several ineffectual efforts to rise, he with a grunt resigned himself to drunken repose.

"'Tis done," said Lucy; "how weak of them to suppose that such a creature as this could keep a sufficient guard. But he was chosen for his known enmity to Cesar.

"Lucy—Lucy," said Cesar, from the room in which he was, and from which he had heard all that passed.

"I am here, Cesar—I am here; you shall be free. Oh, Cesar, do not suppose that what Mr. Deal said is all you have to dread. It is the baffled revenge of Tobias Slankey, of John Grubson, and of Adolphus that will contrive something against you yet more fearful. But you shall be saved."

"Oh, Lucy—Lucy, dear Lucy, if I could but hold you in my arms one moment, I should be paid well for all de suffering and for all de great anxiety."

"Hush! hush! Cesar, try your strength against the iron bars. Do they yield —do they move?"

Cesar made a vigorous effort, but the iron bars of the window moved not in the least, and he said, "Lend me de gun, Lucy; I may, perhaps, wid dat move one ob dem. Lend me de gun."

She handed him Bashi's gun through the bars, and that became a powerful lever as he used it, and broke one of the iron bars short off close to where it was inserted in the stone cill of the window. To wrench that bar away was now the work of a moment, and an opening was left which was nearly large enough for him to get through. Without, however, making the attempt, he set to work upon another bar, which he soon, by the assistance of the one he had already removed, got rid of, and then there was ample space. But at the moment he was about to avail himself of it, Lucy whispered to him,—

"Cesar—Cesar, quick, drag me through the opening. Quick, Cesar, quick."

Not comprehending what it was that induced her to wish to come into his prison at the moment that he thought of coming out of it, Cesar hesitated for a moment, during which, with great agility, Lucy sprung through the opening into the room. She then caught from his hands the two iron bars he had removed from the window, and crouching down under it, she held them up so that in the imperfect light they seemed to be in their proper positions.

"Lie down, Cesar," she said, "and be fast asleep; Grubson comes."

He now in a moment comprehended the necessity for these precautions; and throwing himself down in a corner of the room, he began snoring away at a rate that would have convinced the most sceptical that he was in the land of dreams.

In another moment he heard the sound of footsteps and voices, and became convinced that two persons had paused outside his prison.

"Why, where's your sentinel?" said Adolphus.

"Upon my word," replied Grubson, "I don't know. I left him here, with a promise of ample reward to-morrow if he kept a good watch during the night; and knowing his hatred of Cesar Bobb, I thought he would do so."

"He i not here. Hilloa—what's this?"

"Damnation! It's Bashi asleep."

"Or drunk. There's a most confounded smell of rum. Why, the rascal has got dead drunk upon his post. Upon my word, Grubson, you have a rare talent in finding out a sentinel. He surely has never been such an idiot as to drink himself the dose you gave him for Cesar."

"Hardly that, for I told him it contained a sleeping draught, which was to keep the prisoner quiet all night in case he should attempt to escape, as he was well known not to be deficient in courage, and not to be without friends among the slaves; but we shall soon find out if our prisoner has taken the potion or not."

"And this Bashi——"

"Oh, leave him to me. To-morrow he shall be flogged within an inch of his life. He shall remember this night as long as he lives; the scoundrel, to dare to get drunk when he was put upon such a task. I thought his hatred to Cesar Bobb would have kept him vigilant.

"You see it has not. But when did you ever hear of a negro who could resist rum? No doubt he brought some with him to cheer him on his watch, and you see the consequences."

"Never mind him—never mind him. Let us ascertain if our prisoner be sleeping or waking. If sleeping, you may depend upon it he has taken the drugged spirit."

They both approached the grated window, and peered in as well as they could by the assistance of a small lantern which Grubson produced, the bull's-eye of which he turned into the room, as he said,—

"Cesar, Cesar, you are wanted. You are free."

CHAPTER XXV.

THE REWARD OFFERED FOR CESAR.—THE SICKNESS OF LUCY NEAL.—INFORMATION OF THE FUGITIVE.

WE need not follow the proceedings of John Grubson and his associates, when they found that the bird had flown, and that the prison in which they had flattered themselves Cesar Bobb was secured, no longer held that much-injured person.

Rather allow us, kind reader, to pursue the more stirring fortunes of Cesar himself, and the gentle, but more affecting, career of poor Lucy Neal.

The first thing that the malevolence of Mrs. Deal suggested, was to make the escape of Cesar conclusive evidence of the iniquity concerning which she could not help perceiving that her husband had his doubts. "If," she reasoned, "he was innocent of the charge brought against him, why did he fly? Innocence," she added, "enpures anything, rather than sanction by flight a supposition of guilt."

In this mode of reasoning Mrs. Deal was, to some extent, correct in the abstract; but the facts connected with the present case were fully sufficient to justify Cesar in escaping, inasmuch as he was the victim of a plot formed for the express purpose of crushing him, let his innocence be ever so apparent; and, indeed, as we know, with a full and a distinct knowledge on the part of his enemies of his innocence.

Under such circumstances, it would have been a species of Quixotism for him to have remained for no other purpose than to have allowed those fiends in human shape to triumph over him. Thus we cannot but consider that without at all entrenching upon the general principle that flight is a sign of guilt, and that natural cowardice which in all places, and under all circumstances, belongs to it, Cesar Bobb was quite right in getting away as quickly as he possibly could.

And, perhaps, after all, Adolphus Deal, so that he did get rid of him, was not so much put out of the way at his escape as John Grubson was, who certainly missed the gratification of the revenge which he thought he should have had against Cesar, by submitting him to some punishment consonant to his barbarous and vindictive nature.

That suspicion should fall upon Lucy Neal was but a natural consequence of the escape of Cesar, and John Grubson urged that she should be questioned. He used this word "question" in so peculiar a manner, and with so strange an intonation, that Mr. Deal was tempted at last to say,—

"What do you mean by questioning, Mr. Grubson? It is not to be supposed that the girl would confess anything."

"I, sir," said Grubson, in an under tone, "have been upon estates where slaves have been made to confess matters they would have given almost their lives to keep secret. There are modes of enforcing such confessions, sir."

"Mr. Grubson," said Mr. Deal, while an angry flush of colour came across his brow. "Mr. Grubson, I am only very much surprised, at your want of penetration."

"Want of penetration, sir? I must confess I do not quite understand you, Mr. Deal."

"Then, sir, to make my meaning more clear, I may add that I should have imagined you knew my character too well to fancy that I would lend myself to the employment of torture on my estates. The proposition is an insult."

"And yet, Mr. Deal, it was my duty to make it to you. But having hinted at it as a means of accomplishing what is desired, I shall say no more about it."

"Never mention such a subject to me again."

"My good sir, but it will be so well known among all the slaves that Cesar Bobb owed his escape to the active agency of Lucy Neal, that I dread some amount of insubordination if no notice be taken of it. In such a case as that, the amount of harshness you would be obliged to practise, would be sure to give you uneasiness."

"It always gives me a large amount of uneasiness to be obliged to practise any harshness on my estates, but it is the curse of this species of property, that it must be attended by such circumstances. I will think, John Grubson, of some means of getting over the difficulty you suggest. Probably I shall part with Lucy Neal."

At this moment a female slave entered the room, but being conscious then of the presence of John Grubson, she paused, as if what she had to say, she did not wish to utter in his presence. Grubson bit his lips, but as this slave was one attached to the domestic service of the family, he had no sort of control over her.

"What is it, Cleopatra?" said Mr. Deal; "you have something to say, I can see by your looks."

"Yes, massa, I hab someting to say. Poor Lucy Neal, she be bery bad indeed wid de fever."

"Fever?"

"Yes, massa. De poor gal be bery bad."

"Oh, that is all nonsense," said John Grubson; "of course, whenever a slave gets into any trouble, the consequences are to be attempted to be warded off by being very bad with the fever. It's all trash, I say, all trash."

A look from Mr. Deal stopped John Grubson from saying anything more upon that head, or he would have, no doubt, further expostulated upon what he considered the dreadful iniquities of slaves, who, according to him, were capable of the worst of conduct; and if they were, what and who made them? What can be the answer to this, but the cruelty and oppression of their taskmaster's, such men as Grubson.

"Go, Cleopotra," said Mr. Deal. "Go to your mistress and say, that it is my positive wish that Lucy Neal should have medical attendance at once,

Cleopatra at the moment went upon her errand, but not before she had cast a look of great triumph at Grubson, which he duly noticed, and made up his mind to revenge on the very first opportunity that presented itself to him to do so ; and he fervently hoped and trusted that that time would not be very far distant. But then John Grubson thought, with a great many persons, that revenge was a good lasting commodity.

But poor Lucy Neal was now most seriously indisposed. The great amount of mental anxiety that she had gone through, combined with violent exercise and frequent exposure to the chilling influences. of the night air, had brought on one of the most serious attacks of the fever, that we have before mentioned as being incidental to the country.

A slight shiver, such as is common in the country, and which many superstitiously induced people say pervades the human frame at the moment that some stranger — is supposed to be walking over the spot that is to be one's grave, came over her, and in another hour she was stricken with the fever.

The whites held this affliction in great dread, but it was not at all contagious, being a kind of malaria fever incidental to the climate, so that Lucy Neal was not removed from Mr. Deal's house, but permitted to be in a small chamber that ooked into the garden.

There she was waited upon by Cleopatra and another of the domestic female slaves, who both tended her with as much affection as if she had been a daughter of their own.

No. 12.

Mr. Deal's order that nothing should be spared in the way of attention to Lucy Neal of course empowered those who were interested in her welfare to send for a medical man, and a mounted negro soon brought the one who was nearest to the estate.

This gentleman, when he had examined the state of Lucy Neal, shook his head with a dubious manner, and then declared that the attack presented some bad features which, although they might not necessarily make it fatal, were still of the most serious import.

Such intelligence was kept of course from her ears, but it filled her and all the attendants with dismay, and had she been but sufficiently conscious to draw conclusions from their looks, she would have soon seen what was the opinion entertained by the surgeon.

But we must, however reluctantly, quit the bedside of the gentle and affectionate and brave Lucy Neal, in order to state a circumstance that occurred one hour after sunset on the evening succeeding the night on which Cesar Bobb had made his escape.

Mr. Deal was seated in a room the window of which opened out to a long little lawn, in the centre of which grew some exquisite flowers in which he took great delight; and he seemed to be engaged in reflections of no very pleasant nature, if any one might judge by the occasional spasmodic actions of his lips, and the contraction of his brow, when, by some unseen hand, a large stone was flung in at the window, which fell at his feet.

The stone was not flung with more force than was sufficient to make it reach its destination, and did not seem to be intended to hurt him, although in the alarm of the moment he naturally enough started to his feet, and laid his hand upon the bell rope.

As all was still, however, he resisted the impulse to call for assistance, and picking up the stone he found that it was merely used as a vehicle to convey to him a note which was folded round it, and the contents of which were these, filling Mr. Deal with surprise:—

"Mr. Deal, you are not more unjust to the black man than your habits and education make you, for you have a good heart. If you wish to preserve yourself fly within twenty-four hours of the receipt of this to the coast, and take with you all that you hold dear, for the avenger is at hand, and if one hair of Lucy Neal's head is injured, woe upon the hand that has been lifted against her.   JACK STRAW."

CHAPTER XXVI.

THE RENDEZVOUS OF THE INSURGENT SLAVES BY NIGHT.—THE COUNCIL, AND THE UNEXPECTED ARRIVAL OF CESAR BOBB, AND HIS RESOLUTION.

THE desolate region of Alabama, in the higher and almost inaccessible regions, afforded an ample and safe retreat for the discontented, and it would, in proper hands, be held in the face of an overwhelming force. It was a wide, dreary moor, or heath, overgrown in many places thickly with different species of furze and broom, in a manner that rendered it impervious to human beings, while here and there were to be seen growing tall pines, and further round were to be seen high and lofty hills, or mountains, which formed a ring, or belt, round this secluded spot.

Indeed, the plain, or moor, was shut up between this range of hills, in which it appeared as a dell, though it was an elevated region with regard to the rest of the country; but now it appeared as a desolate scene of waste moorland of great extent, and furnished with a very stunted and starved vegetation that, while it clothed the land to a certain extent, did not make an available growth for any human purpose.

The approach to this desolate tract of woodland was dangerous, and narrow the ascent up the mountain side, which was clothed with different species of vegetation, and was well calculated to conceal a number of men.

The moon rose late that night, but it was a calm, quiet night; the stars shone out clearly, and there was enough of light to permit a man to travel, though it could not enable him to distinguish the many holes that beset the path; for the road, or country, in the waste was exceedingly fertile in all that kind of deceits, that nature sometimes delights in showing.

Every here and there you might perceive a deep hole, or steep descent, down which you might suddenly be pitched to the danger of your limbs.

It was a dreary amphitheatre, which might have served to herd a whole army in silence and secrecy, where no human sight would have intruded upon them. It was a wilderness of a place, and was very well calculated for the purpose which it was made use of on the present occasion, by the insurgent slaves.

The evening had scarce set in, before there were some signs of life observable in the moor. Dark and dusky figures of men were seen stealing from the bushes, and coming forth from their hiding-places, and assemble on the moor.

After a time, several figures were seen running to and fro in the gorges of the mountain pass that led into this amphitheatre, and many more were seen pouring in from that quarter, who were met in silence by those who lay there.

This lasted for the best part of an hour, and then, there being a very large body of men, amounting, perhaps, to near two thousand or more, they collected together in groups, and held conversations together in low, but earnest tones.

This went on for some time, and the subject of every one's speech was the object of their meeting each other in that lone spot.

"Cato," said one tall black to another, who was a most imposing-looking individual, as far as the head and shoulders went, but very bandy and splay-footed, so that he was very much at variance with himself, the upper portion of his person being very incongruous to the lower.

"Well, Scipio," replied Cato; "what you want with me?"

"I want to know the news."

"I have heard none to-day," replied Cato; "I have lain in the bush all day, and have seen no one but our own people."

"Then you know not how we are to be joined on one route? All the Africans will join us; they will all be glad to be free—they will be glad; we will be as we were before we were brought from our African homes; we could hunt, and fish, and work, and do what we chose."

"And so we will again."

"I hope so. I would sooner suffer the worst tortures these whips can inflict than I would return to slavery again."

"No slavery: black man equal to white."

"And that we will soon teach then," was the reply which the negro made, with a gesture not to be mistaken, for he passed his hand over the lock of a gun he held in his hand, and half held it up to his shoulder.

"Yes, yes, Scipio; I will myself, show them what it is to oppress the black, but we shall bear them back, they cannot stand against us, we shall be too many, and shall have too much courage to be overcome."

"The white men will learn, when too late, that we are not to be their drudges, —that men are not mere beasts; moreover, Cato, they will see that, though we can and have endured much, yet we can, when forced to it, endure much more for our own sakes; for I am sure the cotton plantation is as a place of torture, and the owners the devils who inhabit the estates."

" And why should they enjoy the surface of the earth, while there are more men than they number waiting for bread? And why, I say, should the greater number be in chains, at the commands of the few?"

"Well said, Scipio," said another, coming up; "why, indeed. Are we not entitled to one share of the earth? Why, they speak of their right of conquest—that will be our claim, by-and-by, but they will refuse to acknowledge it, I dare say."

"They cannot choose to do so, but should they do so, what will it matter? Are not our people as good in peace as in war, and are they not capable of making good what they obtain, and of keeping what they have got?"

"So they will, I warrant you. A black man can load a gun, and pull a trigger as well as any white that steps."

"Yes, yes, we are all convinced of that. We can push on, and can obtain more arms at every estate we overrun."

"Those who have the courage to face us will, at the best, but serve to whet our appetites, and we can profit by the arms they lose. We shall not only diminish the number of our enemies but we shall be able to add to our own strength, by increasing our arms, for we have none too many."

"There is some hope in that. We shall be better armed as we go on, but the hour grows late. When does the council assemble?"

" I expect the signal every moment," said Scipio.

" Hark! what is that?"

" That is the horn that calls us together. I will away and take my way thither; the council are about to assemble; be in readiness, my friends, for you will hear of us soon, and I doubt not instant orders will be given to advance."

" We have expected a skirmish."

" But it will depend upon the notice some of them may have received respecting the slaves that have not yet quitted their plantations, who, perhaps, cannot do so, but who are willing to join us when we are near them in full force. Men will not run the risk of torture for the chance of an escape, which makes him a fugitive for life; but they do not mind casting their lives upon the hazard of a die, when the prize is well worthy of the stake played for."

There was a level spot, a kind of mount, upon which a number of the slaves congregated together, and who were now assembled in goodly numbers. These were the leaders of the movement that was to take place.

Around them had collected, at a short distance, a number of slaves, who appeared in such vast multitudes that any one not acquainted with the objects in view might readily have mistaken them for the spirits of the nether world, assembled in grand conclave, debating what mischief they could inflict upon mankind.

But the sable counsellors no sooner saw themselves assembled in force than one of them arose, saying,—

" Brother slaves! I hope this will be the last time that I shall address you as slaves, and that you will be free."

" Yes, yes—free, free! We are free!"

" We shall win our freedom. Wrest it from those who have hitherto plied the scourge upon our bodies, without resistance upon our parts, or mercy upon theirs."

"Shame, shame!"

" Ay, brothers, 'tis a shame; and shame be upon those who exerted their power upon us so—but they have taught us our power. They never had any but what was wrung from our fears and our forbearance; and this shall be no longer. We are strong in numbers, and are strong in our cause. What more would you have?"

" Nothing, but the opportunity of measuring our strength."

" And that I hope, we shall have to-night. For this is the night we have appointed to descend into the plantation, and there set free those who have not as yet been able to quit the plantation and blockhouses."

"That," said another slave, who ranked as counsellor,—"that must be done to-night. We have many of us subsisted in these places for some months, and now there are too many to remain here longer, with any hope of provisioning them We must descend upon the plantations, and there take what we want most."

There was a long argument held forth for the purpose of vindicating their assembling in arms, which was, they declared, to recover the liberty of which they were deprived of by violence, murder, and fraud.

These arguments were assented to most eagerly by those present, and industriously repeated from throng to throng, and highly received and approved of. Not that the slaves were masters of very good English, but we have taken the trouble to translate it for them, for their own language was made up of broken English, mixed with many words which seldom or ever reach the ears of the inhabitants of this country.

Here another of the slaves arose, and declared that they, the oppressed, were even as their oppressors, and had in nature the same rights and privileges, and it was wrong to deprive them of their rights; but since they, the masters, had taught them the rights of conquest, let them look to it, and take their account in it, for they, the slaves, would seek the same right to the land they lived in, and would retort then their right of conquest.

This was approved of too, and many more speeches also. Some were much more violent and inflammatory than others, and breathed nothing but vengeance and destruction upon their foes, and their implacable enemies, their owners.

Thus it was they continued to harangue for more than an hour, when one, who appeared to possess all the confidence of the rest, rose and said,—

"Brethren, are you all unanimous in your resolves to give battle to your enemies; to rush from your hills and places of strength and security, upon the unsuspecting and insidious foe, who now lies almost at your mercy?"

"We are, we are," shouted many voices.

"Then let this instant be the time for the attack; let the signal be given to the slaves who have promised to join us when we march to the attack, and many of whom will be well armed, my brothers."

"Hurrah, hurrah, for the attack," shouted hundreds of throats.

"Then light the torches and let the bearers be posted in the proper places, so they may be seen from the nearest plantations, and then they will give information to those who are farther off; so our coming will be known to all."

This was at once assented to, and they were in the act of giving orders to the effect, when some one was observed to come through the pass into the amphitheatre, where they were assembled.

It was well known that no one could approach from that quarter save those who were friends, without meeting with opposition and resistance from the slaves, who were posted there to protect them against a sudden interruption from any party, and the pass was capable of being defended against a vast number of men.

"It must be some friend," said one, who watched the motions.

"Come to give us intelligence," said another.

"Of what character?"

"That is what we shall know from himself," said another, "when he comes; but we cannot tell until he is here. He appears tired, and hardly able to stand."

"He must bring us intelligence of a hostile character—perhaps we have been betrayed by some one, and they have got the soldiers ready to meet us."

"It matters not, we have men enough to meet them, and push all the soldiers they can get into the sea; but it matters not, as I said before. We have plenty of men if they be but true—we have by far the greatest in numbers."

By this time the stranger, who was one of their own colour, arrived, almost exhausted, and entered the ring.

"Cesar Bobb!" they one and all exclaimed.

"Yes, my broders, it is Cesar—him 'scaped from him blockhouse, and him run and run till him no breath left in him."

Cesar threw himself upon the ground to regain his breath, while those around forbore to ask him any questions relative to the cause of his coming until he should somewhat recover from his distress.

From one of the slaves present, he received some cordial, which had the effect of speedily restoring his strength; for he had made such speed thither, as had well nigh deprived him of the power of reaching them.

"Tell us, Cesar, what do you know that we should learn—what news ?"

"None in particular."

"What brings you here in such a state ? Was it to join us, or did you fear that something would happen to us ?"

"No, no, you shall hear," said Cesar, whose oddities of language we will discard, "you shall know why I am here now. You shall know my wrongs, and then you shall be the judges of the wicked tyrants who oppress us,'

"Go on, Cesar. We know you to be one who will be stanch to us."

"I have always loved the land of freedom, but I never wronged another man of it, even though I had every tempta ion to be violent and to take life; but now I will hold my hand no longer."

"What has happened, Cesar ?"

"You shall hear," said Cesar, almost choked by his own feelings, which however subsided, and changed to others of a sterner character. "You shall hear. You all, at least many of you know I loved Lucy Neal. You also know, or may do so now, that she attracted the attentions of my master's son, and there is no wrong that he did not do us, and no misery that he did not inflict upon us, aided by two infamous men known to some of you—the preacher Slankey, and the inhuman overseer, John Grubson."

"Death to such tyrants," said one.

"Ay," said Cesar, "they give death to all who resist the vilest oppression they may deem it right to inflict, because it is their pleasure."

Cesar Bobb went on to narrate all that happened at Mr. Deal's, and how he had been accused of stealing from his master, and how the article had been secreted in the thatch of his dwelling.

Loud were the execrations that were uttered by his hearers at the oppression which he had suffered, and they applauded to the echo his escape, and his threats of vengeance against those who had thus unjustly abused and oppressed him.

CHAPTER XXVII.

THE MARCH OF THE INSURGENT SLAVES.—THE STATE OF THE PLANTATIONS, AND
THEIR FRIENDS IN THE BLOCK-HOUSE.—THE FIRST ATTACK AND VICTORY OVER
THE VOLUNTEERS.

THERE was a pause of some moments, during which Cesar appeared to be recovering himself from his fatigue, and his companions seemed to be considering something in their own minds, when one of them said,—

"Cesar Bobb has been greatly injured—none amongst us more so than he. I speak my mind, my brothers, that he should be a leader—he knows the country—he knows the plantation—and he has been cruelly used."

"He has been cruelly used. We have known him long; and those of his colour will follow him, for they have confidence in him, and they believe that he will lead them on to victory; and that he will not spare himself—he is not afraid—he is a brave man, is Cesar Bobb—we will follow Cesar Bobb."

"Yes, yes—Cesar Bobb is a leader !" exclaimed a dozen voices, among the most influential of the insurgents. "What do you say to it, Cesar? Will you march at the head of a part of our host ?"

"Ay," said Cesar, "I will—I will fight—I will die in such a cause. I cannot return to them—they have disgraced me—they have injured me, and have endeavoured to rob me of the love of one whom I value more highly than life ; and I know not to what extremity she may not be reduced to."

"Then you are one of us."

"I am, while a white man stands with arms before us."

"Hurrah! hurrah !" shouted the slaves. "Freedom or death !"

"Freedom or death !" shouted the insurgents, from hundreds of voices in tones that awoke the dull echoes of the place, and startled the night-birds from their lairs, while the wild animals were awakened from their sleep with fear and trembling.

"Let the signal be given—light the torches, and let men stand on the highest points until all have marched out."

There was a general acclamation at this order, which was immediately obeyed, and a hundred torches glared from different points, shedding a strange and fearful glare, that might have been seen for many miles from the spot.

This was a signal which was intended for the information of their friends, who lay scattered about in different quarters of the country, over different estates, and who were interested in the secret of their rising.

This was a measure, too, that had been settled and agreed upon, and would be looked for by those who expected them, and who would do all they could to prepare for them, and join them in the most efficient state they could.

There was now only the arrangements to make that had been partially agreed upon before, and now they arranged themselves into different bodies, disposed under different leaders, and a regular plan of action laid down.

Among those who led the foremost bodies was Cesar Bobb, who was armed with a sword and a fowling-piece.

"Brethren," he said, "be firm. Let no man fear facing any opposition, because there is none that can be offered to us. There are no soldiers, or at most but a few of those irregular bodies, the militia, who are good at nothing except using the cart-whip or the thong, which they exert on your own backs."

"Death to the overseers! death to the overseers !" shouted the enraged blacks, as they remembered the smart that invariably accompanied the application of the lash, and fire and fury seemed to flash from their eyes.

"On, on !" they exclaimed, in deep, determined tones.

"Then follow me," said Cesar Bobb ; and he led the way up to the defile, through which they passed, and found their comrades posted on the hill sides with their torches, looking like so many spirits of darkness engaged in some devilish incantations, and lighting the earth to entrap some traveller to his destruction.

They paused not, however, but continued on their road, and pursued their rugged descent, until they reached the plain below, where they took up an advanced station, and awaited the approach of the other bodies who were to join them.

This, of course, occupied some time ; and while they waited for the arrival and the formation of the other bodies, they gained their breath, and conversed upon their plan, and the security in the execution of it that was afforded.

"When," said one of the leaders to Bobb, "do you think we shall reach Mr Deal's plantation ?"

"I am in haste to get there," said Cesar.

"But how soon do you calculate upon arriving there ?"

"Not to-night, certainly."

"No, no ; that would be impossible."

"Exactly ; because, were the distance forgotten, such a body of men cannot march on as if they were but one individual ; indeed there must be halts on the road : there will be work to do on the road ; and, what is more, there is, no doubt, ome opposition to be overcome, and we have our friends to look to, to the right and left of the line of march."

" There are many things, I know, to do, but there will be no opposition that can at all withstand our rush."

" That is as may be : the whites have arms and ammunition in abundance, but then their men are the most cowardly that they could choose, because they are the most cruel, and cowardice and cruelty always go hand in hand."

" They do."

" There will be a few burnings," said one.

" Ay, the flames will make a dark night like this look as red as if the very earth gave out a fire."

Thus the men conversed together, but in deep under tones. Their thoughts and feelings were wound up to such a pitch, that they were fit and ready for any desperate deed—they had but to be shown what was required of them.

The word to move on a further distance was passed along, and silently, but swiftly and steadily, did they push forward.

Their course was unmarked save by the tramp of the feet of many men ; but it was not the sound that usually accompanies trained bodies : the step was irregular, and produced a tumultuous and hurried vibration.

They pursued their way for some miles, and upon looking back, perceived that all the torchlights had been extinguished, and those who bore them formed, no doubt, part of the hinder portion of their forces.

It would have been a fearful sight, had any planter been present, to have witnessed the silent, steady march of these determined men. He would then have called to mind the many acts of cruelty and oppression that he had been guilty of, and his cheek would have been blanched with fear as the thought rose to his mind that these men were discharging what would be but a just retribution upon him.

He, in fact, would be answerable for the blood that would be spilt—he would be the cause of the loss of many a life ; indeed, who else could have changed the natures of those who were thus driven to seek their own safety in aggression and bloodshed ?

But how few were there who would do anything in the way of justice ! There were, it is true, some kind masters, but very few, and those few had not the happiness to have such men as themselves about them.

A severe and inhuman overseer often marred the humanity and kindness of an owner ; indeed it seldom happened that their slavery was more than merely bearable by the unfortunate blacks.

They now came to the plantation. It was an outlying one, and in advance of all the rest, and this was the object of attack.

" Burn and destroy," was the order given.

" Burn and destroy," repeated the slaves. " Ay, and well he deserves it ; one man lately has been flogged—scourged to death."

" Death to the tyrants!"

" Search the house—search the house !"

These exclamations were made in consequence of no one appearing, all being quiet, and no appearance of resistance being offered.

" They do not know we have come down upon them. They sleep in security, but danger will knock at their gate," said Cesar Bobb. " We will let them into the secret. Give a shout, a wild hilloa, my friends, one that shall awake them if they slept anything this side the sleep of death."

Then, at his command, there arose such a wild and terrible shout that would have awakened the unfortunate inmates, if any there had been, to a state of distraction and fear impossible to describe.

There was a pause of a few moments, but no one appearing, Cesar took his gun, saying, as he levelled it against the windows,—

" Give them a few shots that will make them appear."

This was done ; about half-a-dozen shots were fired at the house, but it produced no effect, and no one appeared.

"They have deserted," said one.

"Let us enter the house and see, then," said Cesar, "what can be the cause of all this. They cannot have taken their slaves with them, and I cannot imagine it possible that they could have murdered them."

There was an intense excitement among the slaves, and in an instant the doors which were secured, were dashed in, and upon running through the house, they found it had been but very recently deserted.

However, they found not their brethren the slaves, and in some consternation a party was despatched to a block-house close at hand, and there, upon breaking it open, they found their unfortunate companions chained, and secured to the floor by means of iron rings, so that they could not get out without assistance.

No 13.

How they cursed the caution of the owners, who would have left them to perish, perhaps, of hunger or of fire, for it was likely enough they might have set fire to the block-house without being at the pains to look into it.

As it was, however, the slaves were liberated, and in a few minutes more they aided their liberators in setting fire to their owner's mansion, thus destroying the furniture and all that was valuable.

The flames soon ascended high in the heavens, and served as a beacon to those around, and they were greeted by wild shouts and uncouth noises, the winding of horns, and other strange sounds that had a fearful character.

When this was accomplished, and the liberated prisoners were added to their own numbers, they proceeded onwards.

"We shall have to meet them soon," said Cesar to one of his companions.

"Do you think so?"

"Yes, they will show fight, I think. I pray God they may, and the sooner the better, for they will be fewer and less prepared."

"They have taken the alarm," said the same man, "and will, when they do oppose us, be prepared to take us at some disadvantage."

"That will matter but little. Yonder are some more habitations and planta-tions. They will barely give up all these without a struggle."

"You see it is impossible they should obtain sufficient men to oppose us. None of our people dare they trust—our men would come over to us ; indeed, we have some friends here who will join us in this rising."

"Push on," said Cesar, "we have no time to talk. We must approach warily and cautiously, and then there may be time, after all is over, to speak about other matters. See, we have some friends coming."

A party of about thirty slaves now made towards them. They were evidently coming from the direction of the estates, and presented themselves to the insur-gents, declaring themselves friends, and bringing arms to them, begging to be admitted among them, which, of course, was at once complied with.

They brought intelligence, too, that the planters had been alarmed, and had armed all those they could depend upon as being opposed to the coloured popula tion. All clerks, overseers, drivers, and every description of servant they could muster, they formed into a kind of forlorn hope.

"And this," said Cesar Bobb, "is the only means of opposing us ?"

"Yes," was the reply ; "they depend upon these men to defend their estates until they can bring up the militia and regulars."

"Have they sent for them ?"

"I am given to understand they have done so, and then you are to be reduced to submission, and compelled to become slaves again; that is, all that are left after shooting and hanging shall have done their work."

"Let them try. We can die but once, and better that once with arms in our hands fighting for our liberty and for those we love."

"Hurrah ! forward !"

There was nothing further said, but the whole body pushed forward at a rapid pace, silently, but few words being spoken.

They were now fast approaching the planters' houses, and had to pass through a narrow roadway, and then through some cane-fields, and had, in fact, got into the middle of the road, which was narrow and difficult, when they were suddenly met by a volley of fire-arms, which laid many of their number low.

For a moment they staggered, but one or two arriving at the spot where the flashes came from, they recovered from their surprise, and, with a loud yell in defiance, rushed at the unseen foe who had surprised them.

The forlorn hope of the planters had placed themselves in a very admirable position, and if they had had courage and resolution, they might have maintained themselves there with little or no loss, while their enemies must have suffered most severely, and been compelled to retreat.

This would have given time, and it would have had the effect of depriving them of their *eclat,* and have caused a feeling of insecurity that would have weakened their cause, and deterred many who would have joined the insurgents.

But, as it was, they no sooner beheld their former slaves rushing towards them, quite reckless of life, than they were seized with a panic, and did not even reload their guns, but, rising up, turned, and made a precipitate retreat.

In their flight they were not willing to encumber themselves with more baggage than necessary, and therefore threw away their arms, and thus lightened themselves, but their weapons fell into the insurgents' hands.

"Hurrah! Liberty for ever! Down with the overseers! No slavery!" shouted the mob of blacks, who looked and fought like fiends incarnate, as they rushed, leaping and shouting about from place to place.

The planters had turned their backs, at least this was their first attack; but then what could this have been called, since it was composed only of those who had been in the habit of frowning upon black men, and who, when they saw them, appeared to look upon as inferior beings, but who now were reaping the bitter fruits of their former conduct.

The blacks gave every token of their joy by repeated shouts, and pressed on to the houses, at which they intended to rest a few hours.

CHAPTER XXVIII.

THE PROGRESS OF THE INSURGENT SLAVES.—THE BURNING OF THE MISSIONARY HOUSES.—THEIR ARRIVAL AT MR. DEAL'S PLANTATION.

THERE was a general feeling of exultation at the first flush of success. It was not so much the value of the victory itself, as the fact that it was a victory; that fact was what they desired, as it would increase their numbers, and render them more feared than before; and the planters would probably desert their houses, and leave them in possession of the open country, where they could maintain themselves.

They had travelled over many miles of ground, and were getting fatigued, and Cesar thought that to pursue their march further would only tend to disorganise their force; he therefore ordered the party he commanded to make for the nearest residence, and there at once established himself.

The other parties as they came up did the same.

"The men are tired," he said, "and we have marched a long way, and routed a body of the enemy, who imagined themselves strong enough to oppose us, and that for one day will, I think, be enough."

"And I think so too," said another.

"We will stay here; provisions are at hand, and they are needed. A few hours' rest, and then we shall all be the better able to proceed."

"Hurrah!" shouted the insurgents.

"Then we had better put the plan in execution."

"And place outposts, so that we are not subject to any surprise; not that those who have made this night's attack will dare venture to return, yet it is certain we ought to take all proper precautions."

These suggestions were all put into immediate practice, and in less than an hour the whole band who had gathered together were safely quartered in different parts, with good provisions and drink in abundance at their command, which, however, was served out only in stipulated quantities.

There was, of course, now a scene of confusion. The houses were all ransacked, and turned, as it were, inside out, and they carried out all the articles of furniture, that they might be able to accommodate a greater number.

After a short and hearty meal—for they slaughtered whatever animals they could lay their hands on, and thus procured excellent provisions—they lay down and took a few short hours of repose, before they should again commence their operations against the whites, who appeared as yet unable to resist them.

  *   *   *   *   *   *   *

The morning broke; and the sun scarcely shone upon the black groups, before they were awakened by their horns and the shouts of the men. Then there was a hearty repast taken by the insurgents, who were now actively alive to what was to be done.

Thus prepared, and well aware that they should obtain what supplies of provisions they should need as they went on, they left all things as they found them, and thus prepared to move forward, and with little or no encumbrance to harass their movements.

The order was given, and the insurgents ranged themselves in bodies as they had done before, and again commenced their march.

It was now a different part of the country they had to pass through, studded by the estates and residences of the planters, and the scene of many an act of cruelty, which caused many a one present to curse the very spot of earth as he trod upon it.

"Here," said one, "my poor wife was whipped to death because she was too ill to work, and was told she was obdurate."

"Here," said another, "my son was ill-used by the overseer, and ran away, but was brought back and flogged, and tortured to such an excess that he ran away again—flogging and imprisonment broke his spirit and his heart. He died!"

"Here my daughter," said another, "was debauched by a planter."

"And mine by an overseer."

Thus the men enumerated the worst of domestic evils that had been suffered by them at different times, and great was the anger and ferocity that their remembrance called into being, and it was not to be wondered at.

The slaves disliked their labour, and they disliked, above all, those who daily held the whip in their hand—the cow-hide thong—and who applied it most unmercifully to their bare bodies, without any fear of the consequences.

They now divided themselves into three bodies, and spread over the country right and left of their march, for the purpose of seizing upon many of those houses and plantations that they must have otherwise passed.

"I think," remarked one of the leaders, "we shall have time to raise the whole state before they can bring a single body of men to oppose us."

"It seems so," said another.

"But," added a third, "they will bring forces from another state and guns to bear upon us; they will bring their men regularly armed."

"What of that? Shall we not be enough to beat them all off, and compel them to retreat? We can surround them on every side; they will hardly concentrate their whole force, and if they do, can we not retreat around them, until they expose themselves to our power on every side?"

"So we can."

"And while we have numbers, and are in the open country, we can refuse battle as long as we please, for in truth it would be ill policy to accept it at a great disadvantage to ourselves; but we must wait until they are too eager, or until we get into places of security, where their big guns would be of no avail to them, and they would be reduced to an equality of arms, which would be what they do not desire should be done by any means. They would not be able to withstand us."

"It matters not," said Cesar; "we shall have possession of the country, and shall be able at least to inflict vengeance upon them. We can ravage the country with fire and sword from one end to the other."

"Ay, and Alabama, would become a howling wilderness which would take ages to reclaim ; even then would our tyrants deserve to be made to live in iron cages."

"Forward, forward !" urged Cesar Bobb, who had his own reasons for getting forward as quickly as possible to Mr. Deal's plantation ; but he knew he should not be able to reach there that day, for large bodies of men cannot travel as rapidly as individuals, and, moreover, they had many objects of detention.

Of course at every estate they came to there was a stoppage from some cause or other. There was an immediate search made throughout the place for the inhabitants, who had taken the alarm and fled.

There were many fires kindled, houses burned ; and especially those places in which they had been greatly tortured were all without hesitation set on fire.

The plantations were all trodden under foot, the trees and plants injured and often ruined, the crops in the houses burned, and as much mischief done as could be on so short a notice.

They could see for many miles far and wide that there was no body of troops to oppose them ; indeed they were alone in possession of the country round for many miles, while their scouts at once declared that there was no one within their range, and they believed none beyond it.

But in another hour one of the scouts came to Cesar, saying,—

"There are white men upon the hills to the left, Cesar."

"Are they in any numbers ?" inquired Cesar.

"No, they appear as if they were merely watching us, and which way we were coming, and what we were doing."

"And much joy they will receive from what they observe."

"Do you not think that they are intent upon watching us, to descend upon us when we are entangled and disordered in some place which we are firing or razing to the earth, and thus endeavour to overcome us ?"

"Perhaps so, or more likely they have the means of offering some resistance from that place, where they have some advantage of position."

"But," said another, "we shall not go that way ; the line of march has been determined on to go another way—to the right of that."

"And why ?"

"Because we shall come upon some of the missionary establishments, where they preach submission to those who have so deeply injured us, and call this obeying the will of God—the besotted fools !"

"Ay, ay ; they got paid for what they did, and what more did they desire ? They would not have done it for nothing."

"Oh no, no, any more than a planter would cultivate his estate for the benefit of others, and not for himself, directly or indirectly."

"That is right enough, brother ; but see, we come now to a difficult road : they might have done us mischief here if they chose, but I suppose they had not the courage to come down and oppose us."

The negroes now marched slowly and silently along ; they knew that they might have been opposed at this place, for they could not well bring their whole force to bear against any opposition that might be offered.

However, they passed through the defile, if such it could be called, and at once began to open, and to make a broader front than they had presented when they were coming through the gorge formed by some rugged ground and a cane brake.

Having come upon the missionary place, they saw the missionaries coming out towards them, but they were warned by several shots being fired at them, which took some effect, and speedily put them to flight.

They ran away with hearty good-will, accompanied with the execrations of the blacks, who were incensed against them for their conduct in general, always taking the part of the owners, and preaching and inculcating their submission to those who had been theives in the first place, by robbing them of their liberty.

There was no excuse, they said, for them, and they would have destroyed them if possible; but, at the same time, these gentlemen had the good luck to escape, some with a few shots which they carried along with them : they had no loss.

The missionary-houses and meeting-houses were, without exceptions, burned, and wherever any show of resistance was offered, it was sure to be crushed, and none of the volunteers dared show the r faces any more.

They had several halts on this day, and towards the evening they came to a spot where they had all halted.

"They all know now," said one of their body, "that we are up in arms; and therefore there can be no surprise in the question ; and therefore we shall be under no necessity to march by night, we may as well halt for the night."

"There can be no objection to that," said Cesar Bobb, who was present ; "but I should propose our halt should not last more than five or six hours; and then we shall be refreshed, and can come down upon Deal's plantation by daybreak, and we shall make some prisoners, and inflict some vengeance."

"That," said another speaker, "will be well, and I give my vote for that object."

"And I."

"Then," said one, "let the men get their food, and in five hours be called, so as to give them time to get an early meal, and then we can resume our march ; for they cannot be expected to bear long, fatiguing marches without proper food, though they could do it; yet it will be unnecessary to do so until we are obliged. Besides, their spirits and strength will suffer ; we shall be ready to resume our march two hours after midnight."

"At the latest ?"

"Yes, at the latest."

     *   *   *   *   *   *

This matter being settled, hasty preparations were made for passing the night where they were ; and in a short time fires were lighted, and provision, as before, was not scarce ; and after they had satisfied their hunger, they all lay down ; after proper outposts had been set, they fell into a sweet and refreshing slumber.

Their exertions during the day had not been slight—far from it. They had marched many miles, and had taken part in more than one scene of violence ; and now they were within about three short hours' march of Mr. Deal's plantation.

This, however, did not appear to have been their obje ct; for they had bee marching in another direction—certainly not in a direct line ; and hence it was apprehended that there would be no fear upon the part of the inhabitants, who were expected to remain in security on the estate, without fear of an immediate attack upon them.

Indeed, there they remained, and did not even know the insurgent slaves were so near them by some leagues ; but the slaves, at about one hour after midnight, rose as one man and marched upon the plantation.

The sun had scarcely risen when the large body entered the confines of Mr. Deal's property, and when Cesar Bobb saw the block-house in which he had been confined a prisoner, he said,—

"There—I escaped from that place, and Lucy Neal was my deliverer."

There was a pause at the block-house, and one of the blacks proposed that it should be fired instantly. This proposal being agreeable, it was at once put in practice, and in a few minutes more there was a tall flame ascending high in the heavens from the consuming embers of the building that had been so recently put to another purpose.

The block-house was fired, and burned brightly in the dull sky, and illuminating many objects around it, and giving a warning to many of the inhabitants of other estates of the sudden irruption that had been made upon them.

The irruption was so unexpected that no immediate preparation had been made for flight, and the whole of the family were thus compelled to abide and become prisoners; for the blacks had surrounded the whole place.

Before, however, there could be anything done, the discomfited volunteers were collected together, and some more aid being obtained, thus reinforced, they were in duced to screw their courage to the sticking place and attempt another attack in defence of their masters.

The blacks were not aware of this determination for some time, and then some scouts whom they had thrown forward saw them, and hastened to give the information, and one of them coming to Cesar Bobb, exclaimed,—

" Oh, Cesar, the whites have come down upon us again ; you must meet them first for they are all armed and in good order."

" How many ?" inquired Cesar Bobb.

" About two or three hundred," replied the scout, " that is all I saw ; but I think they must have a yet larger force."

" They would hardly make any attempt upon us," said Cesar Bobb, " with so small a force as that—we are many times as strong ; but still they are venturesome, and will hazard much upon the presumption that they can frighten us into submission, or scare us away, and thus become an easy victory for them."

" Well, but we have already beaten those ranaways once, and it will not take much to do so ; they will be up in a quarter of an hour, I dare say; they must be met, and for that purpose, men must be posted, so as to line the way through which they come ; one volley then will be enough, and they will be scattered to the winds, for they have not courage to fight."

This was approved of, and immediately put into practice, and two bodies of blacks were at once marched towards them, and were so placed that they could attack the whites upon the flanks, while another body was marched to meet them.

These were scarcely parted, when another body was sent to meet the whites in front, but a much smaller body, so as to induce them to come on with the hope of vanquishing them, and thus lead them into the ambuscade.

This was easily accomplished, for the whites were composed only of that part of the population which had been connected with the slaves, drivers, overseers, and others—in fact, those who had, on the previous occasion, been dispersed almost by a panic, having fired a volley and then run away, before there was any opportunity of coming to a trial of strength.

There was not much of an expectation that they would meet the small body which was sent against them, though that was ostensibly the only enemy they had, at that moment, to deal with.

However, they came on within half a musket-shot, when a mutual volley took place and was fired, and then the volley of those in ambush ; the slaves then showed themselves, and as soon as the smoke cleared off, there were no whites to be seen, save those who lay on the field, for they had fled.

The whites no sooner saw the flash, and heard the bullets whistling around them, than they turned round and fled—they believed they were all slain, and a complete route was the consequence, and, they threw away their arms in the flight, which of course became the spoil of the victors, who desired no better spoil than good muskets.

" This," said they, " is not a victory alone, but it will arm at least from one hundred to hundred more men : this will at all events enable us to defend ourselves from the troops should they bring any into the field."

" And now," said Cesar Bobb, " let us return to Mr. Deal's house. I fear that some great misfortune will attend me there unless I at once proceed to release her who saved me and enabled me to escape and reach you."

" Indeed, Cesar, we will go at once, and see what we can do, but you may depend upon it they will not dare to injure her, because they are in our power, indeed they would fear to lose their own lives by any such acts."

" I hope not."

" You may be sure of it—but what is the matter ? You see they are all in a great commotion. I wonder what has happened."

CHAPTER XXIX.

THE CHASE AFTER THE PREACHER SLANKEY.—THE CANE BRAKE.—THE DISCOVERY
OF HIS RETREAT AND HIS DEATH.

CESAR looked in the direction in which his companion pointed, and beheld a
number of the insurgents remaining and shouting, and occasionally firing at some
object which they could not observe, but which appeared to be moving. They
immediately hurried forward to ascertain the cause of this commotion which was
wrapt in mystery.

When they came near, they believed they saw some human being running with
tremendous speed from a party of the insurgents who were pursuing him—he
doubled and turned and threw them out repeatedly, and was evidently making for
a cane-brake near the cotton plantation, from which the pursuers were desirous
of cutting him off.

Now and then they headed him, and when cut off from one quarter he would suddenly make a divergence in another direction, then he would turn, and wind about ; now
go right into them, and then give them the slip, on this side and on that, until he
became so entangled that they could not fire at him without danger of shooting
their own companions, which was so great and imminent that they did not
attempt it.

"What is the matter ?" inquired one of those who had just come up, of some
those who had been present when the chase commenced.

"It is a wild man running away."

"Running away. Where did he come from ?"

"He came from some place close at hand. He was concealed, I believe," replied
the black, "and, when discovered, they were about to hang him, but somehow or
other, he got away and made off, after he began to preach."

"To preach," said Cesar. "Was he a preacher ?"

"Yes," replied the other, "I believe so ; but here comes one who saw the
whole of it, from the beginning : he can tell you more about it."

"What is this affair about ?" inquired the other, turning to the new comer, who
was a tall, thin, but overgrown black.

"Why, you see," he replied, "that there was seen, after the missionary-house
was set on fire, a man creep out and run away. There were only a few who saw
him go away, and they were determined that he should be overtaken and brought
to punishment.

"They noted his course and bore down upon him. They resolved that he should
not escape, but marked him down, but when they came up, there was no trace of
him whatever. He was lost, or laid so close that he was not to be found, but
seeing no place of concealment thereabouts, they gave up the chase.

"However, being tired, they rested themselves, and one of them threw himself
on a small hillock of tangled grass and weeds, which he had no sooner done,
than he felt it all move under him, and suddenly vanish, and he was thrown
down.

"The terror of the unfortunate man was very great ; indeed, he roared out as if
he had been put to the torture of the lash, and many of us were alarmed, and could
not think what was the matter ; and when he could speak, he said,—

"'An earthquake—an earthquake !'

"We none of us felt the shock, but we saw the motion ; but yet we thought
he must have been seized with a sudden fit of illness, or madness, and yet we
looked about, and he did the same, when he suddenly exclaimed,—

"'There he goes—there he goes !'

"'Who?—what ?' we all exclaimed.

"'The—the—the——' He could not speak, but pointed to a certain spot, and there we beheld the form of Slankey, the preacher, running away as fast as he could towards the cane brake, for the safety of his life."

"Slankey, the preacher!" exclaimed Cesar, suddenly.

" Yes, it was him—I am sure of that."

Cesar said no more, but darted off in the pursuit of the man who had done him so much evil; whose evil counsels, whose evil turn of mind, and whose malignity had been one of the knot of circumstances that had beset him, and caused him so much misery, and who had aided in oppressing Lucy Neal.

But though Cesar was fleet and animated by hate and revenge, yet Slankey was equally so by the love of life and the instinctive feeling that if he were caught, he would be a sacrifice in the hands of a people whom he had not treated in a manner that would at all conduce to their happiness, or to procure their good-will.

Away went Slankey, and away went the blacks in pursuit of him ; but they did not gain fast upon him —on the reverse, he continued to elude them at every turn ; nothing was left undone that they could do : some threw things at him—one great black threw a large hatchet at him, while another cast a pebble at him, about the size of an ostrich's egg, exclaiming, as he did so, with great energy,—

" Cuss you—you longrbacked snake, take that."

However, it fell on one side, not many inches from his head ; but still he escaped and could the will have performed the fact, he would have been dead ere this.

No. 14.

"Shoot—shoot him," cried one.

"No, no; not shoot," cried another.

"You will shoot somebody else," said a third.

"Damn rascal—kill him—beat him down!"

"Cut him head off."

These and divers other menacing cries were uttered, and the unfortunate hypocrite felt himself becoming more and more environed by his foes, and felt convinced that his life was forfeited if he were taken; though exhausted with exertion, he yet contrived to dive and rush about, with the hope of keeping his foes behind, and at last breaking through them, and then hastening to the cover of the canes where he had every reason to hope he could conceal himself until an opportunity of a further escape would be offered to him.

In his progress, however, he had many narrow escapes. There was at one time a couple of guns fired at him, and the shots flew up from the earth, and struck him, but he continued on.

Then, on another occasion, a desperate blow was aimed at him with the but of a musket, which, had it taken effect as intended, would have smashed his skull; but the black struck a moment too soon, and fell himself with the force of his own blow.

Another time, some part of his clothing was cut off by a blow from a sabre, while one had absolutely seized upon his person; but his grasp being scarcely made, Slankey eluded him and got away.

At length every move he had been making, led towards the cane brake, and he made a sudden rush for it, but was met by a gigantic black, who stood right in his way, but Slankey endeavoured to turn, but it was no use; the black placed himself right in his way, ready to intercept him.

"You rascal," he exclaimed, "you wolf in sheep's clothing, you shall not escape; you shall be hanged, you dog, you shall."

Slankey, terrified to death, made a desperate effort, and ran quite in upon the black, who was taken by surprise. The shock sent him off his legs, and he was thrown down with great violence; and Slankey, closely pursued, now made direct for the brake, which was scarcely two hundred yards in advance.

All his foes were now behind him, and he some thirty, or forty yards in advance; he ran for his life, and absolutely flew. He was within a few yards of the place of refuge, and a yell was uttered, when they saw him gain it.

"Fire—fire!" they one and all shouted.

Twenty guns in a moment were discharged just as he was entering the canes; they saw him limp, but he disappeared.

"Hurrah,—hurrah!" they shouted, "he's hit."

This was indeed the fact, but then he was in the brake. That, however, was not of much consequence, they thought; he could not go far, and would be sure to leave a trace behind him, they would be sure to track him."

"Keep up to him, never mind loading," said one; "we shall take him alive now; he must be taken, and made an example of."

This was obeyed, and away they went; a few of the foremost dashed into the cane brake without a moment's thought or hesitation.

"Catch the preacher." They shouted. "Hurrah! there is blood; we shall have him. He has been hit, the black thief—the wolf's not far off."

"He cannot make his way far in this place, with a loss of blood."

The terrified Slankey rushed on and on; for he heard the voices of his pursuers behind him, and he heard their shouts. He could distinguish their voices, nay, he could hear and comprehend their threats, and he felt that he was losing strength.

Dreadful as his situation was, yet he mechanically rushed onwards; he was almost insensible to the sufferings he really endured. Fear and terror had deprived him of all sense of these, in the terrors he endured on the score of what might be.

But there is a point beyond which nature cannot endure. Physical sufferings presents physical impossibilities and one of these was the certainty that Slankey could not keep up his present flight with decreasing strength, and increasing exertions.

The canes were a difficulty to push through, and he sunk down almost without knowing it; but in endeavouring to rise, only rolled about. Presently however, he crawled near a mound of earth, near a fallen cane of great dimensions, and that in some sort concealed himself like a creature that has been wounded by the sportsman, and crept into some hedge or cover, for the purpose of concealment.

Here the unfortunate but bad man crept with the hope that he might thus lie hidden, and escape from his pursuers, who thirsted for his blood.

He lay fainting with heat; his pulsation was audible; every throb of his heart completely shook his whole frame; and he felt as if momentary dissolution would be the consequence of the exertion he had gone through to escape.

His tongue hung out; his eyes were bloodshot, swollen, and protruded to a degree that would have been terrible and painful to behold; but what he felt, was the horrible fate that seemed to await him. He was not sure he was safe, and that to a man like Slankey was truly horrible.

His wound, for he was wounded, was painful, and he had lost blood as he came along, which weakened him; and the anguish of the wound itself was aggravated by the exertion he had made, and which he had not been sparing of, to escape and force his way through the canes, to the spot where he had fallen.

He could hear his pursuers, their wild shouts, and their hurrahs; he could hear their exclamations, and tell the thirst for vengeance that had taken possession of them, and their determination to track him out of the canes.

This to him was dreadful; yet he could not move—he was too weak, and by far too much spent for such a purpose; he was completely powerless, and lay panting like an over-wrought dog.

" Hurrah!" shouted or yelled the blacks, " here is the track—blood—blood— here and everywhere ; he cannot be far off."

" Push on—we must have him down."

" Down with the villain—down with the hypocritical preacher!"

Slankey shrank at each of these exclamations, as if a knife had been thrust into him, and would have crept further away, but he could not ; he was by far too spent and exhausted ; so much so that he could not move.

Neither had he regained his breath, but lay panting on the earth, unable to move his hands; his eyes scarce enabling him to see, but yet his hearing was singularly distinct and clear, and he heard every word that was uttered by his pursuers, who were within a few yards of him.

" Have you lost the track?" inquired one.

" Yes," said another.

" Why, here are the marks of blood."

" I see them, but I don't see any more. Which is the next place he has gone to ? I cannot see any more."

There was a pause, during which, they were engaged in examining the place to discover the lost track ; and Slankey began to hope for a moment he might yet chance to escape ; though only for a moment, because he well knew that those who pursued him were so numerous that they would divide themselves, and search it all through.

" I can't find it," said one.

" Nor I," replied another, " it appears to have vanished."

" Ay, but he cannot have gone far, you know; he must be somewhere hereabout he had not strength enough to go far; he could not—besides, he was shot, and h evidently felt it."

" Good ! so he did."

" Well, then, we had better divide ourselves, and beat the canes until we discover him, for here he must be."

" Never leave him—never leave him."

"No, no; we must have him, and then he can sing hymns to the winds from those topmost branches of the trees."

The preacher shrank within him, when he heard this; for he well knew to what they alluded to—his mode of death; and to such a man, death, a violent death, was the most awful and terrifying thing that could happen.

However, he thought there was a cessation of the search, or his pursuers had gone off in another direction, and left him there behind; he began to imagine there was yet a chance of life left him, but he was painfully convinced of the contrary.

He heard some one coming through the canes.

This was doubtless one of his pursuers, and he was there unarmed, and without any means of resistence; but had he been ever so well provided, he would have been unable to have used the means of defence; he was completely powerless, and helpless; if he had the chance of safety in flight, he could not have accepted it; he could not have risen to attempt a flight.

The sounds came nearer and nearer, and he could even see the canes pushed on one side as the individual came forward; but he now saw the figure of a tall black, which, however, was not of such a character that it gave him any hope. He feared to look—to keep his eyes upon the object, or the spot where he had appeared; but yet the black had disappeared from the spot.

He breathed again, as he muttered to himself,—

"He has passed, and he has not seen me; he was looking another way. I am safe for a short time at least."

This was a pleasing reflection, if aught could be pleasing to one so prostrate as he was at that moment; he was quite helpless, and had he felt the rope secured round his neck, he could not have asked for mercy.

But when he was about to congratulate himself upon the apparent safety he was in, he heard a noise in the brake, not very far from him, and which increased very quickly, and came nearer and nearer.

Again did the fear of immediate death take possession of his soul; he trembled and shook like an aspen leaf.

The noise grew more and more distinct; it became more definite, and he could hear and distinguish the voices of men, who said,—

"He must be about this spot; he cannot have gone far; he had not strength; he must have dropped down where he was, and crept forwards to some hole, or concealed himself in some place or other."

"Yes; I will not leave a single place that will conceal a rat unexplored, for sure I am that he must be about here somewhere. There is nothing that shall escape my search."

"Push on, and break the canes down, so that you may know where we have made a search, and can hunt him quite out."

"Hang him—a dog!"

"Yes, curse him, for a long-legged villain, who would betray any poor wretch to evil, and then help to punish him."

"He will preach submission to the planter's blockhouse, and to the overseer's whip. Yes, yes, he will preach for all that; but will he preach for the submission hanging when we have caught him?"

He will be made to submit."

' Ay, and swing like a dried leaf from the tree top."

"Hurrah! hurrah!"

"What now?"

"Why, here is more blood; we are upon his track now; he cannot have gone ; he was too exhausted to go far."

They now came upon the track, and the wretched Slankey felt that they had discovered him, and turned over upon his side with the intention of crawling a little further away, from an instinctive impulse rather than any hope that he should be able to succeed in running away.

A loud shout and the cracking of the canes assured him that he was seen by his pursuers, and he shook as he heard one of them say,—

"See, see, there is the black sheep."

"Ay, the wolf."

"The fox," said another, who now came up; "here is our prize."

There was a shout of execration, and he was in an instant surrounded by six or seven tall blacks, armed with cutlasses, who had thrown aside their fire-arms in the pursuit as cumbersome.

"You dog's whelp!" said one, "you are doomed to die, and die a dog's death too—you hypocritical villain!"

"What shall we do with him?"

"Drag him away—drag him away," said one.

"No, no—beat his brains out where he lays; he does not want any time—he's a missionary man; he's a preacher too, and therefore ready to die at a moment's notice. Beat his brains out!"

"Mercy," shrieked the miserable Slankey, "mercy!"

"No mercy for such as you, you do not deserve it; you ought and shall die as a warning to others," said a tall negro, brandishing a musket over his head, and was about to bear the but with his utmost strength upon the prostrate Slankey.

"No, no," said the others, "don't do that—don't do that; drag him away to the tree where we will hang him."

This appeased the other, and despite the cries for mercy of Slankey, they dragged him—for he could not walk, to the spot; he was too weak and exhausted to stand, much less to walk, and they pulled him along.

They dragged him along the earth among the broken canes to the edge of the brake, until they got clear of it, and then shouted to their companions.

These no sooner saw the wretched man dragged along than they gave a shout of triumph and of exultation.

"We have him! we have him!" was the answering shout of those who had him in their grasp, as they dragged him along towards the spot where the others had collected in a body to receive him.

There was a tall tree growing in the middle of the place with tall spreading branches, and they looked at Slankey, and then looked up at the branches. The wretched man knew his fate and trembled, whilst a cold sweat bedewed his limbs.

"Slankey," said one, "your hour is come."

Slankey looked at the speaker, and saw him grin horribly at him, and point with his fingers to the tree above, and there he saw a tall black busily employed in passing a long rope over the stoutest arm.

"You will be up there in another moment."

"Mercy—mercy!" shrieked the terrified Slankey; "oh, have mercy upon me, as you hope for mercy hereafter yourselves."

"No, no—no mercy, Slankey; you must die. You know you teach we must all die, and you may as well do so now."

"Oh, spare me! give me time for preparation. I am a poor miserable sinner like yourselves. I want time—I want time to make my peace with Heaven."

"You have had time enough for years past, Slankey, to do that, you know; you have been in the constant practise of preparing others; you cannot have neglected yourself. Oh no, Slankey, you are too good, too merciful a man, and too much the friend of the poor black, to require any time."

"Have some mercy—be merciful! give me time to pray—do not kill body an soul."

The rope was, however, lowered at that instant, and instantly fixed with a running knot upon his neck.

"Mercy—mercy!" shrieked the wretched man.

"Run him up," said the voice of one he knew well, and the order was obeyed n an instant, and the wretched man, whilst shrieking for mercy, was swinging in the air, struggling and clinging with his hands to the rope; but his efforts did not last many minutes, for the rope was too tight, and he was soon dead.

The body was then secured to the tree as a warning to others, and a mark of their just vengeance upon one who had acted at he had done.

CHAPTER XXX.

THE TERRORS OF MRS. AND MIS' DEAL.—THE ENTRY INTO MR. DEAL'S HOUSE.—
THE INQUIRIES.—THE DREADFUL DISCOVERY.

THE dreadful fate of Slankey appeared to give the negroes a taste for excesses, for they set up a loud shout when they all, far or near, saw the body of the preacher swinging from the tree, high in the air, free from all struggling on his part, but dangling quite free from all endeavours, and dead—quite dead.

This shout was echoed by many who were coming up, for the execution had been done so suddenly, that all the blacks were not aware of it, or had even come up from the different parts of the cane brake, where they had been searching for the fugitive.

"Who is that?" inquired one of those who had returned from the chase.

"Slankey, the preacher," was the reply.

"Then you have taken him—I thought he had got clear off?"

"No, or he would not be dangling up there in the wind. No, no, he's safe enough. Where is Cesar Bobb?"

"Here," said Cesar, who had at that moment returned from the search among the canes, but had taken a wrong track in the first impetuosity of the chase, and had been thrown out of the final discovery.

This was, however, compensated by the result; and when the speaker turned round, he saw that Cesar had not heard of the death of his enemy.

"We have taken and strung up the preacher."

"Have you?" said Cesar. "I should like to have spoken to him; I should like to have reminded him of the many lessons he had taught, and the few he had practised. I am sure he could not have had the conscience to demand mercy."

"But he did, Cesar, ask mercy in the most abject and pitiful manner."

"Which you refused to extend to him," said Cesar Bobb, looking upon the figure of the deceased preacher.

"No we gave him no mercy; for he deserved none."

Cesar, said no more, but there he stood, observing the swinging to and fro from side to side of the inanimate body, which had so lately been the object of his hatred and his abhorrence. Even now Cesar could not look at him without the strongest feelings of unquenched hate; for it was not his evilmindedness and counsels against himself that he disliked, but that they had affected one who was dearer to him than his own life; and as strong as was his love for her, so strong was his hatred against those who oppressed or aided in oppressing him or her on his account.

Turning from the contemplation of this object, he said to his companions,—

"This is not all we have taken up arms for, there are other traitors beside such as he; we must not stand idle, and permit them to get forces together; we must overrun the country, and then we shall have the slaves from every plantation joining us, and then our numbers will be overwhelming."

There was something so true in all this, that the insurgents instantly set about forming their dispersed ranks ready for an immediate march.

"Which way is it proposed to go," inquired one?

"I do not yet know, but I suppose we shall follow the main road, and proceed onwards, where we shall meet with more estates."

"But shall we leave Mr. Deal's?"

"By no means ; we are upon his grounds now, and we shall not leave till I have seen some in safety whom I owe my liberty to."

"Mr. Deal is on the estate, I hear ; what shall be done with him ?"

"I would not have him harmed."

"But he has injured you."

"True," said Cesar Bobb, "I know that ; but he was made to believe I injured him by that vile preacher yonder, the overseer, and Adolphus Deal ; but for them I should not have suffered what I have."

"Death to them both !"

"I should not have been oppressed but for their machinations ; I might have been reasonably happy even as a slave ; she would have gilded many a sorrowful hour ; and with her, sadness would have been transformed to sunshine."

There was, however, no time to lose, and the whole party proceeded towards Mr. Deal's house, which was but a short distance ahead of them.

It was well for Mr. Deal that it was Cesar's party that came against his house, for there were several bodies under different leaders, who were not so much inclined to spare any, but who committed all to the flames, punishing all without any discrimination whatever ; but it was not so with Cesar Bobb.

Mr. Deal and his family, consisting of himself, and Mrs. Deal, and Miss Deal, thought they had better make a virtue of necessity, and remain quietly within doors ; they could not escape ; they could not get away ; they were surrounded on all sides by their enemies ; and therefore any attempt of that sort would be madness.

"Dear me, Mr. Deal," said his good lady, "dear me, what will become of us ? What shall we do amongst all these dreadful black people ?"

"Why, my dear, I don't know that we can do anything ; we have not sufficient force with us to resist them."

"There, it is all very well talking in that way, Mr. Deal ; but you don't seem to think what we are to do. What can we do ?"

"Yes, my dear, the last is what I am thinking about, but I cannot see any easy solution to it—far from it."

"Then, what use are you, Mr. Deal, since you can do nothing, or think of nothing ? What will become of us ? You are a very useless person, Mr. Deal, and ought to have provided for our safety."

"How could I, my dear ? Did I know these men were coming down upon us ? I had no idea they were coming here."

"You never have an idea, pa," said Miss Deal, very dutifully, "when you ought. What ma and I are to do, gracious only knows."

"Well, my dear, you must be as patient as——"

"Patient, indeed ! I have no patience."

"Well, my dear," said Mr. Deal, perplexed out of his wits, "I do not mean to say you have, but it is necessary to have it ; or, at least, you will have to do the same without it as you have with it ; but in that case you will be much more incommoded ; if I were able to do anything, I would, and the best and only thing I can advise you to do, would be to act with as much care and caution as you can."

"A pretty thing, indeed," began Mrs. Deal, when her daughter interrupted her, saying,—

"Oh, ma, look yonder ; I declare there they come ; but what is that hung from the great tree in the middle there ?"

"Why, as I'm alive," replied Mrs. Deal, "that is a man. Oh, the monsters !"

"Oh, oh !" said Miss Deal.

Mr. Deal looked grave, and taking a glass, he surveyed the object, of the nature of which he was pretty well acquainted, though he hoped there was room for doubt.

"What is it, pa?"

"Why, my dear, I fear it is the body of some unhappy man whom these savages have murdered."

"Oh, we shall all be hanged, ma, if no worse happen."

"Well, we have nothing to do," said Mr. Deal, gravely, "but to trust in the protection of Divine Providence, because human aid will not avail."

"Oh, goodness, are we to be——"

"My dear, you will have less to fear than you apprehend; they will hardly injure you, if they should me. But I have not acted unjustly towards them, and, therefore, if I have any hope, it will be on that score; though they may injure my property, yet they will not murder all men indiscriminately."

However, all argument was cut off, and a loud shout heard from without, which caused them some accession of uneasiness from the nature of the shout, because it came from those whom they looked upon as enemies.

"They come—they come," muttered Mr. Deal, in great perturbation.

"Yes, they do come," echoed Mrs. Deal, much terrified at the bare idea of the embraces of a black man. "Lord have mercy upon us!"

"Oh, ma," said Miss Deal, "I declare I don't know whether we shall be ravished or roasted first. Oh, isn't it horrible!"

"Oh, oh!" said Mrs. Deal.

At that moment the doors below were burst open without any ceremony, and the house in a moment afterwards filled with negroes, who ran about from place to place with the utmost unconcern, and none of that care they were in the habit of exhibiting when approaching the private apartments of the planters, their masters.

Mrs. Deal and her daughter shrieked as the head and shoulders of a black man suddenly intruded themselves into the apartment, and was immediately afterwards followed by the body and several others in a moment.

The room was soon half full of them, and a gigantic black, grinning in the face of Mrs. Deal and her daughter, said something about being her brother.

"My brother! Oh dear, did you ever hear the like of that? my brother!—as if ever I had a brother that colour."

"Ah, missy," said the man, "we be all broders and sisters now."

"Oh, my gracious!"

As she uttered this exclamation, the big black man took Mrs. Deal round the waist, and whisked her off the couch, and took the liberty of putting his hideous grinning cavity of a mouth, armed as it appeared to be by a curly moustache of the deepest black, close to her lips, and without ceremony kissed her with such an astounding report, not unlike that of a pistol, to her horror and amazement.

"Oh, oh! do you see this, Mr. Deal, and let me put up with it? Oh, murder; have mercy upon me! Mercy, mercy!"

At that moment a tall, huge, black fellow, with bandy legs, and a nose like the wrong end of a cricket-bat, made a seizure upon Miss Deal, whom he instantly lifted up, and carried out of the apartment, to her unspeakable horror and anguish.

"Oh, spare me! save me," she cried; "have mercy upon me—oh, have mercy upon me! Pa will do anything you ask him, if you will spare me."

"Don't kick and scratch so, then," said the black, giving her a shake that almost dislocated her joints, and reduced her to a state of instant subjugation.

"Mercy," she said; "spare my life! Do anything, but spare my life!"

It did not appear that the negro intended any evil, for he put his burden down in another room, and placed her upright in a chair, and, grinning with mischievous delight, chucked her under the chin, and kissed her immediately afterwards.

"Oh, my gracious!"

"Nobody wants to hurt you, but you must be quiet," said the tall black man, and he grinned hideously. "If you make any noise, it will be of no matter—no matter at all; but, at the same time, you will make us be a little rough with you; we shan't think of eating you."

"Eating me," said the young lady; "oh, dear!"

At that moment Mr. Deal was seized roughly by some of the blacks who had entered the apartment, and who sought to bind him with cords without any cere·mony, and with some degree of roughness, when Cesar Bobb entered the room.

Mr. Deal protested against this invasion of private right, but his remonstrances were not heeded by the man.

"Cesar," said Mr. Deal, "is this the way you return to your old master's house—you who have wronged me?"

"I have never wronged you," said Cesar.

"You have, Cesar, and now you come back with fire and sword. One unhappy wretch you have sacrificed, I myself have seen; how many more Heaven above knows! but can you expect this to prosper?"

"I hope so," said Cesar Bobb; "this much I know, that there are many just causes for what we have done; and we have been compelled to do what we have done in our own defence. As for myself, I have been cruelly used by your son, Slankey, the preacher, and the overseer, John Grubson."

"What do you intend to do, Cesar? You have here a house on my estate, and those who have served me have had their due. I have never treated any with severity, nor have I allowed any one to treat my slaves with rigour."

"You are not a bad man, Mr. Deal," said Cesar; "'tis not you whom I complain of—it is those who act under your orders. You have falsely accused me, but you may think I am guilty; there are others, however, who know I am not; and not only do they know that, but they can tell who is guilty."

"Well, Cesar, who are they?"

"I have already named them, and I believe one of them hangs on yonder tree."

"Who?" inquired Mr. Deal.

No. 15.

"Slankey."

"Is that Slankey, the preacher?"

"Ay, it is," said one of those who were present; "he will not be the only one who will pay the penalty of his crimes."

"If my life is to be the sport of your resentment," began Mr. Deal,——

"Your life is not sought," said Cesar Bobb, interrupting him,

"What is it you desire?"

"The destruction of some things which we will take upon ourselves to destroy, and the punishment of certain persons, whom we will punish, having the right to retaliate upon them, and to put an end to slavery."

"And my life?"

"Is safe, if you resist not, but you must be bound."

He was bound by the negroes who were waiting for the word, but not so as to put him in any pain, but at the same time he was safely secured.

"And now where is John Grubson?"

"I have not seen him since he went out with the volunteers."

"He was among them, was he?" said Cesar.

"Yes, he was called upon to go out with them."

"Where is your son?"

"I know not; he was with them, I believe."

"Where is Lucy Neal?"

"I have not seen her this day."

There was a pause of a few moments, when there was a commotion down stairs, Cesar Bobb went out to see what was the matter; before doing so, however, he gave orders that the house should be searched from one end to the other, and then proceeded to ascertain the cause of the disturbance.

"Cesar Bobb," said one of the insurgent negroes, "come with me—come with me."

"What is the matter, Scipio?"

"I will show you," said Scipio, with a grave countenance; "something you will be sorry to see, I am sure."

"Do not keep me in suspense; tell me what has happened. I fear, Scipio, from your countenance, that something dreadful has happened."

"Something dreadful has happened," said Scipio.

"Then tell me, have you found Lucy?"

"We have."

"And ——"

"Dead!" was the answer.

Cesar Bobb staggered a few paces, but by a strong effort, he aroused himself and walked towards the spot, where he saw a number of his companions resting on their arms, and looking intently upon some object, but what that object was his heart too easily suggested to him—it must be, he thought, the body of Lucy Neal.

CHAPTER XXXI.

THE DEATH OF LUCY NEAL, AND THE DISAPPEARANCE OF CESAR BOBB.—THE DEATHS OF JOHN GRUBSON, AND ADOLPHUS DEAL.—THE BOAT ON THE WATER-FALL.—THE LAST OF CESAR.

WHEN Cesar Bobb came up to the crowd that stood around, they made way for him, and looked up in his features as he passed, and sorrow was painted in their's; and he was permitted to stagger up to the dead body of her whom he so much adored, and for whom he had suffered so much.

She was stretched out a lifeless corpse. The fire that shone from his eye was no longer there.—There she was, dead!

Cesar bowed his head, and fell upon his knees before the inanimate corpse. He looked upon it with a look of tenderness. His eyes poured not forth those streams of grief which lovers are represented to have in store for such occasions. No, Cesar Bobb's griefs was not vented in outward signs—his heart bled, and his spirits and strength forsook him.

He took her cold hands; he pressed her bloodless lips to his own; and then, with a deep and bitter groan, that seemed to find an echo in the hearts of the throng who stood around him,—

"The only tie," he said, "that binds me to my fellow mortals is gone. I have nothing more in common with the world. There lies my only hope, my only joy. You shall no more hear of Cesar Bobb—farewell!"

He paused to take a last look upon the corpse, and was about to turn away, when one of the insurgent negroes placed his hand upon his arm, and stopped him, saying,—

"Cesar, you are not going to leave us?"

"I am," he replied. "I have nothing more to live for."

"Live to restore liberty to us."

"I cannot; my heart will burst. I shall not be able to aid you—I cannot do you any good—I cannot give counsel—farewell, friends, farewell! Attempt not to detain me. I am unable to go on with you."

"Your race have claims upon you, Cesar."

"All claims are buried with my hopes there," said Cesar, pointing to the dead. "Bring her to life, and my power will return. I have nothing in the world, and the world will have nothing from me."

Cesar spoke in sadness, but there was a moody resolution expressed in his brow, that none present would attempt to interfere with him, but looked after his receding figure, as he quietly stalked from among them.

* * * * * *

When Cesar Bobb was gone, the negroes were determined upon prosecuting the war, and, having nothing to detain them on Mr. Deal's plantation, whereas the owner was known for a humane and moderate man, but a strict search was made for those in his employment, who had acted otherwise, and they were resolved that they would avenge Cesar's wrongs."

It was from these motives that Mr. Deal was left to himself, and his lady and daughter were put to no other inconvenience than that which they sustained from extreme fright, and the uncouth attentions and handling of the slaves, who appeared to torment them from design, knowing them both to be somewhat vicious. They then gutted Mr. Deal's house, and plantation afterwards.

In all their search, they did not succeed in finding either John Grubson or Adolphus Deal, both of whom they swore should share the same fate as Slankey, the preacher, for they were all alike steeped deep in the same crime.

However they were not to be found, and it had more than once been suggested by some of them that they should burn down Mr. Deal's house and buildings around, and so force them out, if they were there, for some persisted in thinking they must both be concealed.

However, that was overruled, and away they went. They had not gone far, before they met a party of the volunteers whom they had defeated.

It appeared that, being dispersed by the fire of the ambuscade, they had made their way back by different routes, and some four or five went towards a neighbouring estate.

The negroes of this place, however, rose up when they heard the firing, and came in a body to join their fellows; these met the retreating volunteers, and drove them back upon the body that was now advancing upon them, and who took them prisoners.

They cried bitterly for mercy. With all the abject meanness of cowards, they went down upon their knees and besought their captors for their lives, but the negroes had been too basely treated. A long series of years of wrongs and brutishness and blows had deprived them of all pity or mercy.

"No mercy for you, John Grubson," said one of the slaves who recognised him.

"Where is Adolphus Deal?"

"There—there! Spare me, spare me! Take him, but spare me."

There was nothing more said; but, Adolphus, finding himself in the hands of those whom he believed could take his life, besought them to spare him for his father's sake—that he was innocent.

"You shall both hang together," said the enraged negroes, who dragged them back to the same tree where Slankey was hanging. Here they besought their captors to spare them, and each reviled the other.

Thus, without any ceremony, they were secured back to back, and one rope was run round the necks of both, and to the middle of that there was another rope secured to it, and run over an arm of the tree.

At a given signal they were run up and secured. They were dead in a few moments, and, after a short time, the insurgents quitted the spot, satisfied with their acts of vengeance.

* * * * * * *

The day on which Cesar Bobb left the presence of his companions he made straight to the great lakes; there he was seen to embark in a canoe, which it appeared he knew where to find; he steered into the middle of the stream and there he sat, moody and melancholy, with his eyes fixed upon the wide waters around him, and steering his boat down the stream, which entered a broad and rapid river. He steered his boat with skill, and avoided every rock, but yet he did not appear to be aware that he was entering a stream that led to a fearful cataract, and that soon he would enter the rapids that led to it.

The water was deep, but the stream ran swift; a boat once entering it could never hope to be released from the vortex, save after it should have passed the fearful fall not far below.

The spectator gazed upon the boat as it was hurried on towards the fall with great rapidity. His breath was suspended in his anxiety, for the occupant of the boat appeared to be only careful to keep his boat in the middle of the stream, with ts head down it.

The roar of the cataract must have been heard miles above. The occupant of the boat approached the cataract within a few score yards; and then, throwing away the oars, stood up; and, crying aloud, held out his arms, as if he were about to be transported to heaven, or expected remedy from thence, but at that moment man and boat were never heard of more, and Cesar Bobb slept beneath the whirl of waters, at the base of the cataract.

THE END.